CW00590003

On The Other Side

Teuta Metra

Copyright © 2023 by Teuta Metra

All rights reserved. No part of this book may be used or reproduced in any form whatsoever without written permission except in the case of brief quotations in critical articles or reviews.

This book is a work of fiction. Names, characters, businesses, organizations, places, events and incidents either are the product of the author's imagination or are used fictitiously. Any resemblance to actual persons, living or dead, events, or locales is entirely coincidental.

For more information, or to book an event, contact:

www.teutametra.com

Cover design by Elidor Kruja

"The whole world is my homeland." – Erasmus

1

When the stranger's hand pushed me under the train, I finally understood that I should never have come to this country. This is what happens to people who are born on the wrong side of the border. The things I did before the tragedy were wrong. Helen would say I deserve all of this.

"Wake up, wake up!" A man's voice keeps calling me. I want to do as he asks but my eyelids are too heavy. I can't explain how or why but it's as if my past has physically landed on me, sealing them tightly shut. He says my name again: "Rita, Rita, Rita."

I can hear you, for God's sake! I can't move, I want to scream. Instead of repeating my name over and over, why doesn't he cover me with a blanket?

Cold hands press my body and I want to push them away, but something is pulling me down. There's so much light, so much movement. I don't know any of the people hovering over me. All I know is that everything is cold, and my body is freezing.

The man's shoulders are shaking, and I hear him sobbing now. "I love you," he whispers, gently stroking my hand, as if afraid of the tubes that hang all over my arm. Do I even know him? Wait. *Why* is he crying? *Am I dead?* I concentrate for a heartbeat, but I don't see Death. Shouldn't I be shrouded in darkness? Instead, it's a bright light that surrounds me. At times it's *too* bright, stretching to the point of blindness.

A woman in a white coat enters the room. She too is asking me to wake up. Her voice is familiar, but I can't place it. What's wrong with these people? Why don't they let me go?

An urge to fly far away from this bed builds in my core, but the man's hand is keeping me anchored to the white room. Even my clothes are white now. I don't like white. It reminds me of the waiting rooms in hospitals; waiting for my mum to get well. She never did.

I can see the tubes attached to my body, and I can hear the rhythmic whistle of the oxygen machine, which is already getting on my nerves, but for some reason I can't see the face of the man who keeps calling me. I see the way his body moves, and I see his hand in mine, but I can't seem to focus on his face.

How stupid of me to come to London though, only to find myself under a train. So much struggle and heartache, just to end up like this. It's so pathetically tragic I could laugh.

But I know somebody pushed me. That much I do remember.

I also know that I was supposed to meet somebody today, but there was a fight – I can't remember any more detail than that, it's so frustrating – and then I was pushed, and everything turned to black. I'll never forget the scream. I'm just not sure if it was my voice, theirs, or somebody else's.

I will myself to focus, but the perpetrator's face is fractured into millions of tiny pieces. If only I could put them together, I'd know who did this to me.

But you can't blame a person without a face.

2

London Southend Airport
Saturday morning, 26 October 2019

"Women like us don't go abroad, my dear. This is our home, and no matter how hard it gets we make it work. Women like us are hated overseas. We are nothing but poor immigrants to them – people who will steal their country, their jobs, and even their husbands."

The words of warning that Rita's mum had given her time and again kept flashing through her mind. It had never occurred to her to ask: Who are *they?* But today, standing in front of a British border control officer at London Southend Airport, Rita Hanas understood: He was one of them.

Fidgeting with her lucky charm necklace, Rita weighed her options. Whichever path she took, there was no way she was going to escape. But she was used to rejection.

A chill ran down her spine as she remembered how

the traffickers had asked her to straighten her dark curly hair. "You should look as much as possible like the girl whose ID card we're using," they'd said. And Rita could do nothing but agree.

She balled her hands into fists to stop herself from crying. She could still hear the immigration officer's voice like sharp nails clawing at her soul. She would never be able to forget the features on his face when he took her ID card in his hands. If he hadn't made that phone call, Rita would have sailed through security like everybody else. Time seemed to slow down, allowing her to memorise every irritating detail about him: the way he raised his thick eyebrows, the way he pursed his lips, the tone of his voice as he asked her to follow him. He didn't say how much time she would have to wait, and Rita couldn't ask.

The female police officer tasked with keeping an eye on Rita focused on her paperwork. She'd probably dealt with so many girls like her before. From the corner of her eye, Rita could only see the bottom half of the officer's body; her black trousers and black shoes, the black uniform jacket belted at the hip. *Who cares what she's wearing?* Rita thought. *This evening, when I end up God-knows-where, she'll probably kick off those big shoes and slip into a warm bed next to someone she loves.*

Chin cradled in her cupped hands, elbows resting on her jelly legs, Rita scanned the room. There was a desk with a computer where the officer was working, a water dispenser, four chairs, a door, and a small window.

Hmm. Maybe she could escape. She'd gone through so much to get this far, she couldn't give up now. Life wouldn't be worth living with the love of her life on the other side of the border. If the British police officers forced her to go home, she'd come back again anyway. She had no choice. She had to find Samuel.

Something had happened to him. She could feel it. Men like Samuel didn't simply vanish into thin air. No, he was somewhere in London and Rita had to get there. First, she would search for him at the London Business School where he was studying for his master's degree. And if that didn't work, she would visit every single London hospital, followed by all of the prisons. He needed her and she had promised she would always be there for him.

Rita's chair was far away from the door, but the echo of the footsteps outside was loud enough to hurt her ears. She was too tense to think. The more she concentrated, the more she failed to come up with a plan. All the motivational quotes and books Rita enjoyed reading only seemed to work when she didn't need them.

Rays of morning light spiked through the windowpane. A new day had arrived. She'd been sitting in the immigration holding section all night but hadn't slept a wink. Perhaps she'd dozed on the white plastic chair, but only for a few snatched minutes. Her back hurt and her body felt like it had been hit by a lorry. She rubbed her eyes, took a deep breath, and stood to stretch her legs. Rita stared at the small window above the officer's head for the hundredth time. From where she was standing, she could tell they were on the second floor of the building. Through the black plate-glass window, she could make out passengers ready to board a plane: easyJet flight 230, destination Milan.

You don't have what it takes to run away, Rita!

She sat back down, not daring to take another step.

The room was silent. Nothing moved apart from the rise and fall of Rita's chest. Her breathing was short, like a frightened bird trapped in a cage. Another half hour passed, then the officer got up from her chair. *It's time*, Rita thought, surrendering to her fate. She clenched her fists so tightly that her nails dug into the palms of her hands, but the pain was nothing compared to the ugly feeling of defeat. Failure has a bitter taste – like a dentist drilling a hole in your tooth, a hole that can never be filled.

To Rita's surprise, the officer turned to the small water dispenser, filled a plastic cup with water, and handed it to her. With trembling hands, Rita gripped the cup tightly and drank the water in one go, without taking a single breath. She wiped her lips, raised her head, and looked the officer in the eye.

"Thank you," she said, handing her the empty cup. The policewoman didn't utter a word, yet her eyes were asking: "Why did you have to ruin my shift?"

Rita hunched her shoulders in silent answer. She was obviously the reason the British officer was having a bad day. The woman returned to her chair and Rita continued her imaginary conversation. It was better to pretend she was talking to a fellow human being than herself. Her mind was its usual echo chamber of inner monologue.

"I don't even know why I did it," Rita confessed to the officer's back, her lips barely moving. *It's not completely my fault,* Rita continued the one-way conversation in her head. *It was Chloe who prepared everything. She chose this place. I told her to try Luton or Gatwick, anywhere else. I shouldn't have listened to her. We're not in the same situation. We might be cousins, but that's the only thing we've got in common. Chloe McCaffrey has a British-sounding name and that changes everything. No police officer would ever scrutinise her. Her surname isn't strange, like mine. Chloe has travelled the world, too. This is the first time I've left my country! Okay, so Chloe has a father who barely sees her – once every six months – but he provides her with a monthly income. I have a father who is* probably *dying to see me.* Actually, *I don't know anymore. Oh, and Chloe has a boyfriend. I'm not sure what I have... The only thing I* do *know is I only have two hundred euros in my wallet and a debt of three thousand pounds, which I have no idea how I'm going to pay back.*

The officer coughed, freezing Rita's thoughts. Her chin quivered and she felt herself tears welling up in her eyes. *All you do is cry*, her mind scolded her.

What do you expect? I'm trapped here inside these four fucking walls and Chloe, just because she's a McCaffrey, is outside inhaling the sweet English air!

The door opened and the voices in her head finally stopped talking. Through her fringe, which had fallen over her eyes, Rita watched a man enter the room clutching a note in his hand. He leaned down and whispered into the police officer's ear.

She rose from her chair, straightened up, smiled at Rita, and said her first words.

"It's time to go." Her voice was soft.

No! They were sending her back home. Rita wanted to scream, but she swallowed the lump in her throat. At a snail's pace, she got up and slung her handbag over her shoulder. Wheeling her pink carry-on case, she put one foot in front of the other and headed for the door. Judging by the expression on the officer's face, Rita's lack of speed was irritating her.

With arms crossed over her chest, the officer tapped the yellow floor tiles rhythmically with the tip of her right shoe. She was still smiling, though.

3

What if the plane crashes?

Perfect scenario! the other voice in her head replied as Rita shuffled towards the aircraft. That darker voice of doubt was always there. It never missed Rita's mistakes. It never missed Rita's misery. Thinking clearly was so difficult when you had two voices inside your head, especially when one never shut up. It was a self-defeating sickness that Rita wasn't strong enough to confront.

I told you this would happen, it continued. Rita shook her head and took another step.

A thick mist shrouded the plane, and soft drizzle fell on her shoulders. Rita broke out into a cold sweat and felt like she might faint. She'd prefer fainting to this. She paused for a moment, but the officer bringing up the rear pushed her along. There was no other option. Rita did her best to hold back her tears. *Hopefully the plane will crash,* she thought again. At least she wouldn't have to pay back her debt. But if the plane crashed, she would never find Samuel.

Two more steps left. One. Two. She placed her right foot on to the plane, aching for a miracle. But there was nothing.

A different member of the cabin crew greeted her today, but she gave Rita the same fake smile as yesterday's flight attendant had when she'd boarded the plane to London. Blonde, with false eyelashes, she stretched out her hand and showed Rita to her place. A window seat.

Okay, better than an aisle seat. Rita didn't like people knocking into her arm every time they used the toilet. Yesterday, she'd hated the way that even when they could see the sign that the little cubicle was busy, people still hung about in the aisle, resting their hands on her seat, pulling at her hair.

A line of people was forming behind Rita, but she took her time as she pushed her small suitcase into the luggage compartment above her head and placed her handbag under the seat in front of her. Finally, she sat down and fastened her seatbelt.

So, this was all she had to show for her efforts. She took another deep breath, then buried her face in her hands, letting her tears fall. She couldn't stop them this time and her body shook as desperation set in. What was the point in bottling things up anyway? Nobody cared.

Rita scraped the tips of her Nike sneakers against

the ugly brown carpet, wishing she could make a hole in the plane. Maybe, once it was airborne, it would grow big enough to suck her out and turn her to dust, thin air, whatever.

Peeking through her open fingers, she saw the female police officer study her for the last time. Once she was sure the unwanted girl wasn't going anywhere, the officer waved goodbye to the flight attendant and stepped off the plane. The door closed. Rita moved her hands from her face and dug her nails into the arm of the seat so hard she was afraid the crew would notice the scratch marks and charge her for damage. She desperately needed to hatch a new plan.

Plan A was to kill herself. The last few months without Samuel had been unbearable. She couldn't go home to a life without him.

But Plan A was fast falling by the wayside as there was nothing on the plane sharp enough for the job.

Plan B… Nothing.

Someone took the seat next to her, making her flinch. Now she could feel their eyes upon her. She must have looked a mess, her face red and blotchy and her eyes sunken with lack of sleep. Fear emanated from her pores. So much fear and loneliness.

She turned her head away and glanced out of the little window. The airport looked deserted, and that's why she and Chloe had chosen one of London's smaller ones. They hadn't counted on the border officers checking every single passenger, but what else did they have to do after all? A busier airport would have been better. *Chloe, such a dumb move!* The plane's engine began to roar, and another stream of tears trickled from Rita's eyes. She tried to wipe them away with the palms of her hands, but they were falling too quickly.

The gentle touch of a hand patted her on the shoulder.

"Are you okay?" the man beside her asked.

Oh, he's English, thought Rita, noting his accent.

Of course, he's English. He doesn't need a visa to travel to most of the world like you do, the cruel voice in her head reminded her.

"I'm fine, thank you," she replied, her voice barely a whisper.

That's all you can say? A person who's crying on a plane is obviously not fine.

Rita had never been ashamed of her English before, back when she was living in her home country. But in less than twenty-four hours, everything had changed.

She pressed her fingers to her forehead. She had to stop this negativity, and she had to stop crying. She needed to focus on what lay ahead, and her desperate mind chatter wasn't helping one bit.

Rita's navy-blue shirt was soaked with sweat and

her face was burning up. She brushed away a final tear beneath her eye with her knuckle.

"Is there anything I can do for you?" the man asked in a raspy early morning voice.

Rita lifted her head, and through her damp lashes shot a quick glance at the Englishman. He looked to be in his early thirties. He had the kind of face she would have liked to photograph – one day, in a different life. Although they were seated, Rita could tell the Englishman was taller than her. His ginger beard was trimmed short, and his hair was sandy in colour. His facial hair made his lips look smaller than they probably were and hid his chin, but Rita could still make out a strong jawline and high cheekbones.

"I'm fine, thank you," she repeated.

"Are you going on holiday?"

He was just being nice to her. Either that or not thinking before he spoke, because no one cries if they're going on holiday.

Rita sighed. There was no point telling him the truth. In less than twenty-four hours, she'd learned the hard way that telling people where she came from was not a smart move. Trying to cover her tracks as much as possible, Chloe had decided not to book a direct flight. When she'd changed planes for the stretch from Milan to London, she'd foolishly told the woman sitting beside her where she had come from, eliciting a raised eyebrow and forced smile. Ten minutes later the woman asked the flight attendant if there was an empty seat elsewhere and swiftly scarpered. Rita didn't want the man to do the same. She was not going to tell him she was Albanian. Not in this lifetime, anyway. Her country was Cuckoo Land – the land of no hope.

"I'm going home," Rita said, not wanting to look him in the eye.

Let him believe her home was Italy. There was no harm in that.

The plane was already taxiing, and before long they would be in the air. That's when she was hit by a stomach-churning thought:

What if this man was plan B?

4

The room is quiet. Bright white light and silence. The voices have finally stopped calling my name. I don't know what day is it, but if I'm dead why should I care? My body is so light I feel like I'm floating. Actually, I am. I'm ten feet above my bed, which is occupied by my empty body.

I can see a doctor, a nurse, and a man – the one who has been holding my hand this whole time. We've switched places. Now I'm the one hovering over them.

The man standing at the edge of my bed keeps my hand clutched in his. An anchor, keeping me close each time I drift off into my past. A way to get back to him.

I rise higher, leaving the room, the building, until I'm floating above the clouds, a warm wind on my face like the mid-August breeze as you come out of the sea. I'm sailing over great billowy white clouds, yet I don't fear falling. I want to stay here and rest. I can't remember the last time life stood still for me.

The clouds are moving quickly now, and I'm lost.

This place is so unfamiliar, like school on the first day. Actually, even that had been different, because Samuel was there. He'd showed me the way around the building, where to put my bag, and where lunch was served. He stayed by my side that day and never left it. Until now.

I've known Samuel all my life. He's two years older than me, and in the beginning, he was my best friend. Later we became more than friends. With no siblings and few friends between us, we soon learned to rely on each other.

But way up high, floating through empty space, there's no one by my side. There's certainly no sign of Samuel. I miss him. So why then, when I think of him, does something sink in my stomach like a heavy rock? What happened between us? Why can't I remember any of my recent past?

I don't even know who's holding my hand!

I must have hit my head hard when I was pushed. Am I brain-damaged? It's strange. I'm struggling to remember what has only just passed, but memories from when I was younger are readily at hand.

The day of my seventeenth birthday is forever branded on my mind. I was going to make love for the first time. Who would forget that?

In my country, March 14th is a strange day to be born. On this day, people celebrate the arrival of spring, and the country is enveloped in a fake veil of joy which momentarily hides the desperation. I never cared about those celebrations. The only reason I loved that day was because I got birthday presents *and* a day off from school.

The days leading up to my birthday had been spent shopping. My mum had persuaded me to buy an expensive floral dress. We didn't have the money to fritter away on such things, but Mum insisted. The dress was blue and had little daises around the hem. I didn't need to buy shoes because she already had a pair that matched the dress perfectly.

On the morning of my birthday, I was awakened by the smell of my favourite chocolate cake baking in the oven. It instantly made my mouth water. When I stepped into the living room, it was filled with balloons and birthday cards. They hadn't been there when I'd gone to bed the night before, and I couldn't work out when Mum had done all this. But she was Luna, my all- things-superlative mother, and she would do anything for me.

Back in my room, I slipped the new dress over my head and studied myself in the mirror. My body had gone through an enormous change that year. I was taller, curvier, and my breasts had become much too prominent. Sometimes the eyes of the boys at school dropped from my face to my chest, which seemed to make Samuel jealous. I liked the look in his eyes when he saw his classmates noticing me. It made me feel important, wanted. Sometimes I felt like the whole city was looking at me, the girl who had everything: the beauty, the body, the happy family, and the handsome boyfriend. And as if life wasn't perfect enough, when I turned seventeen my parents gifted me a Canon camera and a new puppy. My life was complete!

I'd been so excited that morning that I'd run into the living room. I found Mum and Dad talking, their heads together and voices low. Mum was wearing a light blue shirt that her sister Angela had sent her two months earlier, as a gift for her fortieth birthday. Auntie Angela was three years older than Mum and lived in London, but they looked like twins. They both had steady grey eyes, fair hair, and short, ample frames. Beyond their outward appearance, however, they had nothing in common; life had treated them very differently. Mum treasured the gifts she received from England. They were different, designed for real people, she would say. As if our country was the dumpster of the world, everything exported to Albania was either counterfeit or expired.

I didn't pay too much attention to my parents, or the pile of envelopes on Mum's desk. Why should I? There were always envelopes and letters lying about there. My mum worked as a translator but because the pay was so

19

low, she also taught Italian to students at home.

As soon as my parents saw me, they stood up, wrapped their arms around me, and wished me a happy birthday. Then Dad opened the door of the balcony, and I met Luk, my new dog, for the very first time.

He was a little Maltese puppy with a silky white coat, straight and thick, which fell all the way to the floor. I jumped up and down in excitement, clapping my hands like a small child who has just heard the ice cream truck outside. Then I fell to my knees and gently lifted the puppy into my lap, where he buried his head in my hands.

Thinking back on his cute black eyes gazing up at me for the first time, and the feel of his soft, droopy ears, makes my eyes well up with tears. Or at least I think my eyes are watery. *Can you cry when you are neither dead nor alive?* There are voices in my room again, and my memories begin to blur with my new reality. The nurse has come to check the chart at the foot of my bed, as I guess she does every morning. I hate it when she checks my eyes, the way she pulls my eyelids up and shines her light into them. She's doing it now, but I don't wake up. I'm here, happy, with my memories of Luk.

I never thought my parents would let me have a dog in that tiny apartment of ours, no matter how much I'd begged for one. We lived in a normal apartment. Two bedrooms, one living room, and a small kitchenette with a door that led to a small balcony that served more as a storage area.

"Now Rita, you know you have to take him out three or four times a day," my dad explained. His eyes looked darker than hazel that day, and for the first time, I noted that he was greying at the temples.

"I can look after him today," said Mum.

She knew I had plans with my friends, so she let me go. I kissed my parents, and with my camera around my neck, I ran down the stairs.

The 14th of March is always sunny in Albania, but I'd put on my light jacket. Samuel used to say the sun was the only good thing we had in our country. I could never understand why he didn't like it here. Samuel had a nice house and a car. Twice a year he went on holiday abroad with his parents. I'd never even crossed the border, but I was happy in that little city of ours. I had everything I needed.

And now that I had the camera, the world was going to know me. I wasn't going to take ordinary pictures just to post them on social media. No, I'd already decided to sign up for photography classes and become a professional.

I spotted Samuel from far away. He was wearing a black shirt with the top three buttons undone, revealing just a bit of his chest. He held a cigarette between his fingers as he leaned casually against the hood of his car. He'd picked up smoking at his private university – as if smoking was the next step to adulthood. When we were kids, I had been taller than him. Now Samuel stood head and shoulders above me. His curly hair was cut short, so you could no longer see the waves, but I knew they were there. When we were in elementary school, I envied Samuel's curly hair, which his mother Hëna had made him keep long. Later, when we grew up, we switched traits: I had the long curly hair while Samuel's was short and dark. But Samuel's eyes were still as green as they had been the day that I'd first noticed them. The older he got, the more I was certain he'd have been a movie star if he'd been born in the USA.

Samuel's family were the *nouveau riche* of our town, but it hadn't always been that way. I remember the days when they used to borrow money from my parents. I also remember when his mum Hëna wore faded dresses – although they were always clean, of course. Everything changed when Samuel's grandfather died, and they inherited his property somewhere on the south coast. Poor old man. His body wasn't even cold when they traded his land, despite him having clearly requested them not to in his will. As if anyone in my country does as they're told.

With the money they received, Samuel's parents opened a restaurant. Soon after that, they opened two more. Before anyone knew it, they ran a chain of restaurants. And now they lived in a much nicer neighbourhood than we did.

It was no secret that Samuel was rich, but he never flaunted it around me. No matter when I saw him, day or night, butterflies fluttered in my stomach.

The day of my birthday I'd styled my hair in a double Dutch braid bun because he'd once told me how pretty it looked on me. When we arrived at his house his parents were out, which meant we got to be alone together in Samuel's bedroom. He could have had his own apartment, but he loved being fussed over by his mum. Besides, his room was big enough to be an apartment. It had its own bathroom, which was the size of my bedroom, and a balcony.

Samuel produced a bottle of champagne and two glasses, and I squealed with delight. I'd never had alcohol before, but I was seventeen, so it was about time. I took a sip and placed the glass on the bedside table, too excited to enjoy the expensive champagne he'd bought. I loved Samuel with all my heart, but I was still nervous. What if he didn't like my body? He'd never seen me naked before, nor I him.

Samuel opened the drawer of his bedside table and pulled out a tiny box. The smaller the box, the more precious the gift, my mum used to say. A *Penelope* logo was printed on the lid.

"The lady at the shop said this necklace would make the perfect gift for someone special. And there's no one more special than my sunshine."

He always called me his sunshine. He said I could light up any room.

"Oh, my goodness!" I gasped, covering my mouth with my hand for the third time that day. So many special gifts! "It's beautiful!"

I nuzzled my head against his chest and listened to his heartbeat, the warm and sensual fragrance of *Acqua di Gio* filling my nostrils. I've never been able to smell that aftershave since, without thinking of my first love.

Samuel fastened the necklace and kissed the back of my neck. Even though we knew his parents could come home at any time, we were in no hurry. I wanted to remember every single second of this magical day.

He pulled down the zip of my dress and then gently turned my head to the side so I could watch him take off his own clothes. I was ready to do anything Samuel asked of me.

We lay down on his bed and he kissed every inch of my body. I could barely breathe, I was floating. It was perfect.

Afterwards, we must have fallen asleep because the next thing we knew there were voices in the hallway. His parents were home! I was gripped with panic and shame, but Samuel wasn't fazed. He kept his parents busy in the living room while I took a quick shower. Then he sneaked me out, the two of us giggling like school children all the way to his car. We thought we'd fooled them, but of course they knew what had happened. As I closed the car door, I raised my head and saw his mum looking down at us from the window of the house.

But I was so happy that I didn't care. Her look of disappointment didn't bother me at all. When I arrived at my apartment block, I ran up the stairs two at a time, my head buzzing and my legs unsteady. It would be impossible to hide my current bubble of postcoital euphoria from my mum, but I knew she wouldn't judge.

When I opened the front door, I heard voices coming from the bathroom. Mum was loading the washing machine. It was the only time of the day there was running water in our house, and if you weren't home at that time, you would miss the chance to fill up on water for the day. In Albania, even the water was strictly regulated. And like everything else people hated about my country, everyone just accepted it. They didn't protest, they didn't negotiate with those in power. They did nothing at all.

I took off my shoes and headed towards the living room, looking for Luk. I was excited to take him on our first walk. That's when I heard the voice of Helen, my mum's best friend. I didn't like Helen. The way she looked at my dad had always bothered me. It was the same way she looked at my mum's handbags when she wanted to borrow one.

"Everything will be okay," Helen said.

"Nothing will be okay. I'm scared. No, I'm terrified. The doctors say it's incurable." That was my mum's voice, and it froze me in my tracks.

"They say I have six months to live, Helen."

For a moment my heart stopped beating.

"Miracles don't happen to me, you know that. And what about Rita? I've always imagined myself standing by her side on her wedding day. I want to be a grandmother one day, Helen! I want to be there for my only daughter, to help her with her own children. I've never wished for grey hair and wrinkles as much as I do now!"

Mum started to cry.

"I always thought I had time to do everything I wanted. We all take time for granted, like the air we breathe and the sun that comes up every morning. Oh, God! Helen, *please* take care of Rita when I'm gone. Will you do that for me? My sister Angela is too far away. When I'm gone, I need you to guide Rita, to see that she stays on the right path."

"Hush, my friend," said Helen. "You will be fine, and you'll see Rita in a beautiful wedding dress one day. I'm sure of it. The doctors don't know what they're talking about. They love to toy with the people who turn to them for help. We'll go to another hospital, get a second opinion. They'll make you better. You'll see. I have a friend who works at that fancy place, the American Hospital."

Whatever I had thought about Helen before, I desperately hoped that she was right. I stood, rooted to the spot, listening.

"Helen, I have acute leukaemia. There's nothing the doctors can do. I just want you to promise me you'll take care of Rita. My husband loves me, but I know Timi, and once I'm gone things will change. He'll marry again. I don't want him to be lonely, but his new wife will be a stranger to me. A stranger to Rita. I will only be at peace if I know that you'll take care of my daughter."

"I promise," Helen replied quietly. I couldn't bear to hear the resignation and acceptance in her voice, so different from the confidence and determination she'd spoken with just moments before.

I wanted to run to them, but I couldn't breathe. It was as if a cloud of fog was choking me. *Leukaemia.* My knees buckled and I fell against the wall, although it too appeared to be shaking. Why was the sky falling on my birthday?

But it's not a ghost mist choking me anymore, it's the clouds moving too fast. I feel dizzy.

"Rita, wake up. *Wake up!* Can you hear me?"

It's that man again, and he's shaking my bed. I'm back in the hospital room. Back in my own body. But I don't want to wake up.

What's the point of waking up when everyone I love has abandoned me?

5

As the nose of the plane plunged into the clouds over London, Rita Hanas realised that she had three hours at her disposal to either find a way to kill herself, or convince the man beside her to pretend to be in love with her and bring her back to the UK.

Even though the idea was utterly laughable, but she might as well give it a go. She had nothing more to lose than what she had already lost.

Couldn't have put it better myself! Pretending to fall head over heels for that poor guy just to reach your end goal would be truly wicked, the voice in her head preached.

People fake love stories to get into the UK all the time. I just need to get back to London and find Samuel. How I do it doesn't matter. Maybe I can pay this man...

Pay?! The voice in her head was now practically screaming at her. *You're stone broke and massively in debt! Or have you forgotten that?*

Rita leaned back in her seat, her left arm firmly pressed against the window, her chin resting on her clenched hands. She could not let the menacing voice derail her.

What if I tell him the truth? I could tell him that I'm looking for Samuel. Actually… no. I'd best not mention Samuel at all.

Why on Earth would he bother to help you? Silly girl! He doesn't know you from Adam. Men don't just go around helping women in need like knights in shining armour, the tiresome voice of doubt interrupted. *You read too many romance novels!*

What if I show him the video? Maybe then he'll help me.

Rita wrinkled her nose. The video, even though it had saved her life, was the most embarrassing thing to ever have happened to her.

The only option she had left was to ask the stranger sitting next to her for help and to be as straightforward as she could.

The border officer might have called my fake warrantor to confirm my identity, but of course a fake person can't answer a phone call. The guy sitting next to me is real though. He could be my warrantor! We could say I'm his girlfriend. He'll never have to see me again. I'll pay him, that's fine, nothing is free in this world, after all. I wonder what his price would be?

Love has no price! the snarky voice in her head replied.

How many times do I have to tell you, it's fake love? Rita silently berated the critique.

That's it. Conversation over. You've lost your mind, the bitchy voice replied.

Oh, how Rita wished it would shut up once and for all! Unfortunately, she knew better.

She dug the heels of her fake Nikes harder into the carpet. The man without a name opened his book to a dog-eared page and began to read. Rita grimaced. She always used a bookmark.

A memory of Samuel walking her to the library years ago made her heart flutter. She let out a deep breath, brushed away a lock of hair that had fallen across her face, and chewed on her lip. Never had she craved a cigarette so badly. She would do anything for a smoke right now. If she thought about Samuel for a moment longer, she was going to burst into tears again.

From the corner of her eye, Rita studied the sandy-haired man. He was wearing Nike sneakers just like hers, although most likely they weren't fake, a pair of faded jeans, and a black short-sleeved T-shirt that accentuated his biceps.

When the seatbelt sign went off, Rita got up and the man instinctively stood up too, letting her pass to the aisle. Attempting to squeeze by without touching him, Rita lost her balance ever so slightly and brushed against him with her body. This random physical encounter produced an unexpected jolt of electricity. *Bitch*, the voice in her head said. Rita ignored it and opened the overhead bin, removing some cleansing wipes, her small makeup bag, and a red shirt from her suitcase. She knew she was going to blush when she asked him for help, but she needed to get back to the UK and this guy might be the only ticket.

Her stomach clenched as she caught the flight attendant's eye. Surely, she wouldn't stop Rita from using the toilet. Even prisoners needed to pee. Before Rita asked her fellow traveller for help, she needed to be sure she looked presentable.

Her plan might be lame, but at thirty-six thousand feet in the air, it seemed to be her only option.

She walked down the aisle to the lavatory and entered through the narrow folding door. Hiding away in the small cubicle, she listened to the cabin crew gossiping outside. Their conversation was dull: clothes and boyfriends. As if it was a perfectly normal day. Well, it wasn't. The rest of the world would go on tomorrow as usual. Everything would be the same for everyone else, as if Rita and her troubles were merely one drop of water in an immense ocean.

She splashed her face with cold water and changed into her red shirt.

Great. She was so nervous her hair was already damp with sweat. To prevent it from getting any curlier, she pulled it back into a simple low bun, revealing more of her soft, pretty features. There was nothing wrong with her face. Everything was aligned perfectly. She had a straight nose and a narrow jaw, with her dad's hazel eyes and her mum's voluptuous figure. Her mum had been beautiful, and with each passing day, Rita looked more and more like her. Rita had her mum's pretty smile, too – when she decided to use it. If she wanted this man to help her, she would have to smile constantly until they landed in Milan.

A knock on the door made her jump. She was running out of time.

Rita quickly applied a yellow-tinted concealer to hide the dark circles under her eyes, foregoing powder to save time. As long as her makeup stayed like this, it would be fine. She didn't use mascara, just in case she started crying again. She didn't need to add a black streaky face to her long list of problems. With one final flourish, she applied pink gloss to her dry lips.

The moment Rita opened the small door of the cubicle, already feeling cleaner and fresher, the plane dipped and began to shake.

The seatbelt sign lit up, and the women waiting to use the toilet were advised to take their seats. The voice of the pilot informed them that they were experiencing a little turbulence and asked everyone to remain seated until the seatbelt sign was switched off.

A little turbulence?

Rita wasn't sure if it was the plane or her who was

shaking more as she moved towards her seat. Her mouth opened and closed like a fish, but no sound came out. Somehow her trembling body made its way to her seat on autopilot. Her hands were shaking so much she found it difficult to fasten her seatbelt. Her small makeup bag was now beneath the crossed legs of the flight attendant. Shit! She must have dropped it when the plane started shaking. The bag contained everything she needed to stay presentable and feel like a lady – all that expensive make-up that Chloe had gifted her. But it was impossible for Rita to retrieve it now, with the plane shaking like an old washing machine on a fast spin.

Her heart pounded in her chest, and a wave of anxiety washed over her. Perhaps her wish was coming true. How selfish of her to have hoped that the plane would crash. How could she pray for the deaths of so many people, just to escape her own fate? It also didn't seem fair that death was now her only escape, when her only mistake in life had been to love too much.

"Are you a nervous flyer?"

The man had closed his book and was watching her. Rita nodded, embarrassed. Yesterday, when she'd travelled with Chloe, the flight had been so smooth, the plane had just sailed through the clouds. She'd seen movies where people were terrified of turbulence, but never in her life had she experienced it. Then again, this was only her second time on a plane.

"Okay, think of it like this," said the man. "Just as ocean waves break on a beach, air also forms waves – or pockets –as it encounters mountains."

Rita glanced out the window. She could see big pillowy clouds, but she couldn't see any mountains. She shivered again. If they hit more turbulence, she would go into cardiac arrest.

"Feeling better now?" he asked.

How can you possibly feel better when you're thousands of feet up in the air?

"Yeah, I think so," she lied.

She kept her sentences short to mask her terror. Just a few moments ago, she'd been trying to find a way to talk to the man, to ask him for help, to potentially use him. She'd quickly forgotten about all of that when the turbulence started.

What had she been thinking? She tried to think in facts: she had two hundred euros in her wallet; she would surely find a solution to her dilemma. All she needed was for this damn plane to land so she could breathe again.

Nervously, she turned her head and glanced around. There was an old couple seated behind her. The man was sleeping, and the woman was reading a magazine. Bizarrely, none of the other passengers seemed to be even remotely concerned about the enormous empty space between the belly of the plane and solid ground.

If they're relaxed, you should be too. Then again, how can you relax when you're a reject? A little turbulence is the least of your problems! You should be more worried about the fact that you're all alone and nobody cares about you.

Rita put her head in her hands, trying to stop the voice from talking. She was gasping for air. She was trapped inside a giant metal tube thousands of feet in the air, and she needed to get out.

"Maybe it would help if you tried to distract yourself?" the man suggested.

How can you distract yourself when the wings of the plane you're sitting in are shaking?

"Just imagine you're somewhere else. How about a beach?"

Following his advice, Rita closed her eyes, but the only thing she saw was the English border officer who had sent her back. She quickly pushed this image aside and racked her brain for something different. She saw Samuel, his dark brown hair a bit longer than it used to be. He didn't look her in the eye. The more she reached for him, the further the distance between them grew. This was a recurring daydream she'd been having for six months now. She opened her eyes again. It was better to be on this rollercoaster of a flight than to be trapped inside her mind.

"It's not working, is it?"

Rita shook her head.

The seatbelt sign switched off and the sound made Rita jump. Even though her seatbelt was so tight that it was cutting into her waist, she had no intention of taking it off again. Then, as if the last few minutes had been a figment of Rita's imagination, a smiling flight attendant started down the aisle, handing out snacks and drinks.

"Coffee?" the man beside her said, pulling out his wallet. "My treat."

Rita kept silent, her body paralysed as well as her vocal cords. The only thing she could manage was a nod, and even that took a lot of effort.

"Would you like anything to drink?" the flight attendant asked in a syrupy voice.

"Coffee, please," Rita stuttered.

With the same smile she gave every other passenger, the woman poured some coffee into a paper cup and handed it to her.

"Make it two, please," said the man next to her.

Rita took a few tentative sips. The coffee was warm and fragrant, but it didn't calm her.

"Time for a game."

What? *Out of all the passengers on this damn plane, why did I have to end up next to the jolly one?*

"What do you mean?"

"I normally bring playing cards with me, but I packed my backpack in a rush this morning. Do you have any on you?"

"Erm, no."

Playing cards were the last thing Rita would have thought to put in her bag.

"Let's play with words then."

Either her English was worse than she thought, or this guy wasn't making sense.

"I don't know any word games," Rita said, taking another sip of her coffee. She'd started counting in her head, but that wasn't helping either.

"It's simple. One of us asks a question and the other answers it. But you have to be as honest as possible."

"Okay." This was stupid. How would he even know if she was lying?

"Ladies first."

"What's your name?" Oh, okay. This would be easy. If he asked the same questions as Rita, she wouldn't have to lie.

"I'm Andrew Holbrook, but my friends call me Andy," he said and held out his hand.

Rita shook his hand, and a small shiver ran through her body. *You're just scared that this damn plane is going to fall out of the sky*, she told herself, taking another sip of her coffee.

"Yours?"

"Rita, and my friends call me Rita." She had just uttered her longest sentence in English since meeting the guy, yet the stupid voice drilling inside her head chimed up: *Your English accent is terrible.*

Rita must have taken too long to come up with the next question, so Andrew broke the rules of the game with a second question:

"When was the last time you sang by yourself?"

"I've never sung by myself, or with anyone else," Rita replied.

Did that make her boring?

"What about you?" She looked into his eyes, which were the same shade of blue as the sky they were flying in.

"I was singing just last night when I was cooking some spaghetti, before she–" Andrew paused, and a dark shadow fell over his face. His eyes darkened now to the shade of the ocean.

"Yes?" For no reason at all Rita was eager to know who this *she* was.

"Oh, nothing."

The plane dipped, hitting another air pocket and this time Rita gave a small yelp. She looked out the window and for a fleeting moment imagined her heart jolting the same way as the wings of the plane. She dug her nails into the armrest.

"Here, hold my hand if that makes you feel better."

Andrew waved it gently before resting it again. "If the plane crashes, we fall together."

Taking in the horrified look on Rita's face, Andrew added, "Sorry, bad joke." He was so close to her that their knees were almost touching again. A beam of sunlight shone through the little window, making his hair look glossy and bringing out the auburn hue.

Slowly, Rita placed her hand over his, noticing there was no ring on his finger. She felt a brief jolt of excitement, followed by a mellow satisfaction.

After her mum's death, Rita had stopped painting her fingernails, simply because she couldn't stop biting them. Staring at her nails now, as she held the hand of this handsome stranger, she felt ashamed.

How could you do this to Samuel? said the voice.

I'm not doing anything. Andrew's helping me calm down a little, that's all.

You must think I was born yesterday, quipped the voice.

"Okay. Next question," Andrew said, mercifully putting an end to the inner chitchat. "Let me think. What do you do for a living?

Other than running away from my country in search of my boyfriend and traveling with another girl's identity card?

"Something very different than what I was meant to be doing," said Rita, trying to keep her voice steady.

He winked at her. "Remember, be honest."

"Okay." Rita shifted in her seat, still holding his hand. Her hands and feet were cold, and her stomach was queasy, but this small talk was helping a bit. "I work in a little restaurant in the city where I live." She had to laugh at that. Rita was born and raised in Durrës. She'd loved her city before her mum had got sick. Located on the Adriatic coast, Durrës was the oldest city in Albania, and the second largest. But she knew that this extra information probably wouldn't matter to the Englishman sitting next to her. "It's a tiny place and not much happens there," she continued. "Anyway, I majored in photography in college, but as it turns out, that doesn't put bread on the table."

Worried that the Englishman would look down on her for her first job, Rita had decided to mention her greatest passion – photography. Her camera, the last birthday gift from her mum, was in her handbag. She nibbled at what was left of the nails on her left hand. Was she giving too much information away to a complete stranger?

"What about you? I mean, what do you do besides rescue nervous fliers?"

"I'm a Crypto trader. Mainly BTC."

Rita must have looked confused because Andrew went on to explain:

"Crypto is digital money, to put it simply."

Well, now she was even more confused. How could you trust in something you couldn't see, especially when that something was money? Few people had money in their bank accounts in Albania; most preferred to hide what little they had under their mattresses. And then there was Rita, who fell into the nothing-to-hide-under-the-mattress-category.

"What does that mean?"

Rita noticed the dark voice in her head had finally gone quiet. Crypto trading was clearly not in the field of its 'expertise.' That was a relief.

"It means I work for myself. I trade. Sometimes I lose, but all in all, I win much more often. There's ups and downs, just like life, but you learn to deal with it. All I need is a laptop and Wi-Fi. I can go on holiday whenever I want, since I only trade for a couple of hours a day."

What if your life is just an endless series of downs and you don't have any idea how to deal with it? she wanted to ask, but that would steer the conversation into the kind of waters she didn't want to swim in right now.

"So, you don't go to work in an office?" Rita asked instead.

"Nope."

"Weird."

"You're not the only one who thinks that." Andrew winked.

Out of the window beside her, the crest of the Swiss Alps was just a dot on the horizon.

"Ladies and gentlemen, we've started our descent to Milan Fiumicino Airport. We expect to land in about thirty minutes." The voice of the pilot snapped Rita back to reality. This little chat had offered her some respite, but now she was about to have to face the real world again.

Andrew smiled at her. "I remember on one flight when a pilot said, 'please don't forget your belongings, and that includes your children and spouses.'"

She laughed. It was nice that this complete stranger had tried to take her mind off her troubles. In the last few weeks, her life had become such an avalanche of misery and fear that she had forgotten how to smile.

"It worked, didn't it? The game?"

It had worked. Amazingly, Rita had forgotten all about the turbulence. However, she'd also forgotten that once she set foot in Italy, she'd have to face border officials again. And she'd definitely forgotten how she'd been planning to deceive the kind man sitting beside her. He didn't deserve that. She'd just have to create a new plan B. She didn't need a man to get her out of this, but it'd sure be nice if he could teach her another game to get her through what was about to come next.

6

Saturday afternoon, 26 October 2019

Milan's rooftops looked like Lego pieces as the plane started its descent, until bit by bit, the buildings grew bigger and bigger, and soon Rita could clearly see the hundreds of cars cruising along the highway. In that short space of time, she'd reached a decision. She would go through border control with her 'new' ID card – the Italian residency card that had been taken from a willing Romanian girl who'd been paid to 'lose' it. The traffickers had told Rita's cousin Chloe that the girl would wait a week before reporting it. Then again, they'd also said that the border officers in London never asked questions and never called the warrantor. Which they had. If the girl had already reported her ID card missing, then Rita could get arrested for theft.

She was gripped by a mixture of fear and anger, but what had she expected? Wasn't a trafficker's job to promise the impossible?

If Rita was lucky today, then she would be able to stay in Italy until she could find her way back to London. Because, no matter what, she had to find Samuel. She also needed to put these last few minutes of craziness with the Englishman out of her mind.

The plane finally landed with a thud. Rita didn't realise she'd been clenching her hands into fists until her nails almost cut through her skin. Her jaw was so tense it ached. She'd survived a turbulent flight. She was back on the ground in one piece, but the ground had different rules than the sky. Rita took a deep breath and glanced at Andrew, who was unfastening his seatbelt. She was strangely sad that she'd never see him again. He was still jabbering away as if they'd known each other forever, but her mind was somewhere else. Now she had to come up with a plan to escape Andrew, too.

I don't understand why you don't ask him for help, He might want to help you. Wow, the voice in her head had changed course. *Unless you're scared that he'll turn you down?*

How people treat you is their karma; how you react is yours, Rita's true inner voice responded, recalling something that she had once read. *I don't want to deceive anyone. It will only come back to Auntie me.*

You honestly buy into that crap? The cynical voice scoffed, back to its usual tricks.

Why hadn't she left her stupid voices up in the air?

45

That would have made all of this a lot easier. Now it was time to act, but her voice of doubt was predictably and deliberately delaying her.

People were already getting up to open the overhead compartments, creating chaos in the aisle. Actually, that was a good thing: The greater the pandemonium, the easier it would be for Rita to slip away undetected.

The flight attendant with the long false eyelashes was talking animatedly to her colleague. "I'm hitting the shops before our next flight."

Rita's little makeup bag was still under her chair. The idea of leaving it behind made her heart ache; the Dior foundation that Chloe had gifted her from London was inside. She'd only used it twice! But she couldn't ask the cabin crew for her bag, lest they remember *what* she was and that *maybe* she should be accompanied off the flight.

Pretending to rub her eyes, Rita sneaked a look outside. No police cars. For the first time in her life, she was genuinely relieved that everybody had forgotten about her.

She looked up to the sky but then remembered she was still on the aircraft. *If there is a God up there, I hope he has my back. I need him now more than ever.*

You can't impose on God's will, her irritable voice muttered. The voice was right.

Over the last fifty years, religion had been expunged

from her country. Her mum and dad had grown up not believing in God. Rita herself had clung to fragments of what could be called faith, but the puzzle was never complete. Time after time, especially after Samuel had left for London, Rita had prayed to God for help, even though she wasn't sure if He would listen to her. Maybe she'd been too late, maybe she hadn't believed enough. She couldn't say if she missed her brush with faith, or if there was a void inside her. You couldn't yearn for something, for someone, you had never really known.

Andrew was still busy putting on his jacket when Rita squeezed past him. She merged with the first passengers dashing off the aircraft the moment the door was opened. It was rude of her to not say goodbye, but she had to get to border control. She didn't want to run the risk of him seeing her get stopped.

She loosened her bun as she walked and fished around inside her handbag for her fake reading glasses, the same ones she had used the day before. An elderly couple was already standing in line at border control, and soon there would be hundreds of people behind Rita. The sooner this nightmare was over, the better. She was taking a risk, a shot in the dark, but it was the only bullet she had.

Sweat ran down Rita's back at the sight of the same officer who had let her go the day before. He hadn't seen her yet. She could still change direction and use

47

the Non-EU Passengers Lane. *Just be yourself, for God's sake, Rita,* the callous inner voice chided her. But what did 'be yourself' mean? Go to the Non-EU Passengers Lane, or reveal her true identity and return to the hell she had come from?

Rita made up her mind and pushed a lock of hair behind her ear. Then she immediately pulled it back again. The officer sees millions of passengers. Why should he remember her face in particular? Her forehead was damp. She could feel her hair curling at the roots.

In a moment of déjà vu, Rita remembered her teeth chattering in London while waiting for the officer to call her. She closed her eyes so tightly it was almost painful, but she knew it wasn't going to help her one bit.

The border control officer's voice jolted Rita back to the present. The old couple in front of her was now nowhere to be seen and he was calling her. Rita shuffled towards him, paranoid that the back of her T-shirt was soaked with sweat. Her hands trembled as she handed over the Italian residency card belonging to a completely different girl. She touched the rim of her fake glasses as beads of perspiration gathered above her upper lip. She was a fake woman, inside and out.

The officer scanned Rita's face as she held up the card.

"I think I saw you yesterday," he said, raising an eyebrow. Rita nodded. It was better not to talk; her voice would give her away. "The one who wanted to surprise her boyfriend for his birthday, right?" Rita nodded again. She was on the verge of tears, and the lump in her throat was growing.

I told you, you talk too much, the voice muttered.

Rita chewed on her lower lip. She could taste the salty flavour of perspiration in her mouth.

"I've got a pretty good memory." The officer grinned, looking pleased with himself. "I certainly didn't expect to see you today of all people." He wasn't looking at the card, or at his computer, thank God. He was only looking at Rita's face. She had to say something.

"Yeah, it didn't go quite how I expected. I got a bigger surprise than he did. I found him with someone else." Her voice shook, but at least this situation gave her a valid excuse to show some emotion. Even though the story was fake, the idea of Samuel betraying her genuinely hurt. "So, I got on the next flight back."

Rita sighed, hoping he wouldn't ask her any more questions. How easily lies were spilling from her lips lately. She rubbed at her mouth, as if trying to keep the truth inside, perspiration now coating her fingertips too. She forced herself to look the officer in the eye. She'd seen this bit of body language in movies. The cooler you came across, the less suspicious you were.

"*Mascalzone*," he said, handing her back the ID card. "*Mi dispiace.*"

"Me too," Rita said, in a lower but slightly more confident tone.

She was free! For the moment, anyway. She resisted the urge to jump for joy, forcing herself to walk calmly towards the exit. Her mind was swirling with possibilities. Clearly the real owner of the ID hadn't reported it yet, which meant Rita still had up to a week to use it. Perhaps in that time she could try another route to the UK. She still had some money left to buy a train ticket. But no more Southend airport, and no more flights. There was more than one way to her island destination.

First, I need to find a cheap place to stay, then I'll call Chloe, Rita thought as she scrolled through hotel websites on her iPhone. But the rooms were all so expensive. Just when she thought she would never find one at a decent price, she stumbled upon Hostel California. Twenty euros per night. She passed her tongue over her teeth.

If I skip lunch and dinner, I can buy myself a few days to put a plan together.

She called the reservation line. The room was cheap because it was a shared room, but that was OK. It was only for a few days, and it was affordable.

"Rita, is that you?"

Somebody tapped her on the shoulder. Rita spun round and found herself nose to nose with Andrew. He still had his passport and wallet in his hands.

"I looked everywhere for you. I thought I'd left you behind on the plane," he said with a grin, reminding her of his lame joke. "I didn't recognize you with the glasses."

Shit.

"Ah, yes, the glasses. I needed to rest my eyes. I didn't sleep much last night."

She didn't need them anymore and went to take them off.

"They look nice on you," he remarked.

"I'll keep them on then," she said with a small smile.

Rita sneaked the scrunchie out of her pocket, and, trying to look as casual as possible, fixed her hair into the same low bun she'd worn on the plane.

"Bumping into you again is a sign we should go for a drink together."

Rita hesitated and he pushed out his lower lip in a pout.

She'd survived her ordeal so far, and she supposed that was enough of an achievement to celebrate.

"OK. Why not?"

7

Milan, Italy
Saturday evening, 27 October 2019

The sun hung low over the magical *Piazza del Duomo*, the majestic white cathedral looming over them. Rita couldn't believe she was in the heart of Milan with a man she'd only just met.

Her eyes flicked from one side of the square to the other. She'd only seen this place in photographs – it was even more beautiful in real life.

"It's amazing, isn't it?" said Andrew, reading her mind. He pointed to the top of the cathedral. "It's like a giant sandcastle. Crazy to imagine how they built that back then without the technology we have today. Simply incredible. Although, being a local, I'm sure you're no longer impressed."

Great. Of course, he would think she was from Milan. He was probably expecting her to show him around. She was just about to make a non-committal comment when two pigeons landed on her shoulder, making them both laugh. She felt bad she had nothing to feed them, but she could take a picture and post it on Instagram. Her followers would love that.

"Would you mind taking a photo?" she asked Andrew, handing him her phone.

"I'd love to!"

Rita couldn't believe how agreeable this man was. For a moment, she forgot who she was and what she was doing. It was more than just the view, the pigeons, and being in the company of a kind, attractive man that was making her dizzy. She hadn't eaten for over forty hours.

"I need a cigarette," Rita said, hoping that would stave off her appetite in the short term. She offered one to Andrew, but he shook his head.

As hard as it was to tear herself away from the sightseeing, her vision was getting blurry. Maybe too much happiness was a bad thing. She certainly wasn't used to it. She fished her cigarettes out of her bag, removed one from the box, and struck a match. She'd been longing for one since the border officer in London had stopped her.

"I'm starving," said Andrew. "I bet you are too. My stomach is rumbling."

He was right. A cigarette wasn't really what she needed. Her throat was sore, and her lips were dry.

After some food and a glass of water, she would be fine.

She took two long puffs, stubbed out the cigarette with the tip of her Nikes, and shuffled after him.

According to Andrew *Il Milano* restaurant was a good place to eat. When the lift stopped at the seventh floor of the building, where the restaurant was located, stars were dancing in front of Rita's eyes. For a moment, she had to lean against the wall just to steady herself.

Andrew was already walking ahead to the terrace, as if he'd been there before. She straightened up as he found a table for two and beckoned her over.

Rita sat down, grateful to be off her feet, and looked at the vista surrounding them. It was a mellow October evening and the view over the *Piazza* was stunning. A soft breeze blew from the south, and far away on the horizon the sky was now the colour of embers.

Andrew took off his jacket and threw it over the back of his chair. Rita didn't want to catch a cold, so she kept her parka on. She was Mediterranean, after all. When she was a kid, her mum never allowed her to dress in a short-sleeved top until May. At the end of August, when summer was officially over, she would always wear a warm jumper, even if the temperature was still above twenty degrees.

"How long will you be staying in Italy?" Rita asked.

"I don't know yet. I just packed and left, but probably a week."

Why am I sitting here in this romantic restaurant with a stranger?

"Have you been here before?" Rita asked, looking at the top of the cathedral.

"Yeah, two years ago. I was here with…" Andrew inhaled deeply. "Rachel."

Okay, so the 'she' who came back last night while he was cooking spaghetti is Rachel.

"Archie was with us too."

"You have a son?"

Rita's voice was breezy and clipped even though she was trying to appear casual.

Andrew chuckled. "No, Archie is my dog, a German Shepherd. Here, I have some pictures."

He handed Rita his phone, and as he passed it to her, she accidentally touched his fingers. The same jolt of electricity ran through her body as before. Good thing she hadn't asked for his help, she'd be ashamed if Andrew knew the truth about her. She couldn't trust this strange pull between them because she'd never been with any other man, no one but Samuel. It was just the adrenaline of having got back into Italy safely, she reassured herself.

A waitress arrived at their table, a big smile on her face. Rita held the woman's gaze for a moment. The rumbling deep in the pit of her stomach was telling her that she needed food more than anything, but her brain was too sleepy to focus on the menu. It was too early for a proper dinner, and lunchtime had already passed. In Albania no one ate dinner before 8 p.m., sometimes even 9 p.m. The clock at the *Piazza* read 6 p.m. How very British of Andrew.

"How about a couple of mozzarella paninis and some beer?"

"I don't drink alcohol," Rita said.

"Really?" he sounded shocked. "Good for you."

She thought back to her dad and the perpetual smell of raki on his breath, but she didn't explain further.

"Orange juice please."

The waitress left and Andrew pointed at the picture of his dog. "He was a little puppy here. But now he's huge."

"Cute," Rita said. "I had a little puppy once too. Here," she pulled out her phone, and opened her Instagram account. Back in happier days Rita had posted hundreds of pictures of Luk. She hadn't looked at her Instagram in the last few days and noticed her followers had now reached 100k.

"Adorable," Andrew said, his face softening as he looked at the picture.

"He died," she added. "In a really bad way."

What was she doing? She didn't have to say anything.

Andrew's face flooded with concern, making her want to tell him everything.

"I think someone I know poisoned him. His name was Luk."

"I'm so sorry," Andrew said, placing his hand over hers ever so briefly. An awkward silence descended upon them. Silence was always dangerous.

Rita's eyes filled with tears as memories of that day flooded her mind, breaking her heart once again, for the millionth time in twenty-four hours. How embarrassing. She was a grown woman crying in front of a man she'd only met that morning. Yet losing a dog was like losing your first love.

I should know. I've lost both, said the kinder of the two voices in her head.

"It's fine," she said, noting the look on Andrew's face.

"Is this your account?" Andrew asked, pointing at her Instagram page.

She nodded.

"Wow! You're famous. So many followers."

"People seem to like my pictures."

Rita took a sip of her juice and resisted the temptation to post the new pictures Andrew had taken at the *Piazza del Duomo*. She couldn't do that. There were people looking for her.

With Andrew's phone still in her hand, Rita swiped on to look at more photos of his dog, but an image of a woman popped up instead.

"I'm sorry! I think I scrolled too far," she said, handing him back the phone. Although not before stealing another glance at the woman's face.

"Don't worry about it."

"Is that Rachel?"

Andrew nodded and ordered another bottle of beer.

"Why is she not with you today?"

Rita knew she was behaving like those annoying busybodies on the bus who keep asking personal questions even though you have your earbuds in, but he looked nervous, and she suddenly wanted to know everything about him.

He took a deep breath. "Because I wanted to be alone. Maybe she *would* be here with me today if she hadn't had a six-month crush on some bloody Australian." His voice cracked at the edges.

"I'm sorry to hear that. I hope she's recovered from the accident," Rita said.

What kind of person are you, Andrew, leaving a woman just because she's been injured?

Andrew looked confused at first, and then chuckled, shaking his head.

"She didn't have a crash. I said she had a *crush* on somebody. They sound similar, but they mean completely different things. Although both hurt a lot." He grinned at his own joke, and Rita was happy she'd made him laugh, even though she still didn't understand what was funny about it. "Anyway, she showed at my door yesterday evening, full of remorse, but I wasn't interested. I packed and left this morning. That's it. But enough Rachel talk."

"She's beautiful and I think you're a lucky guy."

Even though Rita had seen the photo for less than a second, she could have given an exact description of Rachel. Rita had the eye of a photographer, after all.

Rachel was blonde. In the photo, she was wearing glossy pink lipstick that perfectly complemented her tanned face. But what Rita liked most was her smoky eyes. Rita had always failed when she'd tried to do that kind of makeup. Rachel's eyes were an ordinary brown, not chocolate but a rich, interesting brown. Rita had also admired the lemon capri pants and black sleeveless turtleneck the woman had been wearing. She was the definition of flawless.

She's way better-looking than you, the voice chimed in.

Struggling to steer the conversation away from Rachel and now herself, Rita put her fingertips to her temples, as if the right words might pour out the side of her head. If she hadn't seen that damn photo, they would still be talking about dogs, for goodness' sake.

"Did I say something wrong?" Andrew asked.

You should leave now, the voice in her head yelled.

"Not at all. I just have a headache."

But that was a lie. She didn't have a headache. What she had was a vile, self-sabotaging voice inside her head that never shut up. It was a constant inner dialogue that had started the day her mum died.

8

The nurse is calling my name, but I don't want to wake up. I'm lost in my memories. My mum died today. Actually, she died twice. Once, after she'd been reduced to skin and bones, and a second time, when my father remarried.

She must have made it to heaven. I'm still floating in a white sea of nothingness, and I wonder if mum is here, with me, in the clouds?

It's not rare in Albania for patients to be misdiagnosed by doctors, but sadly, that was not the case with my mum. The doctor had been right. The illness progressed so fast that within three months, Mum was dead. Helen came every day to visit Dad and me. In the beginning, Mum refused her help, but it eventually got to the point where she needed help just to get out of bed and take a bath. Helen and I hid all the mirrors in the house. I wanted Mum to remember herself as young, strong, and beautiful. What remained of her now was nothing but a skeletal frame so fragile I was afraid to touch her. When Mum attempted to smile, I could see the skin stretching over her cheekbones, her face a dull shade of yellow.

Dad too was reduced to half the man he'd once been. There were no more jokes, no more smiles. At night I heard him crying.

When Auntie Angela came from London, Helen retreated into the shadows. No one saw her, but she made sure that the house was kept clean, that we had fresh flowers, and that there was a home-cooked meal on the table every day. If any of us needed more sleep or some fresh air, Helen was always there to take over. Mum had been right: I'd misjudged Helen.

The day my mum died the sky wept too. It rarely rains on the last day of July in my country, and people interpreted it as a miracle. Dad knocked on my door at 5 a.m., as if he was Death himself. I could already feel Mum's absence. I ran to her room and stopped at the threshold. The world – at least the world I had known up until that moment – stood still. Mum looked at peace, as if she had merely fallen into a deep sleep.

I fell to my knees and howled to the heavens, hoping my voice would wake her up. But nothing happened. I pushed my clenched fists into my mouth until I tasted blood. Bit by bit, Mum's body had gotten smaller, weaker. And although I had known this moment was coming, deep down, I'd refused to believe it, always hoping for some sort of divine intervention.

How were Dad and I supposed to live without her?

Dad wrapped his arms around my shoulders and gently tried to ease me away from Mum's body. He said my name, but his voice faded away before it left his mouth. Neither Mum nor I moved.

"Please, open your eyes. Please!" The man standing by my bed is calling my name again, but I'm too far away. I remember saying the same thing to my mum the morning of her death. Begging her. Putting my ear to her cold chest and praying for a heartbeat. But there was nothing.

This was the first time the ground shook beneath my feet. After that, I stopped counting the tremors.

The news of Mum's death spread like wildfire in the city. Friends and relatives – people I had never seen before – rushed to our small apartment. I'd seen movies where funeral directors went to collect the bodies of the deceased from their homes, but in my country that was out of the question. According to tradition, the body had to be washed by a close relative, but I wouldn't allow anyone to go near my mum's bed. She was *my* mum.

I locked the door of her room and bathed her as if she were an infant. I'd helped Helen and Auntie

Angela bathe her before, but that was when she was alive. Now it was different, she was naked and staring into nothingness. I thought I was going to faint, but instead I bathed her in my own tears as I whispered all that remained unsaid between us. She'd promised to be by my side for as long as I needed her. Well, I needed her now.

When the words and tears finally dried up, I hugged my mum for the last time. Then, possessed by a strength I had never experienced, I opened her wardrobe and took out a black floral dress I'd never seen her wear. She would get to wear this dress, after all.

An envelope fell to the floor and my knees buckled at the sight of it.

I picked it up. 'To my Rita, when I'm gone,' it read, in Mum's handwriting.

Tears, cold and dense like hail, rolled down my cheeks. All the colour in my world instantly vanished and the bedroom took on a plutonian hue. Through my bloodshot eyes, I glanced again at Mum's bare body. I had to dress her first, otherwise she'd get cold.

I was *mad* with grief. The man standing by my bedside, holding my hand is also going *insane*.

He's called my name so many times it's beginning to sound strange even to my ears. Last night he tried to open my eyes, gently pulling my eyelids up as if it would wake me. I remember trying that trick with

Mum too. It doesn't work, but I can't tell him that.

I drift back to my past, placing the envelope on the nightstand and choosing the best pair of shoes in Mum's wardrobe. I put a bottle of lavender fragrance and a folded white handkerchief close to her right hand, just in case she needed it on her journey.

It takes me over an hour to dress Mum for the last time.

I double-check that I haven't forgotten anything, then kneel close to her body. Taking her stiff hand in mine, I promise that no other woman will ever replace her. I will take care of Dad, and I will take care of the home she has made for us too. I might only know how to read books and take pretty pictures, but I will learn to do all of the things she used to do.

Knowing that this is my last moment alone with my mum, I lay my head against her chest. I would trade the world for one more hug. But Mum's arms don't move.

I stay there, just like this, with no sense of the passage of time. Has it been an hour, or just a few minutes? Death likes to toy with time. A knock on the door yanks me back to reality. Dad, Auntie Angela, and Helen are outside begging me to open up. My time with Mum has run out. I lift my head and slowly wipe away my tears. The envelope is still on the nightstand. I pick it up, and I can tell from the weight and shape of it that there is more than just a letter inside. I tear it open and find a silver necklace with a cherub pendant.

'May this angel look after you when I'm gone'.

That's it? One sentence? No guidance as to what I should do now, how to live my life without her?

I take off Samuel's necklace and replace it with this one.

I pull myself up using the metal bed rails, but my legs give way. The room tilts, and I have to grip the bed rail firmly now to steady myself. There is another knock at the door.

"Bye, Mum," I whisper, dragging my feet towards the door.

The moment I open the door, I'm bombarded by the sound of women crying, solemnly recounting various moments of my mum's life. They rub salt into my wounds, asking repeatedly what will happen to me and Dad now that Mum has gone.

People swoop in and out of my house like ravenous crows.

I squeeze my eyes shut, hoping that when I open them, they will all have disappeared, and Mum will be back. Unfortunately, no matter how long I wait, everyone is still there, except for Mum. Dad is surrounded by a group of men. Their cigarette smoke blurs my view, but Dad's hair is greyer than it had been that morning, his shoulders are hunched with the weight of grief, and his face is etched with despair. He isn't crying though. Custom doesn't allow it. A man should never cry for his woman, not in public, anyway. He nods silently at everyone who speaks to him, but I can tell his mind is miles away.

I bite my nails, one by one, and when I am done, I walk aimlessly around the house, staggering from one room to another. I am searching for Mum, waiting for her to come out of the kitchenette holding a tray of cups filled with my favourite strawberry pudding. In my mind's eye, I see her greeting all the people in the room and telling me that it's all been a bad dream. A dream I get to wake up from. But Mum's dead body lies motionless in her bedroom and I'm afraid to go in.

The man by my bed asks me to wake up. There are other voices in the room today. Women's voices. They are familiar, something tugs at my heart, but I'm too far away.

I float out of the room again because the call of the voices from the past is stronger than those in the present. The strangers in my house on the day of Mum's funeral look at me like I'm a ghost.

"Poor girl," they say.

Maybe I am a ghost now. My body is still lying in the hospital bed but I'm not in it. I'm here, trapped somewhere between my now and my then.

Some of the strangers step on my toes as they hurry

to get out of my house; others bump into me on their way in. Nobody cares about my pain.

All I want to do is cry, but I have no tears left.

It's still pouring when we put Mum's coffin into the ground. The earth devours her instantly, but I can't process a thing. She can't be in that black, ugly, and now dirty coffin. I thought someone would save her, that someone would save me too. I look at Dad. His shoulders are shaking. He *is* crying. I want to say *'Go and pull her up, Dad. She can't stay down there! What are you doing to her?'* But the words won't come out.

Samuel hugs me. I give myself over to the comfort of his embrace, burrow my head into his chest, and sob.

The sun breaks through the clouds, as if heaven now has what it wants and is rewarding us with its warmth. People scatter like birds, looking for shade. Albanian summers are hot, and the sun shines bright as ever, scalding the earth again until steam rises, as if the earth's core is about to burst into flames.

Only when we return from the cemetery do I fully accept my loss; Mum doesn't open the door like she always did. Overcome with grief and anger, I storm into her room and fling open her wardrobe. Her clothes are neatly folded: her summer dresses and her winter ones, her favourite scarf, her shoes, her coats. They're all here.

Everything is here except Mum. I touch the fabric, and tears stream down my face. The pain is cracking open my chest.

Dad, Auntie Angela, and Helen are still taking care of the last visitors when I pull Mum's favourite dress out of the wardrobe and head to my room. I lie on my stomach, inhaling her scent as I sob. My heart is shattering. A crystal glass smashing on the linoleum floor.

After a while, I hear footsteps approaching.

"Rita, honey," Auntie Angela says, her voice full of sadness. She too has lost someone: her sister, her best friend. I know that, but it doesn't stop me thinking that Mum belonged only to me.

Auntie Angela and her daughter – my cousin, Chloe – lived far away from us. When she was younger, Auntie had fallen for a young guy, a Londoner who had worked at the British Embassy in our country. Soon afterwards they were married, and Chloe was born. I remember when they still lived in the city. Chloe was my best friend until I met Samuel. We had days out on the beach with our mums and ate big chocolate ice creams. But the happy times didn't last. My uncle's role at the Embassy came to an end, and Chloe's family moved back to London. By that time, Chloe was five. Not long after they settled in London, my Auntie filed for divorce. She and Chloe have been living in between the two countries ever since.

But in their case, misfortune had been a blessing in disguise. Auntie Angela now had a British passport, and as part of the divorce settlement, she got half her ex-husband's assets. She set up a business of her own with the money and was now a self-confidence life coach.

Every time she and Chloe came to visit, they would bring me the most wonderful princess dolls; nobody had those in our town. But nothing about my life would be wonderful again, and no amount of my Auntie and cousin's beautiful gifts from London could ever change that.

I want to be left alone, but Auntie Angela keeps talking. She sits on the edge of the bed, patting my shoulder. It's not mum's hand, but at least it's warm and familiar.

"Rita, you have to be strong. Do it for your mum. She's watching you."

"How do you know that?" I turn and look my Auntie in the eye.

"I'm sorry," she blubbers. "Luna was my sister, my rock, she was my everything. I'm alone too. I'm lost without her."

Not true. You have Chloe.

"I'm the one who's alone," I say. "I don't care about anybody else's pain. I don't care how difficult this is for you. Without Mum, I can't even breathe, Auntie! Do you understand that?"

The question hung in the air. Where was my mum with her wise words about getting back up and brushing yourself off after being knocked down by life?

My Auntie holds me tightly and our grief becomes one. I bury my head in her chest and whisper, "I'm sorry."

"Shh-shhh-shhh, that's okay, honey." Auntie Angela strokes my hair. "When my mum –your grandmother, died it was as if the entire universe had collapsed. Luna's life and mine fell to pieces. I thought the sun wouldn't rise the next day. But it did. Life goes on, my dear. Luna and I found the strength to carry on. We grew up, we fell in love, we had children. You will find the strength too. You will get older. You will have your own family. Time heals."

"But how can time heal this giant hole in my soul?" I thump my chest with my fists as hard as I can. It feels like someone is rubbing my heart with sandpaper until it bleeds.

Alone.

It was the first word the horrible voice in my head whispered that night. From that moment on, the negative mind chatter wouldn't stop.

Now I realise the voice is wrong. I'm not alone. A man and a woman are by my bed.

"You need to eat," the woman says to the man, handing him a flat square box.

Snatches of conversation fill the room along with an aroma that tugs at something deep inside of me. The smell of baked cheese, basil, and tomato sends me back someplace. *Have I ever been to Italy?*

9

Milan, Italy
Sunday, 27 October 2019

Despite Andrew's insistence on accompanying her, Rita walked alone to her hostel. She didn't want him to see her cheap accommodation, and she needed to call her cousin and tell her what had happened. Let her know she was safe.

They reached his fancy NH hotel and Andrew kissed Rita on both cheeks before she headed toward Via Lambrate and her destination, Hostel California.

They'd shared a few special moments, she could tell Andrew had felt them too, but she was thankful he hadn't invited her to his room. She'd seen a lot of movies about tourists and girls who had one-night stands. It wasn't something she knew anything about, nor could she imagine doing it herself. The question was, had he asked her, would she have said yes?

Every now and then she touched her cheek, to

check if the kiss was still there. They'd agreed to meet tomorrow, and Rita had promised herself it would be just one more day, just one last time, and then she would disappear from his life. So much in Rita's life had chugged along like an old steam engine, and at each station she'd made a long stop, overanalysing every detail. Yet now, in less than twenty-four hours, her life had become a high-speed train. Was she ready to board it?

On the other hand, she'd never done anything spontaneous in her life. Let this be the first and the last, and then she would figure out how to get to London.

Rita knew Durrës, her own city, like the back of her hand, but she didn't know Milan, and she had no idea how to get to the hostel. Despite the best efforts of her phone's GPS, she managed to get lost. After turning this way and that, wandering along unfamiliar streets, she finally found the entrance to a subway station. She knew she'd be able to orientate herself from there.

There was no subway in Albania, so using the underground was another new experience for Rita, but Andrew had made it look easy enough when they'd travelled from the airport to *Piazza del Duomo*. Rita hated the idea of racing through underground tunnels, but according to her GPS, that was the fastest way to reach her destination.

She hadn't slept a wink in that plastic chair at

Southend airport the night before, so all she wanted to do now was get into bed and pass out.

Rita took a seat in the almost empty carriage and as soon as the train rushed into the dark tunnel, she instantly found herself panicking and gasping for air. It hadn't been like this with Andrew. He'd made her feel safe.

The only other passengers in the carriage were two boys who were deep in discussion. With a jolt of alarm, Rita realized they were slowly moving closer to her.

She couldn't understand the language they were speaking – it wasn't Italian – but she could tell from the looks on their faces that they were up to no good. Instinctively, she wrapped her arms around herself. Maybe it would be better to get off at the next station. Without a second thought, she stood up and moved in front of the doors. As she waited for the subway to stop and the doors to open, a feeling of dread washed over her, sweat dampening her palms and coating her forehead.

The boys watched her, a predatory look in their eyes, like hungry wolves sizing up their next meal. They said something in their incomprehensible language and then laughed, pinning her with their gaze.

Rita inhaled a deep breath then tried to let it out slowly, afraid that even the sound of her breathing might trigger them to pounce.

Please, train, stop now. Please! Let me get out.

But no one could help her this deep underground. It was late, maybe even God was sleeping. Rita gripped the cold metal pole beside her so tightly that her knuckles cracked. She wished she could yank the pole free, so she would have a weapon to defend herself.

Just when she feared her legs would give way, the train door opened. Rita snatched her luggage and took one step towards the platform. But before she could take another, one of the boys cut the strap of her handbag with a knife. Then the other slammed her in the back with his elbow and she collapsed on the floor like a dead bird falling from the sky and splattering on the pavement. Her suitcase fell on top of her, slamming into her ankle. Before Rita could figure out what had happened, the door of the train closed. The boy grinned. He held her bag up like a trophy with one hand and stuck his middle finger up with the other. Angry tears streamed down Rita's cheek – the same cheek Andrew had kissed just moments earlier.

"*Zot, çfarë të kam bërë?*" she yelled to God in her own language.

When everything is falling apart, no other language but your own will do. The voice inside her head reminded her to be quiet. She couldn't afford to call attention to herself. She also couldn't report the theft to the police. She too was a criminal, after all. A woman on the run.

Shit! Her whole life was in that bag! Her camera, her real passport, her fake identity, and what little money she had to her name. Damn it. She hated that suppressing her anger and hatred had become her new way of life.

Kneeling on the floor of the Metro, Rita couldn't stop shaking. She touched the charm on her necklace. *I'm sorry, Mum. I'm so sorry they took your camera.*

Luckily, she still had her phone. Like most people her age, Rita kept her phone in her hand or her pocket. The charger was in her handbag, though, gone with the rest of her things. To conserve what little battery remained, Rita turned her phone off. *What the hell am I going to do now?* She couldn't call Chloe and she couldn't go back to Andrew's hotel. She couldn't ask for his help without admitting who she was and what she had done. Today had already been difficult enough, and now this.

Wiping away her tears, Rita scanned the platform. She put her hands on the metal bar close to her and stood up, shifting her weight from one foot to the other to steady herself.

In the corner of the station, she caught sight of something.

Rita, have you lost your mind? her inner voice cried. *Don't go over there.*

But her curiosity got the better of her. Someone might be hurt. She had nothing to lose. She was so exhausted, mentally, spiritually, and physically, that she wasn't even afraid of what else might happen to her. She'd hit rock bottom and felt like nothing could harm her anymore.

A person lay on the floor with a few pieces of cardboard beneath them serving as a mattress. Rita couldn't help but sniff as she took a step closer, catching a whiff of some unpleasant scent. It wasn't a man, but a woman. She breathed a sigh of relief. A woman couldn't harm her, right?

The stranger's pale flesh was visible through the holes in her clothes and her toes poked out the ends of her socks. She didn't appear to have any shoes. From the grey mat of hair plastered to her scalp and the wrinkles around her eyes, Rita could tell that the woman was old. Either that, or life had aged her faster than normal.

As Rita came closer, the foul stench of body odour filled her nostrils, making her stomach turn. Rather than recoil, however, Rita knelt down about a metre away from the woman and waved her hand back and forth in front of the woman's face. Still, the stranger didn't move. Was she dead? No. Rita could see the rise and fall of the woman's chest. She sighed again with relief. The last thing she needed right now was to discover a dead body.

Trying not to make a sound, she gently pulled a piece of cardboard out from beneath the woman's body and sat on it.

What if she wakes up and kills you?

Rita had run out of words and energy to argue with the voice in her head.

The platform was dark, cold, and reeked of urine, yet the expression on the woman's face was peaceful, as if she were sleeping in a five-star hotel. A mouldy duvet covered half her body. Well, this was a zero-star room. Rita slowly opened her suitcase, putting her hand over the zip to muffle the sound. She stopped several times until it was open just enough that she could reach in and pull out a cotton sweater. She folded it up and placed it on the suitcase. That would have to be her pillow tonight. The woman certainly didn't have anything better. Rita's parka would serve as a blanket. She threw it over her body and tugged her arms into the sleeves, just in case the woman woke up and tried to steal her winter coat. She pulled her knees to her chest, her kneecaps almost touching her chin.

The floor was icy cold, and Rita was shivering. She pulled her winter jacket tighter around her, but it didn't help. The hard concrete tiles beneath her ribs made it impossible to close her eyes. Nearly forty-eight hours had passed since she'd slept. *How long can you go without sleep?*

Eventually her eyelids drooped shut, and she began to dream. Someone was covering her with a warm woollen blanket, and beneath her, a feather mattress cocooned her body. A soft spring breeze wafted through white curtains. She had never seen this room before, but she recognized the aroma of chamomile tea. Rita reached out her hand to grab the porcelain mug that was on the bedside table, but somebody coughed, knocking over the mug and spilling the tea. The warm room gave way to cold, dark squalor. Rita's body ached. She couldn't tell how long she'd been asleep. It could have been minutes or hours.

She rubbed her eyes. Where was she? There was a dark, mysterious face looming over her. She pinched herself beneath her winter jacket to wake herself from this nightmare, but the face didn't disappear. The woman's eyes were like two grey marbles, her flesh stretched taut over her cheekbones. A fly buzzed around her matted hair.

Rita cried out in alarm.

"What's the matter with you? Why do you jump like a snake bit you?"

Rita stared at the stranger, her heart pounding in her throat.

"Relax," the woman said, smiling at Rita. Her teeth were yellow and there was a big gap in the place where her two front teeth were supposed to be.

How the hell can I relax in a place like this? Rita pulled her knees even closer to her chest and buried her head in her hands. Trying not to turn her head, she searched for a weapon, something she could use to defend herself against this suspicious stranger. Broken shards of memory flashed through her mind, and Rita saw the boys who stole her handbag containing her worldly possessions, followed by the woman sleeping on some dirty cardboard on the floor of the subway station.

"You stole my cardboard," the woman exclaimed suddenly, her eyes fixed on the piece of card Rita was laying on.

"I'm s-sorry," Rita mumbled in Italian, sitting up and starting to pull it out from under her.

"Keep it. I just wanted you to know it's mine."

Rita nodded.

Of course it's yours. What would I want with this nasty piece of cardboard anyway?

Immediately, she was ashamed of her thoughts.

"I saw you last night," the woman continued. "Those boys." She shook her head, her filthy hair swinging from side to side. "They always pick on girls like you. Girls who are alone. Girls who look like tourists. *Stupid tourists.*"

She handed Rita a cup of tea, then turned back to prepare her own on a camping stove. She held a dirty old Turkish-style coffee pot in her left hand and was shielding the dying flame with her right.

Rita blinked. Am I still dreaming? Where did she get all this stuff? She warmed her hands with the small cup, then lifted it to her parched lips. The edge of the mug was filthy and sticky, but Rita didn't see any point in complaining. As she sipped the lukewarm tea, a large teardrop fell into her cup.

Staring at Rita, the old woman drew closer.

"You know, it's dangerous to wander the streets of Milan, late at night, alone. The night is not ours, my dear. It's better to stay home," she said, her voice whistling between her missing teeth. "Where are you from?" The woman asked.

Rita sipped her tea and kept silent. She hated that question.

"Welcome to my home," the woman continued, lifting the cracked cup to her lips.

"Do they let you stay here? I mean the *carabinieri*, the police, the council?"

"Sometimes they make me sleep outside," said the woman, not expanding on who 'they' were. "But when I see they've forgotten about me, I come back. I have nowhere else to go. During the summer, I sleep outside on the streets, here and there. But when the birds fly south, I know it's time for me to head back to the station. It's not that bad." She grinned again, wrinkles creasing at the corners of her eyes. "I don't run myself ragged to pay rent, electricity, or gas like most people. I have nothing to worry about."

"How long have you been on the streets?" The moment Rita said the words she regretted it. That was not her business.

Other people's misery soothes your sorrow.

"Who knows? Now you drink your tea, otherwise it will get cold. I won't light that thing up again. Besides, I have no more tea for today."

Rita lifted the cracked cup to her lips. *Then it is already a new day.*

"What time is it?" Rita didn't dare check her phone. What if the old woman snatched it from her hand and ran away? She thought of the video she had stored on her phone and shuddered. She should have deleted it ages ago. It wouldn't help her now. No one cared.

"It's still early." The old woman stepped back and checked the platform display. "Five thirty," she called out, then sat next to Rita, pulling her big sweater tighter around her and reaching for her tea. Rita stifled a grimace at the sight of the woman's dirty clothes and unwashed hair.

"Will you report those boys to the police?" the woman coughed, making Rita turn her head away. "They've been arrested many times, you know, but as soon as they hit the streets, they do the same thing over and over again."

Rita went to bite her nails but thought better of it considering she'd not washed her hands in hours. "I'm not going to the police. Nobody will care about my bag. I didn't have anything valuable in it anyway." As she said the last words, she took a deep breath and sniffed to hold back her tears.

People were beginning to move in and out of the station. The working day had begun. Filled with shame and anger, Rita kept her eyes on the floor, staring at the shoes of the passers-by. There were stilettos, men's loafers, filthy sneakers, ugly boots, and small, colourful children's shoes. The higher the heels, the more noise they made. Then there were the men's shoes, they were more practical. And the cute little children's shoes, always stepping on their parents' polished ones.

"Time to move! We have to get out of here."

"Where are we going?" Rita cried, still looking at the shoes.

"You go your way, I'll go mine."

"Can I come back here tonight?"

Rita couldn't rely on Andrew's help. *I need some time to figure this out. A few hours and a place to sleep. I will find a solution.*

The derisive laughter in Rita's head made her determination fade away. *Are you really going to find a way out of this mess?*

"Do what you want. The station isn't mine." The old woman winked at Rita and poked her arm. And with that, she gathered up all her clothes and cardboard sheets, put them on her back, and headed towards the exit.

"Wait. I can help you," Rita said, running after her. Her carry-on bag banged against her good ankle, and she remembered her bad ankle the moment it tried to keep pace. It was then that Rita saw one of the wheels on her case was broken. *Those bastards!*

"Don't worry. I'm used to carrying stuff. My job isn't far from here," the woman shouted. As she made her way through the crowds, she looked like a paper boat sailing through a storm.

Her job?

They left the Metro and crossed the main road, Rita bumping into the woman's back as she unexpectedly stopped and put down all her belongings. As if she were pulling up a chair to sit at a desk, the woman carefully set a sheet of cardboard on the ground and sat on it.

"What are you doing?"

"This is my job, *cara*. If I'm lucky and make some money, maybe we'll drink more than tea tomorrow. We might even splurge on a big breakfast."

Rita smiled encouragingly, but her heart sank at the sight of the old woman.

I need to get away from here, from her. I'm not homeless.

Pivoting one-hundred-and-eighty degrees from her previous thoughts, she simply had to meet Andrew. She couldn't live like this.

"Can I leave my bag with you, please?" Rita asked. "It's heavy and the wheels are broken." *There is nothing valuable inside, anyway.*

"Sure, love." The woman pointed at a place next to her bundle.

Rita was *so* embarrassed to be meeting Andrew wearing the same clothes as yesterday. She was desperately in need of a shower, too. Judging by the unruly lock of hair falling in her face, her head had turned into a ball of frizz. But maybe, just maybe, Andrew would understand her predicament. She had to believe that. Okay, she had to at least hope it. It was all she had left. *If you're stupid enough to tell him who you really are and what happened to you, he will hate you,* the voice said.

Rita raised her head to the sky. She was a fool to expect her dead mother to whisk her away from all of this, from the voices in her head. And yet, she always turned to her.

10

The same man is *still* by my bed. I recognise the warmth of his hand in mine. The doctors and nurses come and go, but his presence is constant, as is his imploring me to wake up. But why would anyone want to wake up and return to a world that has always pushed them away? Pushed them under a train! I'm safer here, in my own dreams. It's a world I already know.

After my mum died, our home became an island of grief. Her flowers on the balcony refused to blossom because I forgot to water them. Dad stopped shaving his beard and became unrecognisable. He also started drinking.

The pain was so unbearable I'd leave him alone in the living room, taking solace in my solitude. The heat at night was suffocating, relentless, and with no air-conditioning, the only way for a breeze to reach us was through open doors and windows.

At night, I heard my father crying. And in my own bed, I cried too. As much as I wanted to console him, I couldn't find the words. The tears and the heat choked me into despair.

One night I awoke to silence.

I tiptoed to the living room. Dad's face was resting on the table, his fingers wrapped around a glass of raki. The bottle was almost empty. I'd never seen my dad drink this much.

I struggled to carry him to his bed. Since my mum's death, I'd avoided that room, where her shadow seemed to flit against the walls. I gently lowered him onto the bed and stroked the fabric of the pillow where she used to lay her head. The smell of her medication still hung in the air, the same smell I detect now as I lie in my hospital bed. Maybe I'm also about to die.

By the time I had tucked my dad in and returned to my bedroom, the sun was shining, promising another sweltering day. The parched earth cried out for rain. The brief shower on the day of my mum's funeral had been like a damp cloth pressed against the forehead of a patient dying of fever. Not nearly enough.

The man standing beside my bed is dabbing my head with a cool cloth also. All night, he's been calling my name and checking the machines hovering over me. Last night, I thought I saw a glimpse of his face, but my mind is muddled. I can no longer tell if I'm in the past or the present. Or, perhaps, I only have access to the parts of my life I choose to be conscious in. Where, among the tangled knots of my life, does this man belong?

Back in my childhood home, I opened the wardrobe and pulled out one of mum's dresses. I brought them back to my room, where I searched for a mirror, remembering that Helen and I had hidden them under my bed. For the first time in months, I saw Mum's reflection smiling back at me.

But as quickly as I saw it, the image vanished, and I turned to my diary. Since Mum had passed, I'd written five letters to her. I'd told her about Auntie Angela and Helen who had been helping us, I'd told her about Dad's drinking. Today though, when I closed my diary, writing letters wasn't enough. I needed to see her.

The bus driver's radio was on full blast, announcing that it was going to be another scorching day. Elderly people were advised to stay indoors and drink as much water as possible. I was far from elderly, but the air on the bus was hot and dusty and I hadn't thought to bring any water with me.

Sweat coated every inch of me, making my mum's dress cling to my back as I stepped off the bus and headed toward her new resting place. *Has she been waiting for me?*

Even with the sun shining, the graveyard was cold. Mum's grave was the newest, the earth already beginning to settle. We hadn't put up a tombstone for her yet.

I had so many things to tell her, but when I kneeled on the ground, I didn't know where to start. I just knew that I missed her so much. Tears streamed down my face, but I didn't wipe them away. A shadow passed over my body. I shivered.

Mum? Have you come back for me?

When I looked up though, I saw Samuel.

He kneeled beside me, enveloped me in his arms, and I breathed in the scent of his cologne.

"Darling, what are you doing here alone? Why didn't you call me?"

Samuel frowned at the dress I was wearing, and I remembered it was my mum's.

"I want to die, Samuel. I can't live without her."

"If you die, I'll die too. You can't live without your mum, and I can't live without you. So don't you dare go anywhere."

He was wearing a clean Tommy Hilfiger T-shirt and his white shorts sullied from the dirt. His stubble was neat, his dark brown hair slicked back as usual. It was just a normal day for him. His mum had no doubt made him his favourite breakfast that morning. Scrambled eggs and a glass of milk.

He gently wiped away the tears beneath my eyes with his knuckle and helped me to my feet.

Dad was awake when Samuel brought me home. He had even made me breakfast.

"Rita." He looked at my dress too, but said nothing, just wrapped me in an embrace. I could smell the raki he'd been drinking all night.

I left Samuel and my dad in the living room and went to take a shower. Afterwards, as I dried my hair, I could hear them talking about me, but I couldn't make out the words. Mum's death seemed to have bonded the two men in my life. Samuel had stepped into manhood and Dad liked that. Or maybe he simply saw him as the son he'd never had.

"Rita, *shpirt*, Samuel wants you to go on holiday with him. A little distraction would be good for you," Dad said as I entered the room. He said that word again, *shpirt*. My soul. It didn't have the same warmth as it had when Mum used to say it.

"No, Dad. I'm not going anywhere. I can't leave you alone." I didn't want to tell him that I wanted to visit Mum's grave every day. She needed me, and I needed her.

"Go with Samuel to his summer house. I won't have to worry about you anymore and can focus on my job. Being at home makes me feel…" His lower lip trembled. "Work will help me. There's a lot of loose ends to tie up. I need to travel for my job and…"

He paused, letting the unfinished sentence hang in the air. He wanted me to leave.

Was I now a burden to him?

"Go. Pack," he urged me.

"Today?" I turned and looked at Samuel.

Is Dad throwing me out?

"Yes. My mum and dad have already left." Samuel said.

But I didn't want to go on holiday, especially not with Samuel's mum.

"No. Dad, I can't. Who would look after Luk?"

No way would Samuel's mum allow a dog in her house.

"Do it for me, Rita, please. I'll take Luk to work with me. He can keep me company while I'm travelling."

Dad glanced at the dog in my arms.

"How can I enjoy myself when Mum is gone?"

"We have to learn, Rita. *You and me.* We will learn. Now go, I'll be fine."

I believed him. But had I known that when I got back, I wouldn't find my father alone, I wouldn't have listened to him. No grieving man should be left to his own devices.

When we arrived at Samuel's house the sun had already dipped into the sea and the sky was now a deep shade of plum. People were strolling on the beach, but all I wanted was to go to bed.

"I love you," Samuel whispered, as we entered the

coolness of his large summer home. I silenced him with a kiss.

That night I fell asleep with my arms wrapped around him. Safe. His hand in mine.

But whose hand am I holding now, in this hospital bed?

11

Milan, Italy
Sunday morning, 27 October 2019

With no money, no bag, no camera, and a phone that was about to die, Rita found herself lost in a city where she didn't belong. Her phone battery was down to just ten percent. It was a risk, but using it was her only way of finding Andrew again. Rita pulled out her phone and a forgotten note fluttered to the ground. Money! Five Euros.

She didn't think much of many of her people's habits, but she was thankful it was customary to hide banknotes in the pockets of jackets and trousers. With a smile, Rita snatched up the money and set off to meet Andrew. Before telling him the whole truth, she could at least buy him a cup of coffee. It took a long time for her smile to fade. Was it the money giving her butterflies or the fact she was about to see Andrew again?

Rita reached Andrew's hotel moments before her phone died. While walking, she had made a mental note of all the road signs so she could find her way back to the old lady without her phone's GPS and gather her belongings later. She'd convinced herself that Andrew was going to help her. She couldn't contemplate any other solution.

Holding her breath, Rita pushed open the glass door of the hotel, the bright lights of the lobby making her squint. It was strange to adjust her mindset from sleeping on the street an hour ago to waiting for her friend at a four-star establishment. Beads of perspiration covered her forehead. She wiped them away, then furtively brushed her damp palms on her jeans.

"Good morning! I'm looking for a guest of yours, Andrew Holbrook. I know it's early, but it's an emergency. Could you please let him know I'm here?" Rita said in one breath.

The man sitting at the reception desk rose from his chair like a sloth. He rubbed his eyes and turned his attention to the computer screen. "What's his name again?"

Rita repeated every syllable, watching his fingers as he tapped on the keyboard, one key at a time.

"Ah, Mr. Holbrook left at 2 a.m.," he said with a yawn.

His words hit Rita like a punch in the gut. "That

must be a different Mr. Holbrook." Her voice caught in her throat. "Andrew and I are supposed to meet today."

A patronising smile appeared at the edge of the receptionist's lips, as if he'd seen this scenario many times before. Another girl dumped by a British tourist. He glanced at the computer screen again. "We only have one Mr. Holbrook staying here, and he definitely checked out this morning."

He left you, didn't he? The voice in her mind was awake. *You had the chance to ask him for help yesterday, but no. You thought you could do it alone. Well, look how far* that *got you!*

"I definitely remember your friend, because he was the only person who left in the middle of the night," the receptionist continued. "I called him a taxi. He had to get to the airport as soon as possible." He said each word slowly, as if Rita was stupid as opposed to merely in shock.

She saw the unspoken words in the man's tired eyes and his tense jaw. Over time, Rita had mastered the interpretation of faces. Then again, she clearly hadn't interpreted Andrew's face very well. All that attention he showed her yesterday was a farce. How she hated him! Not because he'd left, but because he'd lied to her, like everybody else in her life.

OK, she'd lied too. But that was different.

"Thank you," she said. She was about to leave when

the receptionist called her back.

"Wait. Are you Rita?"

She nodded.

"He left something for you." He handed Rita an envelope.

He does care!

Rita tore it open and pulled out Andrew's business card. Could the receptionist read the disappointment in her face?

On the back of the card, in neat writing, it read: *Call me, please.*

No more, no less. No explanation as to why he left in such a hurry.

The receptionist looked at his watch. "Why don't you call him? Although, he may already be on the plane."

"I will. *Grazie*," Rita whispered. She walked towards the exit, then stopped in the middle of the hotel lobby and turned around.

"Do you have a phone charger, by any chance? I forgot mine."

The man dipped under the reception desk and pulled out a Samsung charger.

"I need an iPhone one," she stuttered.

"Look, lady, this isn't a phone store."

He turned away from her and fixed his attention on a woman who had appeared behind Rita. Standing in line with two pieces of luggage, she pushed by Rita and placed her elbows on the desk. The jingle jangle of her bracelets reminded Rita of her former boss, Lizbeth, and the hell that working for her had been. She shuddered at the memory.

Back outside, Rita sat on the curb, her knees touching her chin. She ignored the lone tear traveling down her cheek. It was stupid to cry over Andrew, she barely knew him. But it wasn't that. She was crying because he'd been her last hope.

The clouds were moving fast now, threatening rain. A heavy wind swirled dead leaves and litter up in the air, and particles of dust crunched between her teeth. Rita pulled up the hood of her parka and thrust Andrew's business card into her jeans pocket. She sighed and pulled out a packet of Karelia cigarettes – one of the few things she had left from her country. She counted, there were twelve in total. They should last a few days. How many days she had left in Milan, she didn't know, but she needed one right now.

Rita glanced at the cigarette between her fingers, as if weighing up the amount of nicotine it contained. *Smoke half. Half is enough.* With a shaky hand, she shielded the cigarette from the wind as she attempted to light it. After three attempts she managed to strike a match. She took two puffs, one after another, without stopping for breath. *What the hell am I supposed to do now?* she thought, tapping the broken tiles of the pavement with the tip of her trainers.

The fear she'd felt yesterday while boarding the plane to Italy was back, but this time, it was even stronger. Andrew had momentarily made her forget her past, giving her a glimpse of an alternative life. But that was just another lie. She brushed away another tear.

The wind blew harder, carrying the scent of damp earth. Rita looked at the sky. It was dark and ominous. Birds as well as people were already trying to find shelter. She took another puff of her cigarette but didn't move.

A procession of ants marched past her feet. Rita watched how they disappeared into a crack in the pavement, following each other in a straight line. When she was little, staying at her granny's house in a small village in the north of Albania, she used to watch the ants burrowing into the cracks of the dark soil. She'd often put her little foot in front of their home, cutting them off.

"I just want to see what they would do," Rita would cry when her granny made her move her foot.

"Leave them alone, Rita. We don't hurt them, and they don't hurt us."

"But how come they get to go underground and show back up whenever they want?" Rita had asked.

"Because that's nature's law."

"So why can't Grandpa come out anymore? We buried *him* in the ground."

Granny had given her a sad smile. "He's also following nature's law," she'd said. "Once you're buried, you can't come out anymore."

You're going crazy. Her tedious inner voice snapped her back to the present, a present she no longer wanted to be part of. *Just give in and go back to where you came from, where you belong. You're nothing but a tiny fish in the middle of an ocean. An ocean full of good-looking but deceitful sharks like Andrew. They'll eat you alive! Forget Samuel too. Go back home!*

No!

But how was she supposed to survive, when all the odds were stacked against her?

The first raindrop hit her face hard. She stubbed the butt of her cigarette out against a lamppost and stuck the remaining half back in the pack. She stood up, pocketed the cigarette pack, and began to run, praying the woman was still at the Metro station, that she hadn't lied to her too.

In an instant, her face was dripping wet, but she didn't know if it was from the rain, her tears, or both.

12

By the time Rita found the Metro station, she was drenched. The old homeless woman was sitting exactly where Rita had found her last night. The cardboard Rita had slept on the night before looked like a tattered old rug, but she was relieved to see that her suitcase was there beside it. She sighed with relief and headed towards the woman, her body shivering, and her hands numb.

"Ah, you're back."

The woman's face beamed, as if she was talking to an old friend.

"Yeah, I couldn't find a bridge to jump off," Rita muttered, kneeling down next to her luggage. She turned her back to the woman and unzipped the bag.

"How was your day?" she asked, rummaging through her belongings. She took out a woollen sweater, her fingers brushing against the jewellery she had hidden folded into the middle of it. *Wait...* The necklace Samuel had given her on her birthday was in that bag!

She grinned. How could she have forgotten? *Because of that delectable Englishman you were fantasising about yesterday*, the know-it-all voice replied.

Rita kept her necklace out of sight as she discreetly stuffed it back into her bag, worried the old lady might steal it. She'd checked the price of her gift on the Internet after Samuel gave it to her – the curious mind of a teenager – and knew it was an expensive gem. Thank God she hadn't put it in her handbag!

Slowly, trying not to catch the woman's attention, Rita lowered the lid of her suitcase.

She changed her wet sweater for a dry one, then sat down and rested her back against the concrete wall of the subway station.

"Terrible," the old woman said. "All this rain meant I had to get back inside early. A man gave me two euros. I don't know what he looked like, I always keep my head down, but I saw his shoes and they were fashionable. I bet he was young and rich. Anyway, he gave us something to eat for breakfast." She rubbed the palms of her hands together and pulled her old, mouldy duvet around her knees. "As for dinner, just close your eyes and imagine we're somewhere fancy eating a meal fit for a king. Trust me, it works." She closed her eyes. Her face softened and she looked happy and relaxed, as if she really was in front of a grand buffet.

The sandwich! Rita fished it out of her coat pocket.

"I bought dinner for us tonight."

The old woman gaped at Rita, as if she'd just handed her a grilled lobster.

"It's been a long time since I've eaten something like this!"

Rita smiled and handed her the sandwich. She'd bought a large one, costing her the full five euros. She had no money left, but by feeding the old woman, Rita knew she had somewhere dry to stay until the rain stopped. Nothing was free in this world, not even a cardboard box at a Metro station.

The woman held out her hand, then quickly pulled it back.

"Cut it in half," she instructed, then stood up to examine Rita. "Poor thing, your hair is soaked. Here, take this." She handed her an old, filthy blanket.

Rita wrapped the blanket around her shoulders like a poncho while the woman cut the sandwich in half and took a bite of her royal meal.

"I'm Maria, not that you asked," the woman said. She wiped the palm of her free hand on her dirty clothes and held it out.

"Rita."

She had no choice but to shake the woman's hand. Sitting this close to her filled Rita's nostrils with the stench of unwashed skin. It took all her strength not to gag.

Aren't you ashamed of yourself? her mind scolded her. *She's the only one who cares about you.*

"So, Maria, why do you stay here?"

She didn't know why she was asking. Clearly Maria had no other option. She had every right to tell Rita to mind her own business and shoo her away for being so direct. But she didn't.

"I like it," Maria said, in an indignant voice.

"I'm sorry, I shouldn't have asked."

"Eat your sandwich, or I'll have it." Maria snapped, looking at Rita out of the corner of her eye. "Where are you from, anyway? You're not Italian."

That last part wasn't a question, but a statement.

"I asked you last night and you wouldn't answer."

"Erm…" Rita took some time to think, as if she had forgotten the name of the country she came from. "Nowhere in particular." She took a bite of the sandwich, hoping to delay any further probing.

Maria raised an eyebrow. "Every country has a name."

Rita didn't say a word, just continued to chew her sandwich.

"You're hiding from something." Maria paused, as if to see Rita's reaction. "Your Italian is pretty good, by the way."

"My granny was Italian, and my mum was a translator."

Rita sighed and tucked a lock of wet hair behind her ear.

"That means you have Italian blood."

"I suppose."

Rita might still have relatives in Italy, but she didn't know them. When the Communist authorities had closed the borders, before Rita was even born, her maternal grandmother had been trapped in Albania. She could no longer visit her parents in Italy, and they couldn't come to see her. Luna had always said that her mother's longing for her country had crushed her soul.

"And why don't you go back to your country, wherever that is?" Maria asked.

"I can't."

"It doesn't matter what happened. There's always a second chance."

"I don't believe in second chances. I've never gotten any." Rita's lower lip trembled. She bit the knuckle of her index finger until it hurt.

"Now I'm the one who's sorry. I shouldn't have asked," Maria said, patting Rita's shoulder.

Her breath reminded Rita of rotten eggs Helen had cooked for her once.

"And you? Why don't you look for your second chance?"

Rita hated herself the second she said it. She was

being mean, taking her troubles out on this nice old woman.

"Maybe because I don't have a second chance. Or maybe, when the second chance arrived, I didn't see it and let it slip away," the old woman replied in a quiet voice.

Rita gave her a tight smile. "Cigarette?"

The old lady's eyes shone at the suggestion. Rita dug a cigarette out of the pack in her pocket and broke it in half. The one with the butt she handed to Maria, the other half she kept for herself and merged it with the butt she already had in her pocket. For a while, neither of them spoke as they savoured the clouds of smoke winding out of their mouths.

"You've given me food and a cigarette, so I'll tell you my story in return," Maria said. "Would you like the short version, or the long one?"

In all honesty, Rita didn't want either. She just wanted the woman to shut up and let her focus on what to do next. Now that she remembered she had a necklace she could sell, there was light at the end of the tunnel. Samuel would understand her decision.

"Okay. I see. How about the short version?" Maria smiled, demonstrating to Rita that while she was homeless, she wasn't stupid. "I was in love with a man. Now, that's nothing new. Everybody falls in love with someone eventually, and everybody thinks that person is the love of their life blah, blah, blah. But I fell in love with this man the first time I saw him. We were both young and enjoyed going out, dancing until dawn. It wasn't like today, where people get to know each other on the Internet." She shook her head and took another puff of the cigarette. "His name was Antonio, or at least that's what he told me." At the mention of his name, her voice cracked like melting ice. "He was the most handsome guy I had ever seen. I was thirty-five years old, yet all my experiences with love had ended in failure. When I was a teenager, the other girls bullied me. I was chubby and I used to cut my own hair because we were poor. My clothes were always a little torn and usually second hand. After a while, I started to believe all the taunts and cruelty, and I became convinced that I wasn't worthy of love. If I was, then surely, I would have found it by then. When Antonio stepped into my life, I already owned my own house and I'd just received a pay raise. They never complained about me at work. I was the first one to arrive in the morning and the last one to leave at night. I never asked for a day off. It wasn't as if I had anything else to do. My job was the only thing I hadn't failed at yet. So, meeting Antonio was like a rainbow after a storm. Silly me, in my mid-thirties, old enough to know better. You're meant to know what you're doing by then, right?"

Rita shrugged. Maybe she would never make it to

thirty-five to find out.

Maria took a deep breath, her voice trembling with emotion.

"I'd never seen eyes like Antonio's. They were blue, but sometimes they would turn grey and green." *Blue like Andrew's eyes.* "Are you listening to me?"

"Yes," Rita replied.

"At some point we started going out every evening. I couldn't wait for the day to finish. Now, I was the first one to leave work. Antonio had no family here in Italy. He'd just arrived from Albania."

When she said the word 'Albania,' Maria stopped and looked at Rita, who glanced away uncomfortably.

"I wanted to look after him, so I let him move in with me. My life was going well, so why not? I could sense my colleagues talking about us behind my back. Every time I mentioned this to Antonio, he would say they were just jealous of our love. And day by day, I became convinced that this was true. I'd hit the jackpot!

I worked and paid the bills while he stayed at home. He told me he was looking for a job, and I believed him. I didn't mind. I liked the idea of him waiting for me at home. When I called him on my lunch break, his voice would be husky from sleep, and all I wanted to do was slide back into our warm bed and in between his arms. He said he was ashamed that I was the one working, and that the moment he found something, I could quit, or at least work fewer hours. I couldn't see the truth staring me right in the face. I only had eyes for him. I worked harder, so I could give him more, scared he would walk out on me – the fat, unlovable, ugly girl.

Anyway, to cut a long story short, he forged my signature and sold my house. He also managed to get his hands on all the money I had in my bank account."

She paused and glanced at her bare feet. Rita didn't know how to reply.

"Want another one?" she asked finally, handing her another cigarette.

"You're spoiling me. Or maybe you're trying to murder me. You know smoking kills, right?" Maria waved one hand in front of her face dismissively. "Bah, I died a long time ago."

She smiled at Rita, her eyes glistening with tears.

"Then what happened?" Rita asked.

"Antonio disappeared and I went to prison for two years. He'd used my signature in more than one place, for more than one questionable transaction. I couldn't prove my innocence. After that, I got no second chances."

Her voice was flat, the wrinkles on her face resembling the twisted, winding roots of an ancient tree.

Rita opened her mouth to say something, then closed it again. She couldn't think of anything better to

109

say than "*I'm sorry*," and she'd been saying that far too often lately.

"Maybe you're wondering why I told you my pitiful life story?" Maria continued. She pointed a gnarled finger at Rita and looked her in the eye. "Listen to me carefully. If there's a man in your life, don't let him ruin it!"

Rita swallowed the lump in her throat, thinking of Samuel. "How can you tell?"

"Ah, *cara*. It's the look in your eyes. I used to have it too, until it vanished along with everything else."

The woman was wrong. Samuel wasn't like Antonio. He didn't lie to Rita – okay, he had, but just the once.

"What's gone, is gone," Maria said. "You can't bring back the dead, and you can't change people. You must steer your future in the direction you want it to go, while you're still on track. If you think you can't be strong, remember my face and stand up for yourself." Maria coughed, blowing out a puff of smoke. Her eyes were focused far away, as if she was talking to her past.

"I never used to smoke," Rita muttered, like the vice was the most important part of Maria's lesson. But Maria had shared so much with her, it was only right she told something of her own life in return. "The first time I smoked was the day after my mum passed away. I knew my mum wouldn't have approved, and that it was bad for me, but somehow I didn't care. It was comforting, almost, to harm myself physically, when emotionally I was in so much pain." Talking about her mum's death was like jabbing at an open wound.

"Oh, you poor thing," Maria said. She stubbed out her cigarette and tossed the butt across the platform.

Then she turned her back to Rita and without saying good night, put her head on her wooden footstool pillow.

Rita opened her suitcase again and reached for her book.

"Aren't you going to sleep?" Maria mumbled.

"I always read a bit before I sleep. I won't make any noise." Rita managed a wan smile, which was the most she could do.

Rita opened her book but the words on the page seemed to blur, and she couldn't focus. She couldn't stop thinking about Maria's story. She'd always perceived herself as the victim and blamed others, especially Helen, for her misfortune. But perhaps she wouldn't be where she was right now if she'd found the courage and strength to stand up for herself sooner.

13

The nurse by my bed reminds me of Helen. Or perhaps it's just that I don't want her there. Thank goodness the man holding my hand doesn't leave my side. The nurse checks the chart at the foot of my bed then places a hand on the man's shoulder. They exchange a look as if they know each other well. How long have I been in the hospital?

"Rita, wake up." It's not the nurse, it's Helen, pulling me back to the past.

It's my eighteenth birthday, but I don't want to wake up. Seven months have passed since my mum's death. I can't imagine celebrating without her, so I stay in bed until midday, writing her a letter. Writing a letter, knowing you will never get a response, hurts.

I tell Mum about Dad's drinking. Last night he drank a whole bottle of that colourless liquid. The stench of raki permeates every room in the apartment. This is his ritual now, every night that Helen is not with us. But at least he doesn't shout or cry anymore.

He has changed so much. Once he was Timi Hanas, a man in love with life, his wife, Luna, and his daughter, Rita. Now he is just a man, Timi, without a last name. Every time he talks to me, it's as if he's addressing somebody else, someone invisible in the room.

I write all this down without stopping. It's easy to tell Mum about all of Dad's shortcomings instead of my own. My heart aches as I tell my mum how Helen is sleeping in Dad's room now. In *her* bed. And it's all my fault.

The day I came back from my holiday with Samuel, it was Helen who opened the front door. She held Luk in her arms. Feelings of irritation and betrayal washed over me. I was furious that she could so easily take the place of my mum, coming and going like she owned the place.

I was so ashamed by my anger that I couldn't invite Samuel in. Luk jumped up at me, but I barely looked at him. I'd missed him, of course, but like Dad, he too had betrayed me by accepting Helen so readily. I locked myself in my room. My dog whimpered on the other side of the door, but I didn't care. I called Auntie Angela and told her how Helen was in our home. To my surprise, she wasn't angry. She said Helen would be good for Dad. She was younger than him. He was still only in his early fifties. He still had a life to live. He needed a nice woman to look after him. I was shocked.

I ended the call and threw my phone down on the bed and decided I would never speak to my aunt again. And I kept my promise.

As soon as I heard Helen and Dad leave the house, I stormed out of my room and drank half of my dad's bottle of raki. The taste of liquorice flooded my mouth and I wanted to throw up immediately.

I have no memory of what happened after that. Time is blank. Empty.

I feel the same right now, my consciousness back in this hospital room. I remember the feeling of being pushed under the train. I wasn't drunk, but *they* were. *I just don't know who they are.*

My past is so much clearer than my present.

That evening after the raki, Helen found me with my head in the toilet bowl. I have no idea how long I'd been there. I don't know why I'd done it. Maybe I wanted to punish my dad and my aunt, or maybe I wanted to punish myself for letting my mum down. All I knew for certain was that my head was throbbing, and my stomach burning.

Helen cleaned up the mess I'd made, washed my face, and replaced the raki so my dad wouldn't know what I'd done. She stayed with me the whole night. She even changed the wet flannel on my forehead every two hours. I don't know what she told Dad, but she said it was 'our little secret'. She wrapped me around her little finger in that moment. From then on, she spent every night in my mum's bed.

I don't put the last part in the letter. I'm sure Mum already knows.

Back to the day of my eighteenth birthday, every second is a painful reminder of Mum's absence. Perhaps Helen is trying, but she could never fill Mum's shoes. She even forgot to buy me a cake! The only thing Helen *is* filling is the boot of Dad's car with a portable grill...

"We're having a barbecue party," she says, knowing full well my mum never liked barbecues.

Luk sits on my lap for the drive to the countryside. I've forgiven him for betraying me. After all, I'd betrayed Mum too. Dad pulls over somewhere on the outskirts of town. There's a little green meadow with two tall trees and a stream of water gurgling close by. We can fill our bottles with the fresh spring water trickling down from the mountain. It's way better than the city water.

Samuel joins us too, and it's nice to see Dad looking so happy as he shares a beer with him. Somehow Helen has managed to hide his bottle of raki, and he is drinking less, but I refuse to acknowledge that her presence has a positive effect on him.

Luk is happy too, chasing butterflies.

Dad fires up the grill. The sun beats down on us, there's not a cloud in the sky. We find some shade beneath a tree and lay out our picnic blanket. Helen has even gone so far as to buy one of those picnic hampers with all the plates inside. I take out my camera, the last gift from Mum, and capture some images.

Since Mum died, my life has been reduced to pictures, books, and Internet searches. I look at the photos other people post online, and I take in all the places Mum is never going to see. If Dad has found solace in Helen's arms, I have found refuge in other people's stories.

Helen is wearing jeans, a T-shirt, and trainers for the barbecue. It's the first time I've seen her without her formal high heels on or an ugly blouse.

She flips burgers and makes sure everyone has a full plate. I hate to admit it, but her barbecue skills are brilliant, and this is kind of fun. *Almost* enough fun to distract me from Helen's ballooning belly. Presumably, she's simply eaten too much like the rest of us.

"Rita, can you hear me?" The man by the side of my bed is calling my name.

"Yes!" I want to say, but as usual, no words come out of my mouth.

14

Milan, Italy
Monday morning, 28 October 2019

Rita tossed and turned on her piece of cardboard all night. Finally, just when it seemed day would never come, light pushed away the darkness. She opened her suitcase, dug out her thickest sweater, and left it beside Maria's head.

The old woman opened her eyes. "What are you doing?"

"Please, take this. I have nothing else to thank you with."

Maria ignored the sweater. "Where are you going?" She sat up on the cardboard, her elbow resting on the wooden stool. "Are you going back to your country?"

"No. I'm not going back to that miserable life again, but I can't stay in Italy either."

Rita sighed and zipped her bag closed. For a moment she stood still, contemplating her next move. Then she gave Maria a hug.

"If I ever get out of this alive, I'll come back and look for you."

Another impossible promise.

"Just go and do what you have to do. I had a nice time with you. Nobody talks to me. But I don't blame them for walking past me. I was the one who treated myself badly in the first place. So please, remember to be kind to yourself."

Rita swallowed down the lump in her throat. She owed Maria the truth.

"I'm Albanian."

Maria smiled her toothless smile. "I know, *cara.*"

"How?"

"Remember the night the boys shoved you off the train? You cursed in your language. I know the word *Zot.* It means God in Albanian. Antonio used that word a lot."

"You knew where I was from and helped me anyway?"

"*Cara*, one rotten apple doesn't mean the whole tree is worthless."

Rita's eyes filled with tears. She dipped into her pocket, pulled out two whole cigarettes, and placed them in Maria's palm. "Remember me for as long as these cigarettes last."

"*In bocca al lupo*," Maria replied.

She'd wished her to be in 'the mouth of a wolf' – the Italian way of wishing someone the best of luck.

Rita stepped onto the street and took a deep breath. Rain had fallen and the night had been long and dark. But now it was a new, clear blue morning. Someone gave her directions to the nearest jewellery shop. She found one that bought second-hand items, but it was still closed.

Rita sat on the pavement and waited.

After about an hour, the door of the shop swung open. The saleswoman's perfume filled Rita's nostrils, a scent that transported her to happier times when she was a woman who belonged in such a store.

"No drifters inside."

Rita spun around. There were no other people inside the shop. Just her.

"Are you talking to me?"

The young girl pointed at the door. "Yes. This isn't a charity shop. Please leave."

She thinks I'm homeless! Well, I did sleep rough. Twice. And my beaten-up luggage makes more noise than a home-made go-kart.

"How much would you give me for this necklace?" Rita placed her jewellery on the glass counter, her cheeks flushed with humiliation. "Just tell me, then I'll leave."

The saleswoman's expression changed as soon as she saw the piece. She picked up the precious stone and peered at it.

"We don't buy stolen goods," she replied after a long examination.

"Screw you! First you call me a vagabond, and now I'm a thief?" Rita shouted. "Two days ago, some boys stole everything from me, and nobody cares. I want to sell the most precious thing I have left, and you accuse me of having stolen it. All I want to do is to buy a ticket and go home."

The saleswoman's face shifted from white to red. "Show me an ID card."

"I just told you my bag was stolen. This is all I have left." Rita gestured to the necklace. "You know what? Forget it. I'll find another place to sell it."

Rita snatched the necklace back and headed for the door. Maybe she would be lucky in another store.

"Wait," the young girl called after Rita. "Okay, I believe your story."

Rita turned slowly.

"One hundred euros."

"It's worth more than four hundred euros and you know it," said Rita, although she knew she was in no position to barter.

"I'm doing you a favour."

"Two hundred." Rita held her breath and crossed her fingers behind her back.

"One hundred and fifty. That's my last offer. Take it or leave it."

The saleswoman was young, but she understood the game. She'd won.

"Fine, I'll take it," Rita mumbled.

One hundred and fifty euros was better than nothing. She dropped the necklace on to the mirrored counter and stroked the gemstone one last time. That was her past, and now she had a chance of a future.

In the time it took her to walk back to the Metro station, Rita had touched the banknotes countless times to check that they were still there. She had money in her pocket, and she had a plan. She bought herself a train ticket and waited for the green-line train. After what had happened to her Friday night, she hated the underground, but it was the fastest way.

The train was packed. It reminded her of all the times she used to travel by bus in her own country. In the span of ten days, Rita had been transformed from an honest girl into a liar. Or was she simply a survivor now? *Maybe I can be both. It changes nothing. If my plan works, I'll be in Calais by tomorrow, and the day after that, I'll be in the UK where I will find Samuel.*

She arrived at Milan's central train station, praying that if the ticket cost more than the money in her pocket, she'd find a way to sneak on to the train.

"One hundred and eleven euros," said the man behind the glass window at the ticket office.

Thirty-nine euros left. Rita couldn't perform any miracles with that, but at least she could buy some food over the next few days. She found the right platform and boarded one of the train compartments, holding her breath until she made it safely to her seat. Now and then, she peered out the window. People were running to catch the train, hugging one another, some crying and waving goodbye. So much emotion. But apart from that, she saw nothing alarming. No police. No obvious thieves.

It was only when her forehead bumped against the cold glass window that she realised the train was leaving. Italy would soon be behind her.

A tear ran down her grubby cheeks, but she didn't have the energy to wipe it away.

She grabbed a newspaper someone had left on the little table in front of her.

Le Monde, 23 October 2019. It was a week old, but Rita didn't care. She didn't know a single word of French, but she could look at the pictures and hide behind it every time another tear trickled down her face. She flipped through the pages. There was a photo of a large lorry, beneath an even bigger headline. Rita scanned the caption and picked out the word Essex, she knew that was a place in England. She also saw the number 29, and the word *victime*.

This word seemed to be common to many languages.

Victim. Whether someone was killed, assaulted, or the target of some other malevolent act, all victims had one thing in common: in addition to whatever injustice they had suffered to earn themselves this title, they were also robbed of their identity, their agency. They went from being an individual with a name and a personality, to merely being a "victim" – the human remnants of some malign deed. A dead body on the sidewalk, a battered woman in a shelter, it didn't matter. Their entire existence was reduced to victimhood, defined by misfortune outside their control which another had inflicted upon them.

Rita was holding back tears. She'd heard that it cost nothing and was relatively safe to cross the French border into the UK hidden in a lorry. She hoped it was true, as this was her only choice if she wanted to get to London.

15

The voices in my hospital room are getting louder and clearer. Today there is somebody else in my room and I can finally make out her face. It's Chloe. I want to shout out her name, but I'm not really there. Although, my heart is certainly beating fast as the nurse looks at the machine beside me – proof that I am still alive.

Chloe is crying. But she isn't the only one. I can hear a baby crying, too. A harsh wail that drags me back into my memories.

As soon as Helen's bump had started to show, my dad married her at the city hall. There was no grand party, just two friends as witnesses. I faked a migraine and stayed home. I think they were secretly happy I wasn't there to sour the mood.

Their son (and my new baby brother), Daniel, arrived exactly six months after the barbecue. Dad was over the moon. I could see it in his eyes. He'd always wanted a son and Helen had delivered. Meanwhile, I was doomed to life in a country where having a son was preferable to any number of daughters.

I still hadn't forgiven Dad for bringing Helen home, and now they had a child. She had spread her roots like ivy throughout my home, my mum's home, and she wasn't going anywhere. It hadn't taken long for her to throw out my mum's bed. It was left outside the door where someone soon carried it away. I watched as new furniture and curtains were brought into the apartment. Everything changed, and all I had left were my memories. Mum's clothes remained hanging neatly in my wardrobe, while many of my own clothes were tucked inside boxes and shoved under my bed.

I was torn, unable to decide whether to hate or love the baby.

"Honey, we're home," Dad shouted. "Come and meet your little brother. He looks just like you when you were a baby."

My heart cracked as soon as I heard those words, and I decided I would not love the baby. He couldn't look like me because Helen was not my mother.

With Luk in my arms, I walked to Mum's room where the baby lay in his crib beside the bed. I peered inside and let out a soft gasp. Daniel was even smaller than I had imagined, no longer than my forearm. How could such a small creature grow to be a man? The baby stretched out his hand, his eyes still closed, and grasped my index finger. The jolt of pure love transmitted through that touch was so great that it almost hurt. My heart melted. Having nobody to talk to, I whispered into the dog's ear,

"Look, Luk. He's so cute. Maybe I can forgive him for having Helen as a mother. It's not his fault. We don't choose our parents, do we?"

Baby Daniel was the only beautiful thing to happen in my house since Mum's death. The older my brother got, the more handsome he became. He'd been born with blue eyes. I'd read that the colour would change, but it never did. Daniel didn't look like either of his parents, and for that, I loved him even more.

When Daniel was six-months-old Helen returned to work doing exactly what Mum had done – giving private lessons at home. They'd both studied Italian. It was how they'd met. And now Helen was teaching Mum's students. She'd stepped straight into her best friend's shoes in every way possible.

She was working, and I was not, so I started to help with the baby.

The first time I changed Daniel's nappy, I felt sick and couldn't eat all day. But YouTube videos helped – not only did I learn how to change a baby's nappy without vomiting from the stench and mess, but I also became a pro at warming a baby bottle. Things got easier every day. After a while, they put Daniel's crib in my room. Now my brother not only occupied my days, but my nights too. I spent a lot of nights cradling him and dozing in the rocking chair. I imagined my mum doing the same for me.

Every night I wrote long letters telling her everything about baby Daniel. I thanked her for all her care when I was a baby. I also told her how Dad had started drinking again.

"Let Rita be!" I heard him shouting one night. "She knows what she wants."

"If she were capable of making smart decisions, she wouldn't have studied photography. It's the most stupid thing she could have chosen. Do you realise how many girls her age are self-sufficient and not living at home with their parents anymore?"

"What do you mean by that?" he shouted.

Daniel started blubbering, so I gave him a piece of bread to chew on.

"Well, perhaps she should be living with Samuel by now? They've been together for a long time. Surely, he intends to marry her, doesn't he? Why doesn't he take her home?"

So that was the reason why Dad had started drinking again. Helen didn't want me under the same roof as her brand-new family. But this was *my* apartment. First, she put Daniel in my room, invading my privacy, now she wanted me out of my home.

Not only did she have an issue with me, but now she was criticizing my boyfriend too. We had made plans, of course we had, but I wasn't going to tell Helen that. Samuel's parents had offered to buy him a house, but he didn't want them involved. I didn't want their money either. We wanted to create something of our own from scratch, like my mum and dad had. Samuel was going to start his own business, but he hadn't figure it all out yet. And I wasn't about to push him just because Helen wanted me out of my own home.

I slammed my fist down on my desk, wishing it were her face. My hand hurt.

Dad too slammed the door behind him as he left the house.

Now there's a third bang, as the man beside my hospital bed slams his hand against the wall.

"Will she ever wake up?" he asks the nurse.

The nurse shrugs kindly. "Keep talking to her," she says.

I fall asleep again.

16

France
Monday evening, 28 October 2019

Rita opened her eyes and winced. Overnight, her body had seized up in the shape of a question mark, and her neck ached so much she imagined her bones might stay set like that forever. She cupped her hands behind her neck, turning her head from left to right, and straightened her back with a crack. Then she noticed where she was, and a chill ran down her spine. Her book was still open, face down on her lap on the same page. All she remembered was switching trains in Paris. Luckily nobody had asked for an ID card at the border, and she'd somehow managed to get a few hours of sleep. Compared to where she had spent the last two nights, the warmth of the train and the soft seat was the lap of luxury.

Not only did she not know where she was, but she realised with a jolt of alarm that she was the only one left on the train. In the past, she would have been cross that no one had bothered to wake her. Now, she saw it as a blessing in disguise. She thrust her hand into her jeans pocket to check that her money was still there, and her fingers brushed against Andrew's business card.

And what are you going to do with that, keep it as a souvenir?

Rita squinted through the darkened window and saw the sign 'Gare de Calais Ville' station. She grabbed her bag, stumbled off the train, and drew in a long, slow breath. French air was different from Italian air, and they were both so very different from the air in Albania. She had started categorizing countries by the scent on the air. Despite the incident with the bag thieves and being forced to sleep on the street, the Italian air had been *dolce* – light and sweet – while the French air was thick enough to crush you.

Not knowing which way to go, she followed the river of people heading towards the exit. Along the way, she learned a new word: *sortie*. She tried to blend in, but her brow was furrowed in worry and concentration. The more she tried to relax, the more tense her face became, the deep grooves in her forehead reflecting the strain and anguish building inside her.

The platform display told her it was 6:35 p.m. Two station controllers sat talking to one another, not looking at anyone in particular yet somehow keeping an eye on every person leaving the platform. Rita lowered her head and let her hair fall over her face, insinuating herself into a crowd of people.

Out on the street, she stopped in her tracks. A large group of gaunt, unnatural-looking people was shuffling towards her. *Zombies?* She stood for a moment, trying to make sense of the situation. Then she remembered the date. It was almost Halloween.

October's nearly through, and here I am, wandering around Europe with London just on the other side. And Samuel too.

A cold breeze nudged her thoughts.

You're lost, the voice in her head sneered. She hadn't heard it for a while but in its absence, it seemed to have grown stronger.

I thought I'd managed to leave you on the train, Rita bemoaned silently.

The plan was simple. As soon as she saw a lorry heading to the UK, she would jump into it. Then the next morning, she would be in London. She wasn't going to allow the doubt in her mind to knock her off course. She joined the group of people in costume and shuffled forward.

The crisp night air stung her nose and ears, and the sky had turned from coral to the colour of a spreading bruise. Rita rubbed her hands together and breathed warm air on them. The mist, which seemed more like a thick smoke, hung close to everyone's heads. She had gone about half a mile when she realised that she didn't exactly blend in, what with her battered suitcase and no Halloween mask. She had to leave this group of people wandering the street, yet the thought of walking alone in the dark filled her with dread.

At the first crossroads, she sneaked away. Nobody had spotted her when she joined them, no one saw her when she left. She headed for some trees, hoping they would shield her, her jaw tense and her pulse racing. The grass had mixed with the rotten leaves and created a mushy humus that her feet were now sinking into. The wheels of her suitcase also became submerged in the slush. When it was clear she was getting nowhere dragging the suitcase, Rita lifted it up and balanced it on her head. Her body sagged under its weight. For a fleeting moment, she considered throwing it away.

She had no idea where she was going, but she continued on into the darkness, nonetheless. Leaves from the bushes smacked into her face, twigs tangling in her dirty hair.

By now, the voices of the Halloween teens had faded into the distance. Fear nibbled at her heart at the sound of footsteps crunching on dead leaves. She couldn't see anything; she was now too deep into the woods. She had no choice but to carry on in the same direction.

Her knees throbbed, and her arms ached from the weight of her belongings. In the end, she threw the suitcase away in anger, relieved to finally walk at a normal speed. What had she lost? A couple of clean sweaters? Some books? She couldn't believe she had let it slow her down for so long.

She spotted a light in the distance and quickened her pace. Then, something slammed into her head, and she fell to the ground. Rita blinked, confused, but she was OK. Her right leg hurt, but apart from that she was still in one piece. Just like in the Milan Metro, she saw white teeth glowing in the darkness. Were they the same teeth? Was one of the boys following her, or was the male standing in front of Rita a real zombie?

She cried out so faintly she doubted he'd even heard, but he reached out his large hand and helped Rita to her feet. Now, from his height, she could tell he was a man, and she was momentarily relieved those awful teens from the Metro hadn't been on her tail.

"Who are you? This is our forest," he said, speaking English but with a thick accent.

Rita had never heard this accent before, not that she had heard a lot of accents.

"I... I..." she spluttered.

"Are you a spy, or a journalist?"

A spy?

"I'll give you everything I have," she stammered,

even though she had just thrown away the last of her belongings. "Just let me go."

She dug into her pocket and fished out the remaining thirty-nine euros. The man stood still. Rita reached out for his hand and placed the money in his open palm. His eyes glimmered in the darkness. No torch needed to count the money, it was only three notes.

"Who are you?" he asked again in a deep voice, shoving the money inside his coat.

"I'm just someone who needs to be on the other side of the border tomorrow morning. That's all. Please don't call the police." Rita's voice cracked.

And don't rape or kill me, she wanted to add, but didn't.

"Follow me," he said, turning around. In his other hand was the suitcase she'd just thrown away.

He has my money and my clothes! What more does he want?

Beads of sweat formed across her brow. If she had to choose, she would rather he killed her straight away. The moon was hidden behind the clouds. Rita was totally alone. Even the moon wouldn't get to witness her death. In all the books she'd read and films she'd seen, the predator raped the victim first and then killed her.

What if I turn back? It's so dark he won't see me.

Without thinking twice, Rita started to slowly step

backwards, holding her breath, one careful step at a time. But the sound of her shoes on the rotten leaves betrayed her. She didn't know how the man could tell she was trying to get away, but he did. He grabbed her arm and pulled her to his side as he marched on. They continued in silence and Rita counted every tree, letting out a long breath with each big bush they passed, knowing it wouldn't be the site of her murder. Her heart thundered so loudly she wondered if the man could hear it. She looked up at the inky sky. Was there a God up there she should be praying to? Even if there was, it was so dark she doubted He could see her.

Wherever the man was taking her, he was slowing down. Rita left God in peace. He hadn't shown up anyway, so why bother begging for help over and over again? She could feel rivulets of sweat running down her sides, and there was mud under her fingernails. She was going to die dirty, and there wouldn't be any of her close relatives around to wash and prepare her body for burial. She thought back to the turbulence on the plane, wishing her life had ended that day. At least she'd have had Andrew by her side.

Rita wiped the palms of her hands on her coat. She noticed the bushes were thinning out and there were lights up ahead. There was an enormous field dotted with campfires. She could make out the silhouettes of people dancing around them. The flames were so high Rita imagined them reaching the sky and waking up God. As they approached the field, the voices grew louder. Now she understood. He meant to share her with his friends.

They're going to take turns raping me, then chop me into pieces!

It had been so dark in the forest she hadn't seen what her kidnapper looked like. She turned to him to beg for her life one more time then gasped in surprise. In the dull light of the distant fires, she could see the man wasn't actually a man, but a boy of no more than fourteen.

And most of the people in the field were women and children. Her pulse was racing. After all she'd been through, now she was going to die of a heart attack!

"This way." The boy pointed to a nearby tent. "You'll stay with us tonight."

A new wave of panic washed over Rita.

"Don't worry. There's only my mother and the kids," he said, as if he could read her mind. "We want to go over to the other side too. We tried many times but we haven't made it yet. You're like us, right?"

Like us? Who are you? But she remained stunned into silence.

The boy led her past the fires to a black tent patched up with pieces of ragged fabric which looked like huge moths in the darkness. Rita froze outside the tent, unable to enter. The boy smiled and waved a hand for her to follow him. Powerless to object, Rita took two more steps until she was standing just inside the entrance to the tent. The boy placed Rita's suitcase in a corner, then bent down and whispered something to a woman, who Rita assumed was his mother. The woman was lying on a mat – there were no mattresses or beds – and she struggled into a sitting position, her elbow resting on the ground. She pursed her lips. Her eyes were small, or maybe they looked smaller because of the large, faded brick-coloured headscarf she wore. She pulled the scarf forward and said something to the boy in a language Rita couldn't understand. The woman waved her hands maniacally, gesturing to the entrance every now and then.

Just when it seemed the woman would slap the boy, he pulled out Rita's money, which he'd tucked in his pocket. The woman clasped her hand over her mouth, falling silent. Her eyes sparkled in the darkness and the wrinkles on her forehead disappeared. This time, she looked at Rita and gestured to her to sit on a nearby wooden stool – a tree trunk. It was better than the concrete floor of Milan's Metro. Silently, Rita sat, her hands between her knees.

"I'll be back soon," the boy said to Rita in English, and disappeared.

It was cold and gloomy inside the tent, yet Rita was

sweating like she was in a sauna. She was paralysed, but she managed to take shallow breaths. They hadn't killed her yet. From the corner of her eye, she saw the woman open a small box, like a rabbit hutch, and pull out an old, dented brass cezve. She wore a long-sleeved dress, the same colour as her headscarf.

The woman pointed at the tent entrance.

Does she want me to leave? Rita considered getting up, but then the woman herself passed by her and left the tent.

Rita looked around and realised that she wasn't actually alone. Two children were sleeping close by. She couldn't tell their ages, but the dim light of the fires outside shown just brightly enough for Rita to make out their skeletal hands, hollow cheeks, and chapped lips. A small dirty blanket covered their bodies, leaving their bare feet sticking out. Rita moved closer to them. The pillow they were using was nothing more than a plastic bag, stuffed with clothes.

I have to sneak away, now!

Two seconds later, the woman walked in through the fabric door of the tent. Startled, Rita sat back down on her tree trunk stool. She handed Rita a plastic cup, steam rising from it. If it was hot, it didn't matter what it contained. Rita cupped her hands around it to warm them.

"Tea, tea," the woman said, pretending she had

an imaginary cup in her hand which she lifted to her lips. Rita understood she had to drink from the plastic cup. Rita also understood it was stupid to ask her host who they were, because the woman clearly didn't speak English. The woman slid back under the torn blanket and wrapped her arm around her children.

The liquid warmed Rita's body. After her first sip, she silently thanked the woman, who was pretending to be asleep.

Deep in her thoughts, Rita didn't know how much time had passed by the time the boy came back to the tent. Her eyes had grown accustomed to the light, and she could see the boy's clothes were just like the tent: patched, torn, and dirty.

She peered up at him through her fallen fringe, as he opened his coat and pulled out a black plastic bag. The smell of baked bread filled every corner of the tent.

The woman jumped to her feet and again they spoke in their own language. From the way she moved her head, Rita understood the woman had said *no*. The boy turned to Rita and handed her a quarter of a baguette. Just a plain piece of bread. But after the last few days, Rita had forgotten that most people ate their bread with a plate, butter, or even jam.

The boy sat next to her and tore a big chunk from his part of the baguette, nodding at the children. "They haven't eaten a thing for two days. I told her to wake them up, but Mother thinks it's better to leave them until tomorrow. Even if it means sleeping with an empty stomach, that way they'll have food for one more day ahead."

Rita peered at the bread in the bag. Three more rolls. "They're cold now," he continued. "It takes an hour to walk from the shop to here. Anyway, bread is bread, cold or warm, and we will fill our stomachs and have pleasant dreams tonight. The shop is like paradise. You should see it! They have pizza, cheese, bacon and..." He took another bite. "And sweets, a lot of them." This time he licked his lips, as if he was nibbling a piece of cake. "I wanted to buy some sweets for the kids, but then I thought how much we need this money." The boy looked at his piece of bread, which he'd already half-finished. "Also, if I buy too many things, the others will notice and wonder where I'm getting the money. It's better to be careful."

The others.

Rita shivered. Who was this family, and who were the others? She took a small bite of her bread and chewed it a thousand times before swallowing. She tore a second chunk off but struggled again to gulp it down. Rita opened her mouth to have another bite but the boy grabbed her arm.

"Only three bites. Save it for tomorrow. I promise

it'll still taste good, just harder. The next day we'll mix it with water."

Using a paper tissue from her pocket, Rita copied the boy and wrapped up her bread.

She put her head in her hands and thought back to when she was five years old. She loved staying at her cousin's house. They would always refuse to eat the soup Auntie Angela had cooked for them and would sneak off to the balcony to feed the birds with their leftover bread. Better bread than this family survived on.

17

Chloe has stopped crying. She is talking to the man and every now and then I hear snippets of their conversation. I hear Chloe saying that everything will be alright, but I don't believe her. The man wipes his eyes.

"Rita is strong," Chloe says. "You have no idea what she's suffered. Getting here. Losing her mum. Then her dog."

Luk. My sweet boy.

And with that, I'm thrust back to the past, back to the day Helen killed my dog. Chloe and the man by my bed can't see I'm leaving again. My body is still there, but I linger on between life and death. It's almost time to decide which way to go.

As soon as I heard Helen telling Dad I should leave home, I started looking for a job. A real one. I didn't tell Samuel, but I'd sent my CV out all over the city. The replies I received were almost identical, as if all the companies I'd applied to had some unspoken agreement that I wasn't fit for any job on offer. As Helen had always said, others were more capable than me.

When I wasn't taking care of Daniel, I was taking pictures, hoping my photography would be good enough to get me a job at a local magazine. I wasn't exactly shooting for Vogue or Hollywood, but I still wanted people to see the stories behind the pictures. Once a week Samuel and I went to the outskirts of the city. I was forever searching for that one evocative face that would be worthy of a magazine cover and make me famous. That's when I knew what I had to do – I had to tell the story of the women in my country. If I could just shoot the perfect picture, no magazine would say no to my work.

So, I took pictures of them, working in the fields, feeding their children, and working in their homes. They kept their households running while their husbands worked abroad. I talked to them. I saw the pain in their eyes. They didn't know if they would see their husbands again. Maybe these men had double lives in these strange other countries that had welcomed them. They rarely came home, but they kept sending money back and the women kept taking care of the children.

Seeing how hard I was working to get noticed, Samuel asked his father to put in a good word for me at a daily newspaper. That's how it is in my country, if you have money, you know everyone.

The editor of the newspaper didn't offer me a job, but he posted one of my pictures on the last page of the newspaper and they paid me a little for it.

I didn't realise that that would be the first and last payment I would get for my photography. I didn't realise that to be successful in that field, it's not what you know but *who* you know.

I wrote a letter to Mum and told her the good news, attaching the newspaper clipping inside my diary. I was over the moon, heady with my own success. Dad was staying in the capital for work, and I didn't want to spend time with Helen, so I sneaked out to meet Samuel.

It was a warm spring evening. The sky was amber. Days were longer now, and I loved to stroll on the nearby beach with him. Beach season had not yet begun, and there were only a few young couples sitting on the sand. The beach in Durrës was not as pretty or luxurious as the ones in Vlora, or Saranda, in the south of Albania, but it was still a beach. The scent of salty air and the sound of the waves were the same.

I hadn't told Samuel that Helen wanted me out of the house. It was too humiliating.

We sat at our table at Chic bar. The waiter always kept our table free because the tip Samuel gave him was half his daily wage.

Samuel drank a beer, and I had a cappuccino. After Helen found me drunk on raki I vowed never to touch alcohol again. After our drink together we walked along the beach hand in hand, talking in excited whispers about our futures – he a successful businessman and me a famous photographer. Life was perfect for those two precious hours.

He walked me home and when I opened the door, Daniel was crying on the couch.

"Rita." He stretched out his arms and ran towards me.

I kneeled down and gave him a cuddle. "What's wrong, sweetie?"

It must be Helen. Maybe she'd slapped him. It wouldn't be the first time.

I ruffled his hair, and all I could hear through his sobs was, "Luk, Luk."

He was pointing to the corner of the room. Luk lay on his right side, his paws limp, his eyes closed. On a normal day he would have jumped up at me the moment I arrived home, licking my face. Sometimes he even got jealous when I gave Daniel attention, wanting it all for himself.

"Is he sleeping?" I asked, although more to myself than my baby brother. I wasn't convincing either of us.

"Oh, you're here finally. I've been calling you,"

Helen appeared, her shoulder leaning against the door frame. "That ugly beast of yours has been lying there for hours. *He won't move.*"

That ugly beast of yours! Those words. I would never forget them. Her shrill voice, like a blacksmith grinding a metal bar, drilled deep into the cracks of my heart. Helen held Luk's bowl. I had cleaned the bowl out only that morning. Why had she just washed it?

She'd poisoned my dog. There was no way of proving it, but I could see it in the curl of her lip as she stood there looking down at me. She'd come into my home like a snake, fooling my father and my aunt. But she hadn't fool me. I'd seen right through her from day one. She wanted me out and she'd played her trump card.

For a split second, I considered killing her. I could say I was defending my dog. That would hold up in court, right? Or doesn't it work that way with animals?

I placed Daniel to one side and stood up, rage emanating from my every pore. My bag and camera fell to the floor. While I had been out taking pictures of the sunset, this bitch had killed my dog!

Chloe and the man are calling to me. Can't they see what Helen has done?

I look at myself lying in a hospital bed, and I look at my dog lying motionless on the floor. I have to make a choice – a choice between two agonies.

I walked over and kneeled beside Luk, shaking him

gently. "Oh, Luk! What happened, boy? Luk, please wake up!" But I knew he was not going to wake up. I cried as I stroked the little dog's head, and then slowly turned to face Helen. "What have you done?" I screamed.

She gave me a cautionary, keep-your-voice-down look, but I would scream as much and as loud as I wanted. This was my home.

Helen shrugged. "I'm not his owner, you are. Take him outside. I've had enough of this nonsense. You've been gone for hours, and Daniel hasn't stopped crying. You're an adult now, aren't you, Rita? Deal with your own dog."

She went to the entryway, put on her high heels, and left the house, slamming the door behind her.

Having missed my opportunity to hit Helen, I punched the wall instead. I hit it as hard as I could, but however much my hand hurt, it didn't come close to the pain in my heart.

I didn't know what to do. I was all alone with a dead dog and a crying toddler. Eventually, I stood up, found a warm blanket, and covered Luk's lifeless body.

In my country, the idea of burying a dog was laughable to most people. Pets were usually just thrown into the nearest bin, or left out in the open for other animals to dispose of. But I wasn't going to hand my Luk over to other animals so they could rip his little body apart and devour him. Burying him was yet another thing I had to do in secret, and now I also had to take care of Daniel. I called Samuel and explained what had happened. I could hear in his voice that he didn't believe Helen could do something like that, that he thought there had to be some other rational explanation.

A few moments later, Samuel arrived. I somehow managed to bottle up my grief and anger as I placed my dog's lifeless body into the boot of my boyfriend's car. My heart was shattered. Since he was a little puppy, Luk had always travelled on my lap in the car, but this would be his final road trip, and Daniel would be sitting on my lap instead.

The darkness had swallowed the city whole, so nobody would see what we were going to do. When we arrived at the cemetery, I left Samuel and Daniel in the car and took Luk's body, along with a small hand spade, from the boot before hurrying towards the graveyard. I didn't know what I was doing, I just knew I needed to do it as quickly as possible. I found a patch of soft soil beside my mum's grave and used the hand spade to dig a small hole, around three feet deep. Sweat and tears ran down my face as I lowered my dog's body into the hole and covered him with dirt. Just like that, Luk was gone. The same as my mother. As if neither had ever even existed.

"Take care of him, Mum," I whispered, before dragging myself away.

Back in the car, Samuel was telling a joke and Daniel was laughing. Life goes on.

I swallowed and opened Samuel's glove compartment, looking for wipes or a rag to clean my dirty hands, when an envelope marked London Business School fell into my lap.

"What's this?" I asked.

"Ah, that. I, erm, applied for a master's degree in Management in London. I was going to tell you."

Exactly when was he going to tell me?

"Are you leaving me?" My voice was stone cold. I'd just buried my dog, and now Samuel was telling me he was off to London. How was I going to live without him?

"Of course not, I could never leave you!" Samuel glanced at Daniel, who was beginning to nod off. "It's for us, our future, me and you in London. Far away from this fucking country."

Samuel had never loved our country like I did. He had always been ashamed of it, and I'd never understood why. Then again, I'd never been abroad. What did I know about the rest of the world?

"If I get accepted, we'll apply for a master's degree for you too. Just imagine! You could find work as a photographer for a fashion magazine in London. Wouldn't that be great?"

"Are you sure you only had one beer tonight? How am I supposed to go to London? Maybe you've forgotten we need a visa and money to go to the UK. I can't afford a master's in Albania, let alone London."

"They have scholarships, babe. I've checked. I can pay for it. My father won't mind. I'll tell him it's an investment. We'll pay him back."

The idea of starting a new life in London with Samuel was both scary and beautiful. Was I ready to live in a big city like London? Yes, I could do anything if I was with Samuel. And after what Helen had done today, I wanted to get away from this place more than ever. But I didn't believe for a minute that his family would foot the bill for my education.

My mind was reeling. I'd just lost my dog and now Samuel was talking about starting a new life in another country. I needed time to take it all in. I needed time to grieve.

Samuel was still talking, but his voice soon evaporated into thin air.

It's not him I'm hearing now. It's another voice, pulling me back. The voice in the present is stronger than Samuel's in the past, and I find myself being dragged back to *the now*. I'm in the hospital room again, but Chloe has gone.

"She's sweating. Is that a good or bad sign?" the man asks the nurse.

Who is this man? Is it Samuel? Is it my dad? I can't even tell what language he's speaking. He's holding my hand. He says he loves me. That's enough to keep me here for now.

18

Hell
Tuesday morning, 29 October 2019

The tent shook from the wind howling outside and Rita sank into sleep, dreaming of bread. Her head on her hands, she didn't remember dozing off. When dawn broke, in what felt like just a few seconds later, she opened her eyes and tried to stretch her cramped legs. There wasn't enough room. She blew on her hands, trying to warm them up. Even the air that came out of her mouth looked like cold puffs of steam.

Rita glanced at the others in the tent. Despite their empty stomachs, the family with no name was still sleeping. Now and then the mother's arm would emerge from under the blanket and envelope the children, as if she was confirming all her little birds were still in the nest.

Rita's mum had done the same. And to some extent, Samuel had too. *What is he doing now?* she wondered, brushing away a tear. He had just vanished into thin air, leaving no trace. It didn't make sense. When was the last time I had waited for him to call her back, the 17th or 18th of June? All his social media accounts had disappeared. She thought it was the 18th. Did it make any difference? She just wanted to find him.

Rita groaned, then put her hand over her mouth. She didn't want to wake the family.

Shaking her head, she tried to push the memories of her mum, her dog, and Samuel out of her mind. Dwelling over all she'd lost was not going to help her right now.

The first rays of sun crept through the holes in the tent and Rita looked around the small space where so many souls had spent the night together. The ground was damp. She rubbed her hands together to warm them and then tightened her arms around her body.

A pile of clothes lay close to the children's feet. She saw a dented frying pan, some plastic cups which may have once been white, and some plastic bottles. Those were cut in half and filled with dirty water. Rita could clearly see the children's fingerprints on them. On the makeshift table was the plastic bag with the bread inside.

Everything was plastic. Everything was dirty.

Rita stretched her body and, without meaning to, touched the woman's feet. She pulled her legs back quickly, as if she'd stepped on thorns. If this wasn't hell – and she was pretty certain that she hadn't died – then where was she? Rita recalled the fires from the night before, the other tents and the people. *Am I a prisoner? If they wanted to kill me, they had plenty of time to do it while I was asleep. It would be better for them to let me go and keep the rest of the bread for themselves. It would be one less mouth to feed.*

Pushing her thoughts aside, she lifted the fabric of the makeshift tent door and stared outside. The ghost village was still asleep. It was so silent that Rita was afraid of her own breath. Not feeling brave enough to leave the tent, she loosened the cloth door instead. It flapped in the wind, so she held it tight.

She was still busy concentrating on her breathing and making and discarding plans when people in the other tents began to wake up. Somebody slapped the tent she was in from the outside, and Rita jumped. The boy and the woman beside her opened their eyes too. None of them seemed worried. The little ones didn't even budge – they only opened their eyes when the woman spoke quietly to them in the language Rita couldn't identify.

Hunger shone in their eyes. Without looking at the uninvited newcomer, the children got up and hurried over to the bag of bread. Rita watched them, noting their skinny legs and their bare feet. Their dark skin was visible through the holes in their clothes. Their faces were brown, but they looked paler than they should be, likely due to poor nutrition... or no nutrition at all. The kids snatched the bread with both hands, their eyes growing larger and brighter with each bite of the dry baguette.

Rita's own eyes filled with tears. She was still staring at the children when the woman disappeared. Before Rita had time to notice her absence, she came back through the door of the tent and handed her a cup of what she called tea.

"Thank you," Rita said in English, grabbing the plastic cup.

She lifted the hot liquid to her dry lips, remembering Maria and the tea she'd given her at the Metro station. *What would have happened to me if she'd not been there to help?*

"Eat now, otherwise the kids will stare at you and beg for your bread." The boy's voice snapped her out of her thoughts.

The kids? He was still a child himself. Rita nodded but didn't have the heart to pull the hunk of bread out of her pocket. She finished her tea in just three gulps and placed the empty cup on the ground.

The suitcase she'd thrown into the forest that the boy had gone back for was in the tent now, covered in mud. Running her palm over the lid, she cleaned it a bit, then unzipped it and dug out three thick sweaters. She handed the biggest one to the woman. Not much else was left in the bag, except books, which she doubted the family would want. The boy's eyes were fixed on the T-shirt still in her suitcase. It was the only thing of Samuel's she had left.

She picked it up, holding it to her nose to inhale the scent of Samuel one last time, then handed it to the boy. It was her way of saying thank you for the bread and the hospitality. Biting her bottom lip to stop the tears from welling up, she looked around her at the misery these people were living in. It almost made her feel guilty for thinking her own life had been hard.

The boy wasn't like the rest of the family though. His face was darker, and he had hazel eyes, just like Rita's. Even though his hair was cut short, the roots were curly.

He put the T-shirt over his head and pulled it down over his scrawny body.

"Hollywood, Hollywood," he said, pointing at the design on the top. "Thank you," he said, spinning around before covering his gift with his shabby coat.

"Come. Let's go out," he said, holding open the fabric door.

Just tell me how to jump into a lorry and disappear, Rita wanted to say. But who could teach that to anyone?

The boy was still holding the fabric door open. Unable to think up a good excuse not to go, Rita followed him. Once outside, she stretched her back, reaching up to the sky as the first rays of sunlight, cold and foreign, stroked her face. *The sun has teeth*, her grandma would have said. She would have been right today – it was bitingly cold.

"Stay here, I'll be back in a minute," the boy told her, before approaching a group of teenagers.

Rita glanced around her and shivered. She'd felt safer inside the tent.

The moment the boy reached his friends, he opened his coat and showed off his new T-shirt. After moving from side to side, he turned round and looked at Rita. All their eyes fell upon her. Rita averted her gaze and looked at the other tents. They were all the same – filthy and threadbare. In every corner of the world, poverty had the same sour smell.

A young woman emerged from one of the other tents. She gave Rita a curious glance and then proceeded to light a fire next to her feet. Using three stones as a fireplace, the young woman put a black saucepan on top and poured in some water from a plastic bottle. A group of children followed her, each holding a small bowl firmly in both hands. They sat around the low flames, little eyes fixed on the meal boiling in the big pot.

Feeling trapped, Rita looked back over at the boy and his friends. They were still staring at her. *What the hell do they want?* She clenched her hands in her pockets. The boys in Italy had done the same thing. First, they'd given her predatory glances and then they'd stolen her camera. They'd stolen everything, but the camera hurt the most. Rita dropped her gaze to the burning flames.

Finally, the boy left the group and trotted towards her.

"I don't even know your name," Rita said the moment he joined her.

"Bashir," he said, holding his thin fingers out to the fire in a bid to warm up. Dirt coated his fingernails.

"Does it mean anything?"

"Yeah." He paused. "The one who carries good news, they say." He said it in a dull, dry voice, as if he didn't believe it. "And you?"

"Rita."

"What does it mean?" He appeared to enjoy the conversation. She remembered Andrew and how he'd tried to distract her with a question game on the plane.

"Pearl." It suddenly occurred to Rita that she had never asked her mum why she'd chosen that name for her. "How old are you?"

"I'll be fifteen next month," the boy said.

At fifteen, I was trying to get out of eating the meals my mum had cooked for me, flouncing around in pretty dresses, and hanging out with my boyfriend. I can't imagine taking care of a family at that age.

"Where do you all come from?"

"Most of us are from Somalia. And you?"

"I come from Cuckoo Land," she said.

"You're joking. Like cloud cuckoo land?"

It might as well be a make-believe place.

"Yeah. Something like that."

Bashir chuckled. "I've never heard of it. It's not in Africa, I'm guessing."

"You're right. It's not in Africa. If I told you I'm from a bit of everywhere, would that be enough?"

"That can't be true. A person has to have a place of birth, a motherland, a homeland, whatever you call it," Bashir replied.

What could she say to a fourteen-year-old boy who looked like a thirty-year-old man? Not knowing what to say, Rita sighed and pulled a cigarette out of her pocket.

"Can I have one?" Bashir asked, pointing at the cigarette.

"You're too young to smoke."

"I've been smoking since I was ten."

Rita cut the cigarette in half and handed him the piece with the butt, like she had done with Maria. She then picked up a piece of burning cedar bark to light his half and her own.

"How long have you been living here?"

"Almost six months," he said, exhaling a cloud of smoke.

If I had to spend six months here, I'd go mad.

"It's difficult to get on a lorry if you're a big family like us." He pointed at the two tents. "Many have been lucky, but not us. We've tried twice and failed twice." He took another puff.

"What is this place?"

Bashir's eyes widened. "Have you never heard of Hell's Jungle?"

Hell's Jungle. *So,* I am *dead.* "Never."

"Strange. We've been on the news so many times. We're famous, you know? Except we're not. They closed the place, but we came back. We have no other place to go. We're all trying to get to the other side. How did you find us if you've never heard about us?"

"I didn't find you. *You* found *me*, remember? I'm trying to get to London."

Rita counted the cigarettes inside the packet. Three left. Was that enough until she got on a lorry? She could go without eating but not without cigarettes.

The flames of the fire quietly crackled beside them.

"Do you know where I can jump onto a lorry?" She finally asked what she'd wanted to since she'd arrived at the camp.

"They're everywhere." He still had the butt of the finished cigarette between his dry lips. "The problem is being in the right place at the right time. And on top of everything else, you must be careful what kind of lorry it is. If you hide in a refrigerated lorry, you'll come out like a piece of ice. Even if they thaw you, you'll be no good to anyone." He snorted. This was his life and laughing at it was the only thing he could do.

Refrigerator? She thought of the newspaper on the train to Paris.

Back in her country she'd heard that all she had to do was jump onto a lorry and the next morning she would be in England. Simple as that.

"How do you know all this?"

"A friend of mine once got on a lorry like that. He was lucky, the police stopped him. Most of the time I know how to tell a good lorry from a bad lorry. The ones that have a tarpaulin cover normally aren't a freezer. Others have the goods they're carrying written in huge letters on the side, so that makes it easier."

"And how do you know if there's space?"

He smiled.

"Ah, once you're inside you find out."

"What about the right time?" Rita laced her fingers together and put them near the fire.

"When dusk falls, that's when you sneak on. The night is our friend."

"Can you take me there tonight?"

"No, you can't go tonight. Remember those boys I

was talking to? They told me that police were on the streets last night. Everywhere. The same is predicted for tonight. Usually, they go around searching the lorries for a few days. You should wait until we know they're gone."

Wait here? No way.

"The problem is," the boy added, "you must leave soon and get to the other side or get the hell out of the jungle. A precious pearl is more valuable than a hot meal."

"What do you mean? Should I be scared?" Rita was already scared.

"Don't worry. We'll defend you, me and my friends. That's why I talked to them. Coming from the same village, we're like brothers. We look after each other. Often other groups start fights with us. They're stronger than we are. We are all here fighting for the same thing, yet it's us they attack."

"Attack?" Rita's pulse doubled.

"It's not called 'the Jungle' for nothing. Life is tough here, only the strongest survive. Mostly, they grab whatever we have to eat. When they find nothing, they get angry and sometimes pick up two or three girls. The girls come back broken, if they come back at all." He inhaled deeply. "A week ago, two girls hanged themselves on that tree over there."

Rita's breath stuck in her throat and her stomach lurched.

"I need to go to the toilet," she said, scanning the campsite, searching for any sign of a bathroom.

Bashir pointed at the trees, the same place the girls had hanged themselves. "Avoid the toilets. You'll shit yourself before your turn comes. There are always seventy people in the queue. Even if you're lucky and you make it, you never know what you might catch there. Nature is better and cleaner."

"I can hold it in. But tonight, you have to take me to the lorries. Please."

"Don't you understand my English? I told you, tonight is impossible. Why aren't you listening?" He stood and looked down at Rita.

"I have to get out of here! What if the guys lied about the police?" Rita forced back tears.

"Okay, I'll show you myself, but don't say I didn't warn you." Bashir shook his head and gave her an exasperated, almost pitying look. He started towards the tent but turned back to her at the entrance. "Also," he shouted, "they're my friends, and they don't lie." He bent down and disappeared behind the flap of the tent door.

Rita breathed in the chilly air. Her stomach twisted again with hunger, fear, and every other imaginable emotion. Bashir didn't understand that Rita was risking her life for love. Then again, how could a fourteen-year-old boy understand that?

19

Today it's not the nurse who talks, but the doctor. He keeps his voice low but I'm past caring. Luk is dead and Samuel wants to leave the country. Past and present memories are piled one on top of the other like a stack of cards.

I remember how confused I was when I got out of Samuel's car. The idea of going to London had come out of the blue. Could we really make Samuel's plan work?

When we left the cemetery, he'd asked me if I was okay, and if he should stay with me, but I wanted to be alone. I'd just lost my dog, and I had to get my baby brother to bed. Of course, I was also angry with Samuel. He should have spoken to me before submitting the application.

With Daniel in my arms, I opened the door of my apartment. Helen wasn't there. I sighed, knowing it was for the best. I was no murderer, but I could have killed her that night.

I put Daniel in his pyjamas and fed him some toast.

"Rita, is Luk going to come back?" he asked.

"No, honey. Luk is not coming back."

Daniel's eyes filled with tears, and I felt bad for telling him the truth. I pulled him closer and kissed his forehead. "Now, let me tell you a story."

I hear my own voice making up a children's story. It blends with the voices in the hospital room. My auntie Angela is there, and with a pang of emotion, I realise how much I've missed her. I'm recognising faces. Isn't that a good sign? The man and my aunt swap place. Why can't I see his face?

20

Hell
Tuesday evening, 29 October 2019

The sun disappeared behind the trees and the temperature dropped. Rita sat beside the fire, listening to the crackle of the burning wood, the crispy air filling her lungs. All day long, different women had queued up to cook for the inhabitants of their tents. The meal they prepared was nothing more than water mixed with wild plants and anything they could find in the woods. Rita tried twice to eat the piece of bread she had in her coat pocket, and both times, she stopped. In the end, she handed it to a little girl sitting beside her.

If I get away from this hell on Earth, I will cherish every day of my life, she thought watching the child gnaw at the dry bread.

Why don't you start now?

Were these the lengths she'd had to go to just to discover her own strength? She put her hand in her pocket, drew out another half-smoked cigarette, and lit it. The cloud of cigarette smoke mingled with the smoke of the dying fire. It was almost time to leave, and Bashir was nowhere to be seen. *What if he isn't telling me the truth?* She kicked a pebble at her feet. The small stone flew inside a nearby tent. Rita couldn't have aimed that well had she tried a thousand times! A girl, around her same age, came out to see who had thrown the stone. As soon as she saw the girl, Rita's heart skipped a beat. She'd read once that everyone has a double somewhere in the world, what the Germans called a *Doppelgänger*. Rita didn't normally believe in that sort of thing, and yet, here she was, face to face with someone who could have been her twin sister.

"I'm sorry," Rita whispered, unsure if she was apologizing for kicking the stone or for being the luckier of the two of them. "It was an accident."

The girl came closer, and Rita saw she wasn't a girl at all. She was a young woman, breast-feeding a small child nestled in her arms.

"It's okay, don't worry," the woman said. She had the same accent as Bashir. "The stone hit our tent and it woke my son up. I try to keep the children asleep. If they sleep, they don't ask to eat." She smiled and rubbed the little boy's hair. Two teeth were missing from the left side of her mouth, but Rita thought her smile was radiant, nonetheless. Despite the cold, the woman wore only a light sweater that covered half her body, a long skirt that reached her ankles, and a pair of sandals. Looking at the woman's red feet made Rita shiver.

The women cradled the little boy with her right arm, and with her left, she smoothed down the hair of a little girl who'd stepped out from behind her. The little girl wrapped her arm around her mother's leg and put her dirty thumb in her mouth.

The lump Rita had in her throat since that morning grew even bigger.

"Are you a journalist?" the woman asked her.

Why did they all think that? "No."

"I've watched you sitting here the whole day."

This caught Rita off-guard. Bashir was right. A girl like her, still in her best clothes and wearing shoes, stuck out like a sore thumb in this place.

"NGO?"

"No, nothing like that," Rita muttered, without looking at her.

"Ah, I thought you were with one of them. Every now and then their people turn up here, ask some questions, leave some food, and write about us. The world sees briefly, but people soon lose interest, move on to another headline." Her tone changed from tired to sarcastic. "Once, someone offered me a chocolate bar. That was generous."

"I'm like you," Rita said quickly. "I'm just trying to get to the other side."

She pointed to where she thought the sea had to be, and beyond that, England. The young woman's face softened. She put the child down gently and adjusted her dress. The boy started picking at some dry blades of grass, but the woman made no attempt to stop him. She stepped closer to the fire, poked the embers, and put a saucepan on it. It was her turn to cook.

"What's your name?" the woman asked, blowing onto the fire.

"Rita," she answered in a low voice, wondering how the woman could be so nonchalant. Had she not noticed that looking at Rita was like looking at herself in the mirror? A lighter-skinned version of herself, but the same, nevertheless.

"Rita. That's a beautiful name."

"Thank you. Yours?"

"Sumaya."

"Sumaya," Rita repeated, just to check she'd understood it properly.

"So, Rita, where did you come from? How did you find us?"

"I came here from Italy. I'm not Italian, though. I was walking in the woods, and somebody stopped me. Turns out the boy lives here. His name is Bashir." Rita told the woman her story in one breath, as if she were afraid of forgetting something.

"Ah, Bashir, he's my little brother," Sumaya replied, and blew again on the fire, which didn't want to light. "Since my father and husband left, all the burden of the family rests on Bashir's shoulders."

Rita gave her a quizzical look.

"If Bashir is your brother, then the woman in the tent where I slept last night is your mother?" She eyed the tent where the rest of the family was.

"Fatima is my stepmother. My mother died two weeks after giving birth to me. I never knew her." Her face didn't show any trace of pain. Perhaps, never having known her mother, her pain had another name. "I was one year old when my father got married. Fatima has been my mother ever since. She's the only mother I know. My father could have never gotten by alone."

I wish I could have been as happy as you when my dad married Helen, Rita thought.

"Your stepmother doesn't speak any English," Rita said. "But I'm glad you do. I don't know how to thank her for letting me stay inside her tent."

"I will tell her for you. Fatima never got an education, she stayed home to tend her father as a child, then looked after my father. I went to school and took some classes until I got married. You see my son over there?" Sumaya pointed at the small boy she'd been nursing, who was now shoving dirt into his mouth. "My husband never met him."

Rita wasn't very good at guessing children's ages, but the boy had to be around two.

"My husband and my father left the village together, before us. I didn't know I was pregnant. We already had two children, and life in our village was unbearable, with or without children. There were days when we had nothing to eat. What little we got from the fields was stolen by the gangs from neighbouring villages. Our houses were falling apart, and we had no money to repair them. One day Bashir came to visit us with good news. My father and husband had paid a large amount of money to traffickers who promised to take us to the UK. They said we'd be welcomed and that all the men would have jobs waiting for them. We believed them. We had no other choice."

Sounds familiar.

"We arrived in France, and they told us it was England. We had no idea. They left us in the middle of the street and disappeared. We had two choices: jump onto a lorry, or dive into the sea, because we couldn't ever go back to our village again." Sumaya opened the lid of the saucepan and threw in a handful of rice. There was no salt, no oil, just plain water and rice. "I've been saving this rice for two months now."

Her face lit up as she stirred, either at the prospect

171

of the night's meal or from the warmth of the growing flames.

"Two days ago, Bashir was able to collect our quota of rice from the Red Cross, but he was attacked on the way back to the camp. This is all we have left."

Rita coughed, not from the smoke but from the fear of what could happen to any of them.

"How long do you think you'll be here?" Sumaya asked, poking the cinders with a stick. Rita couldn't believe how calm she was, as if they were having a conversation in her own kitchen.

"I'm going to try to leave tonight." *If I stay one more night here, I'm going to fall apart. I had no idea I wasn't strong enough to wander the streets of Europe without anyone looking out for me. Samuel has always been there for me, until he left. But I can't push my luck any further.*

Rita couldn't say this out loud. She didn't want to cry in front of this kind woman.

"Well, good luck," Sumaya said. She looked Rita straight in the eye but didn't flinch. Maybe she saw the similarity between them but didn't care. Looking the same wasn't going to help either of them.

"Thanks, I'm going to need it."

Silence hung in the air between them.

Now it was Rita's turn to poke the wood. Staring at the charcoal, she grappled for the right words. When she found nothing, she lifted her head and glanced at the sky. The way the clouds moved promised rain. Two light-grey clouds fused and turned into one darker cloud.

"I hope it won't rain tonight." She couldn't find anything better to say.

"Well, if our prayers have fallen on God's ears, it will. We're running out of water, and we don't have many buckets left," said Sumaya.

One person's disaster is another person's blessing.

Holding the hem of her skirt with one hand, Sumaya rose and herded the children inside her tent. A cold breeze blew from the north. Dirt and leaves swirled in the air, making Rita sneeze. When Sumaya didn't immediately return, Rita began to wonder if she had somehow offended the young woman.

Of course you have, said the voice in her head.

But I didn't even say anything! Rita yelled back silently.

Exactly! You just sat there doing nothing.

But what can I do? I gave Bashir all my money, Rita quipped.

Money isn't everything.

Maybe the voice was right. These people had given her shelter. Instead of toasting herself by the fireplace she could have done some chores to repay them for their hospitality.

Then, Sumaya appeared again, this time carrying a small bowl.

"Here." She handed it to Rita and grabbed the saucepan that was still steaming. "Be careful not to burn yourself," she said, slanting the pot. Then she poured hot soup into the bowl. Some of the droplets splashed Rita's hand. Clearly, a ladle or a spoon was a luxury that no one in the camp had. "Enjoy, and good luck tonight," Sumaya repeated, then turned to leave.

"Wait, you need this for the kids." Rita tried to hand back the bowl of soup. She hadn't eaten a thing all day, but those children needed it more than her. Plus, she would be leaving tonight.

Sumaya smiled, "There is plenty for everyone. I added some extra water, it's fine."

Tears filled Rita's eyes, the words tightening in her throat. These people had nothing, yet they still shared all they had.

She blew on the soup and took a sip from the bowl. It was hard to eat without a spoon, but the small amount she got filled her stomach. It ought to tide her over until she got to the UK.

Bashir, where are you? Please don't desert me now!

As if hearing her silent plea, a tall male figure stumbled out of the bushes and headed towards her, his face hidden behind a huge pile of dry branches he was carrying. He flung them down, and relief flooded through her at the sight of Bashir's familiar face.

"We'll need them tonight. There's going to be frost," he said.

Rita pulled her knees up to her chin, moving away from the dead logs, making the rest of her soup spill out of the bowl.

"I'm not going to be here tonight. You know that," she said resolutely.

Bashir looked calm as he put more wood on the fire. It didn't take long for the flames to send glittering embers up into the sky like fireworks.

21

I think I heard fireworks last night and the man whispered Happy New Year to me. Does this mean it's already January, or am I still dreaming?

After I lost my dog, the atmosphere in my apartment grew worse, the cloud of grief became a permanent fixture. Dad said he would buy me another pet, as if I was a little kid. Of course he'd say that, considering he'd replaced Mum with Helen so quickly. I knew Helen wouldn't tolerate another dog. Not that she had anything against pets, just mine.

During the nights that followed, I heard them arguing again. I could hear snippets of their conversation, but Helen kept her voice low. I was still looking for a job. I wasn't at all convinced that Samuel's family would pay for me to get a master's degree in London, let alone that he could get me a scholarship. These things were for other people, not the likes of me. But Samuel was a dreamer. He'd always been like that, never taking life too seriously. A luxury of the rich. I, on the other hand, took life more seriously than I probably should have. That's why we were together, I guess. Polar opposites who kept each other on track.

I was still job hunting but had my heart set on winning the grand photography prize for my final college project. I'd taken a photo of an old woman holding a child's hand while she crossed the street. The child was squeezing a big teddy bear in the crook of his skinny arm. It had been hard to capture the precious moment, both of them smiling at each other. The kid had kept moving his head from side to side and it had taken over thirty attempts to get the perfect shot. Samuel loved the photo as much as I did, and he was sure I'd win.

Perhaps an editor would see my work, and just like that, I would get a job. Surely it wasn't that difficult if you were in the right place at the right time. I'd never been in either, but I could dream.

I hadn't counted on falling into a dream from which I couldn't wake up, though. The man beside me is sipping a coffee and telling me he loves me for the millionth time. But I'm too far away to open my eyes.

I'm in my classroom now and it's empty. My classmates have all gone. Even my friend Magda. Magda is short for Magdalena. In my country, the first thing people do is shorten your name – whether you like it or not. Even if it doesn't suit you, people think it's their right to give you a nickname. And so, Magdalena is her name only on paper, and only her parents, her professors, and I know her full name. She is the only friend I have left, and the only person who hates Helen as much as I do.

My other classmates make fun of me for spending so much time on the project because they are all certain who will win – and it's not me. It's always the same person, the dean's current favourite. The prettiest girl, or at least, the most willing.

I thrust my camera and some of my books into my backpack and carry the rest in my arms. I always take more books than I need to school, as if I'm scared Helen will burn them while I'm away. I wouldn't put anything past her after what she did to Luk.

The city is steeped in cold January drizzle. It's that time of year, when days tiptoe into darkness quicker than you realise. I zip my parka up to my throat, put on my warm woolly hat, and walk along the corridor.

Outside, it's dark and wet, the kind of rain that soaks you to the bone, catching you unawares. But I have no intention of taking a bus. I would rather get wet than arrive home early to Helen.

I trudge along and my phone rings, rescuing me from my cruel thoughts about whether Helen has been right all along. Samuel's smiling face appears on the screen of my iPhone.

"Hi, hon." His warm voice is like an embrace against my cold body. "I have some wonderful news. Remember the master's in the UK? Guess what?" He paused for greater effect. "They accepted me! Isn't that amazing? We're going to London!"

London.

Bang! Like a sudden crash of thunder and a flash of lightning somewhere out at sea, it dawns on me: things are going to change. I am losing him. They will never give me a scholarship. I don't have that kind of luck. In the hope that I've misheard or misunderstood him, I press the phone harder against my ear, tiny raindrops soaking my face. Or maybe they're tears.

"Rita, are you still there?"

"Yes! I'm so excited for you!" I swallow down the lump in my throat. "It's just... I can't imagine my life without you."

"What do you mean? The moment I settle in England, you'll join me. We've talked about this."

"Yes, you're right," I whisper, saying the words more to myself than to him. Who are either of us kidding? I am losing those I love, one by one.

"Shall I pick you up tonight at eight-thirty? I haven't seen you all day, and I've missed you."

We have so few days left.

We arrange a time and place, and he tells me he loves me, calls me his sunshine. I do the same. But it's mechanical, an old habit, because if you truly love someone, you don't let them go. I thrust my phone into my pocket and look at the sky. Maybe I can get a visa. Times have changed. It can't be that difficult anymore. *Albanians can travel without a visa in Europe, but not in the UK*, the voice reminds me. *Keep your feet on the ground, girl. His parents are paying for his master's. Even if you can get a visa, who's going to pay for you? You don't even have anything valuable to sell.*

As usual, my cynical voice is right. With my hands in my pockets to protect them from the cold, I hurry towards my apartment to get ready.

I'm a few minutes from home when the streetlights go off. That's nothing new in my city, it's always happening unexpectedly. The people on the street drift into the shadows like ghosts. I can't see where I am treading, then I slip on a puddle of water and fall. This isn't the first time I've fallen into an open manhole. People are so desperate for money that they remove manhole covers and sell them for scrap. On dark rainy nights, it's easy enough to fall into them. Luckily, I've only tripped, and I'm not injured too bad, even if my leg hurts and my hands are filthy.

I finally arrive at my apartment block, where the lights are shining, and the prospect of a shower and a hot chocolate keep me going. I hobble up the stairs slowly, and on the fifth floor, I steady my breath and knock on the door. Brushing the mud off my clothes is pointless, but I straighten myself up. The last thing I want is for Helen to see me so filthy and start nagging me.

It's taking too long for her to open the door. Maybe she isn't home at all. I fumble through my pockets for my key and insert it into the lock. But it doesn't turn. It doesn't make any sense. I knock on the door again. Nothing. I wait for ten seconds, then knock again. I take a step back and check the name on the door, just in case I have somehow, bizarrely, mistaken where I live.

Timi Hanas.

It is definitely my apartment.

Then it hits me, and my chin begins to tremble. Helen has done it again, only this time, in a statement louder than words. She's changed the locks. She's finally, totally, utterly, and completely gotten her own way, ejecting me from my dad and Daniel's lives. A tear runs down my face, carrying the dirt and landing on my lips. The taste of salt and mud mixes with my saliva. I didn't cry when I fell in the manhole, or when Samuel told me he was leaving, but I'm crying now. I swallow it all down. Daniel's yell breaks the silence behind the closed door. Is Helen spying through the peephole, enjoying the theatrics she has orchestrated? I go back down the stairs, counting each step until I reach the ground floor. Then, I stop and look back at my apartment for the last time.

My packet of cigarettes is soaked through. It takes three attempts to light one. I take a puff and blow out a cloud of smoke. I decide to text my dad, my hands trembling like leaves on a stormy night. The screen has cracked from my fall, but it still works. I write half of my message, then delete it. Why bother? He kicked me out already when he brought Helen into my home. He kicked Mum's memory out of his life the very same day. Dad has done nothing to defend me. He doesn't want me in the apartment either, and the truth breaks my heart.

Men are all the same, Rita. That tiresome voice pops into my head.

No, Samuel isn't the same. Samuel would never do this, I cry silently.

Samuel is leaving you too, the voice reminds me. *Soon, you will be totally alone.*

I shake my head in defiance, but the voice is having none of it, saying the word *alone, alone, alone* over and over like a drill boring deep into my skull. Maybe I've jumped to conclusions. Maybe I'm just all worked up after my fall and Samuel's news.

I call Samuel, although deep down, I don't want him to answer.

"Hi, love. I'm not there yet."

"She locked me out of my own house."

"Helen?"

There's a pause. Is he finally on my side?

"Where are you now?"

"Still on the ground floor. I'm soaking wet, I fell in a manhole and my leg is throbbing."

"Is it broken? Shall I call the doctor?"

"No, my leg isn't broken. But I can't take this anymore."

"Anymore? Has she hurt you before?"

I stay silent. I've tried to explain to him many times before that Helen is mean, but he thinks I'm just jealous, that because of the promise I made to my mum, I don't want other women to come near Dad. It might be partly true, but Samuel refused to acknowledge the extent of Helen's cruelty.

"Go to Eden's Garden café. I'll meet you there," he says, his voice full of concern. "I'm stuck in traffic, but I'll be there as soon as possible."

Eden's Garden. Even the bars and restaurants have weird names in my country. Eden's Garden, Heaven, Paradise – who were they trying to fool? As if giving heavenly names to businesses trapped in this place would change anything. Even the food from our stores is out of date. We check the labels, of course, but the vendors think they're smarter than us and simply erase the old date and apply a new one. Nothing is safe.

Anyway, Samuel is not leaving Albania because of the food, the infrastructure, or the open manholes. He wants adventure.

I don't feel like going out with Samuel now. I'm cold and filthy and can't stop thinking about how I am going to get my belongings from my apartment, and where I will sleep tonight. Despair is choking me.

Instead of walking towards Eden's Garden, I head for the sea. The cold, salty air fills my lungs. I glance behind me at my city twinkling in the distance, although I know that fairy-tale effect won't last long. The lights will go off soon and plunge the city back into its usual gloominess. My tired city with all its false promises; it lived, laughed, wept, and bowed down accordingly. And the next morning, the city would rise once more and do it all over again. Well, I can't. I am buried beneath the weight of all the hardship, and I don't have the strength to stand up.

My heart pounds and goosebumps cover my body as I look out at the murky sea. I'm tired of trying and failing. It wouldn't take much effort to do what I'm thinking about. A little courage and I could be with my mum forever.

But courage is something I don't have. Perhaps if I did, I wouldn't be in this mess.

Raindrops continue to fall on me, as harsh as Helen's words. With every passing minute the sea gets angrier, and the wind blows my hair into my face. Determined not to turn back, I take a few steps forward. My shoes are already wet, the crests of the waves dying at my toes. A few more steps and the water will be up to my knees. Then I hear a familiar voice coming from the heart of the sea. I don't notice the beam of car headlights on my back. Nor do I hear Samuel crying at the top of his lungs. Just a soft voice coming from the sea, calling my name. Long ago I heard that call, but I can't remember where. It's like I'm in a trance, and all at once, it feels like everything is going to be okay. Two more steps, and my heart skips a beat. Finally, I recognise it. Mum. Oh, how I've missed her! I stretch my arms out in front of me. What is she saying? Keep going, or turn back? Damn the waves!

"Rita, please! Wherever you are, come back. I love you!" The man is calling me again. He puts his head in the palm of my hand, soaking my skin with his tears.

22

Hell
Tuesday night, 29 October 2019

The sky had grown even darker, and the base of the clouds hung closer to the woods. Rita walked one step behind Bashir, putting her feet where his had been a moment earlier. She too could see in the dark now. The only sounds in the deathly silence were her pounding heart, the dead leaves, and the dry grass crunching beneath their shoes. Every now and then Bashir stopped to get his bearings.

The night was quiet, the moon their only light. Once, there had been many moons in Rita's life. Luna, her mum, whose name means moon in Italian. Hëna, Samuel's mother, whose name also means moon in Rita's own language. Neither moon was in her life anymore. Rita had only one moon left, and it was watching over her now. The chilly breeze coming from the west pushed the clouds away, but the smell of rain still hung in the air.

Once again, Rita went over what Bashir had told her earlier. She had to hop into a moving lorry. The parking lots were where most crimes took place, so naturally, they had the most surveillance cameras and guards. They had to avoid them.

Rita wiped her brow. Throwing herself into a *moving* lorry had never crossed her mind. It was difficult enough to do it when the lorry was standing still, let alone going down the road. She had two possibilities: go back to the Jungle or keep moving forward to where the police and the lorries were.

After an hour of walking, they stopped.

The little toe on her left foot throbbed every time she took a step. Her mouth was dry, her throat too. In contrast, streams of sweat ran down her body.

"Sit down," Bashir said. It was the first time he'd spoken since they'd set off.

Rita did as she was told, nervously glancing around her.

"That's the place." He pointed at a street in the distance. "We will stay here. The police, if they're here too, are doing the same. If in thirty minutes nothing happens, then we'll approach the edge of the main road. If you're lucky, your lorry will come soon." He blew on his clenched fingers to warm them up.

Luck wasn't usually on her side. Rita pushed the negative thought aside, remembering the promise she'd made about leaving tonight. She had to stay positive. Intentions became words, and words became reality. *Okay, I've got to be lucky tonight.*

After squatting for more than ten minutes, it felt as if hundreds of ants were crawling over her legs. Trying to stretch her right leg, Rita lost her balance and fell over. Bashir pulled her up, but not before her face hit the ground, filling her mouth with the taste of mud.

"You okay?" he asked, keeping his eyes locked on the road.

"Yeah," she mumbled. Was she okay? She didn't know.

The whole night — or what felt like it — passed by, and nothing happened except the passing of a few cars. They saw neither *gendarmes* nor lorries.

"It's time to move," Bashir said, keeping his voice low.

Once on the road, Rita shielded her eyes to protect them from the beams of the headlights. The first lorry showed up and Rita's heart began to beat hard against her ribcage. She wiped her clammy hands on her trousers and rubbed her cold cheeks. She was so close to the other side, yet so far away.

From behind the bush that they were hiding in, she saw other people walking towards the lights. They were all waiting for the right moment. Only the lucky ones would make it tonight.

A lorry stopped at a traffic light, and everything happened in slow motion. A group of boys, maybe five or six, broke the handle of the back of the lorry using a crowbar. They opened the door and scrambled in. But the last boy didn't make it. One of the lads inside the lorry pushed him out and slammed the door shut. The red light changed to green. They were free.

"*Connard!*" the young man shouted, running behind the lorry.

Rita was gasping for air. *I can't do this.*

"Did you see how they did that? You will have to do the same."

It was like watching a movie, and she wanted to switch to another channel.

"That one is yours." Bashir pointed at a lorry moving towards them. "The moment it stops, I'll open the door and you jump in." His voice was firm. "Remember, we have just thirty seconds to do this."

Rita gave him a firm nod. So, my future is going to be determined in the space of thirty seconds? Her eyes widened as Bashir pulled a crowbar out of his filthy coat.

I can do this.
I can't do this.

The lorry got closer, and Rita dug her nails into the

flesh of her palms, repeating what Bashir had told her. Suddenly, however, Bashir yanked her arm and pulled her to the ground. For an instant, thinking of the crowbar, she squeezed her eyes shut. But surely, Bashir wouldn't hurt her.

His voice dropped to a whisper. "They're here."

"Who?"

He put his finger to her mouth, holding her down with his free hand. French *gendarmes* swarmed onto the street. They opened the door of the lorry, shouting out orders. One after the other, three men, two women and a child stepped down from the vehicle.

"Let's get out of here. We'll try again tomorrow," Bashir said, pulling Rita back into the bushes.

Rita waited for him to say, "I told you so." But he didn't.

23

Hell
Wednesday, 30 October 2019

Rita and Bashir walked back to Hell's Jungle in silence. The temperature had dropped to freezing, and even their breath cracked in the air. It was almost morning when they arrived at the camp. The closer they got, the more their silence thickened. Although everybody appeared to be asleep, shadows of flames flickered in the sky. The fires were the only way to stay warm on nights like this, so the boys took turns tending the flames, keeping them stoked and under control.

Rita had no idea how Bashir found their tent among so many identical ones. Everywhere she looked, it was the same – hunger, squalor, and hopelessness. He opened the fabric door, and they ducked in. The tent was warm inside compared to the biting wind she'd been standing in all night. His family was sleeping, their faces so close together they were inhaling one another's breath. Without a sound, Rita settled into her place on the wooden stool.

Bashir fell asleep immediately on the ground beside his mother. From the gloomy light of the fires outside filtering through the tent, Rita could see his chest rising and falling rhythmically. She wrapped the small blanket the woman had left for her around her legs and shoved her hands into her pocket. She couldn't sleep, and she couldn't stay here forever. How many more nights was Bashir willing to help her? Rita glanced over to where the last of their bread was supposed to be. There was none left. What if the others came, as Bashir had warned her? The entire camp was illegal, full of desperate people trying to find a way to get to the UK, as though it was the Promised Land. Bashir had told her the others were stronger than them. No. Rita wasn't going to wait until they raped another girl, stole another child, or killed another man for his ration of rice. It might be her turn next.

Yet, what could she do?

Her eyelids were growing heavy and before she knew it, she'd fallen asleep. When the rays of morning sun crept through the holes of their tent, Rita could have sworn she hadn't slept a wink. The family slept on while the camp slowly came to life.

Rita peered outside and saw Sumaya heading somewhere with a bucket in each hand. Without thinking twice, she ducked outside.

"Good morning," Rita said in a low voice.

"You're still here."

Sumaya didn't look at all surprised. She clearly knew what it took to escape this hell.

"Yeah, no luck last night."

"Don't worry. The right moment will come."

I certainly hope so, she wanted to say, but her words were lodged in her throat.

Sumaya wore the same clothes as yesterday, and the same slippers. Although today she'd put on some socks. Rita looked at herself. She too was wearing the same clothes she had been wearing in Italy. She was in desperate need of a shower. She suddenly realised that the last time she'd taken one was at her aunt's house in Albania before she'd started out on this sorry journey. She couldn't figure out how long ago that was.

"Is there somewhere here I can take a shower?" Rita asked. Her voice was full of guilt, like so much as thinking about cleanliness was some sort of crime.

"You can take a bath in my tent, although probably not the type of bath you're used to. Here take this." Sumaya gave Rita a big steel bucket. "Let's go". The young woman took two more buckets and they headed towards the exit of the camp where there was a dirty ditch. Sumaya filled two of her buckets. Trying not to fall into the ditch, Rita did the same. The water was black, but it was the only water they had. Was she expected to bathe herself in this?

"It's important to fill up the buckets before everyone else wakes, otherwise it's too crowded and you don't stand a chance. I have some washing to do today, but first, your bath."

They staggered back to the camp, and Sumaya placed the buckets on the fire. It was down to its last embers, so she poked the wood some more.

But the water is filthy, Rita wanted to say. She must have been making a face.

"Don't worry. If the water stays still, all the dirt will sink to the bottom. Then we'll pour carefully into another bucket. It's as clean as we can get here."

The water began to steam and Sumaya told Rita to fetch her clean clothes. She entered the tent where she'd spent the night. Fatima and the kids were awake, while Bashir was still asleep. Rita opened her suitcase and pulled out her last items of clothing – jeans, leggings and a turtleneck. Only books remained in her bag now.

Then, she peeped into Sumaya's tent, and the woman beckoned her in. Her tent was the same as Bashir's, but cleaner, with two small blankets serving as mattresses on the ground. The one where Sumaya had been sleeping still showed the imprint of her body. A thin blanket covered the kids who were huddled together. There was no other blanket for Sumaya, she must have been using her clothes to cover herself during the night. A pile of clothes was neatly stacked close to the door of the tent along with some plastic bottles. Two were empty and the third one was half full. There was no space for Rita to bathe, but her own stench was getting too strong to ignore any longer.

The kids woke up and looked at her like scared birds. Rita tried to plaster a smile on her face. Her mum had once said it was important that children saw a happy face each morning.

"I'll take the kids outside, so you can have a relaxing bath," Sumaya said.

Was she expected to fit in the bucket?

"Here." She laid a plastic bin bag on the ground. That was supposed to be her shower mat. "There's no shampoo or soap. Sorry."

Never in her life had Rita imagined people living in these conditions, least of all herself. She placed her clean clothes at the far end of the tent, then peeled off her dirty ones. The wind pierced through the holes of the tent, licking her shivering body. She hadn't realised how much weight she'd lost until she splashed water over her body and felt her ribs poking through her grimy skin. Even with no soap, she did the best she could, enjoying the warmth of the water. Then with her dirty sweater she dried her hair and body and put her fresh clothes on. To stay as warm as possible, she put on her leggings and her jeans.

When she came out of the tent she was still shivering, but at least she was clean. Well, cleaner.

"I prepared you some tea," said Sumaya. "I always need tea after washing. You soon get cold again."

Rita took the plastic cup and lifted it to her trembling lips. "Thank you for everything," she whispered, edging closer to the fire.

"We help each other. That's how we survive. Don't worry, you'll get used to it."

I don't ever want to get used to it.

Rita was on the verge of tears, but she had to compose herself. She couldn't cry in front of this woman who was doing so much to help her.

They spent the whole morning washing the clothes, bashing them against large stones. Rita felt guilty for all the times she'd complained about loading the washing machine in Albania.

When they were done, her back was aching and her hands were red and sore. But she was happy. She was helping the people who had helped her.

Bashir was with the boys from yesterday. He was still wearing the shirt Rita had given him. How she wished she had something for Sumaya too. The only things left were the necklace her mum had given her, which she never took off, and her silver bracelet. Rita had spotted it a few months back on the black market. She'd haggled a good price for it, mesmerised by the letter S on the charm. It had made her think of Samuel, but now the S would be for Sumaya. Rita took it off and handed it to Sumaya.

"I don't have anything else."

"I can't accept that!" Sumaya exclaimed.

"Please. To remember me, or to sell. Get the children some food."

Sumaya nodded and smiled, her eyes filling with tears.

Then Rita remembered she had something else they could sell. She called Bashir over and pressed her iPhone into his hands.

"What are you doing?" he said, shielding it from view from the gang of boys.

"Sell it. Feed your family and help me get out of here."

It was her only remaining connection to the world, but if she didn't get out of this hell there would be no world left for her. She'd only come this close to ending it all once before.

24

Samuel pulled me out of the sea the night Helen locked me out, grasping my cold hands in his, just like the man in the hospital is doing right now. Is he Samuel? Has he come back for me?

I try to move my head to see his face, but as always, I can't. I'm floating back to my past.

Samuel holds me tight until my body warms up again, staying awake all night and chasing away my nightmares. We are lucky his house is so big. His parents didn't see him carry me in.

When I wake up the next morning Samuel is gone, and in his place is a pile of new clothes. Not everything is bad in my country. Some cafés stay open until 5 a.m., and if you have money to spend, you can call any shop and they will open it for you after hours. That's what Samuel must have done for me. Memories of what I'd tried to do the night before flood my mind, much like the sea water filled my mouth and nose. *You're a failure*, the voice in my mind says. *You can't even kill yourself properly.*

I decide to drown out the voice with a shower. I stand beneath the scalding water, my skin turning red, thinking of my dad, my little brother, and my diary. I long to write to my mum, but it's probably for the best that I can't. How could I tell her what I tried to do last night?

I am just putting on my new, clean clothes when I hear voices from outside the door.

"Was she drunk?"

I cover my mouth. I can't bear the idea of Samuel's mum talking about me like this.

"No, Mum! Rita just had a difficult time last night. That's all."

"Look, I didn't say anything when you brought her on holiday with us. She'd just lost her mother, poor girl. But now she's all grown up. She has to take care of herself."

"But I love her, Mum. You know that."

"Yes, well, you'll be in London soon. The distance will do you good, give you some clarity. Maybe you'll find another girl... better suited to your social standing."

My heart sinks. By 'social standing' his mum means a girl with money. As if money is everything. I am clearly not wanted in Samuel's home – or my own, so I call Magda.

"You can't stay in a dorm room with your friend!" Samuel shouts as soon as I got off the phone.

"What do you care? You're leaving soon."

"Of course I care."

"Where else am I meant to go once you're gone, then?"

He looks down at his feet. Silence.

My hospital room is silent too, nothing but the soft beep of the machine beside my bed and the squeaking of the nurse's shoes against the tiled floor. The man is still there. But I am not.

Flitting back to the past again, for the next two weeks I share a bed with Magda in her dorm. My dad is upset that I've left home, but I don't mention what Helen has done. What good would it do? I meet up with Dad once a week, and every time he begs me to go back home, I tell him I won't even consider it. I'm a grown woman. And the walls of that old apartment hold nothing but grief and bad memories. It's time to move on.

But I do ask Dad to send me pictures of Daniel. I miss him. I even think of sneaking into his kindergarten to see him, but I'm too scared of what Helen would say if she found out.

Samuel left for London at the end of March. That was the day my world fell apart. I hadn't ever kissed another man in my life, but our last kiss felt so final. *You're being stupid*, I told myself. *You will get a visa too and join him soon.*

I didn't have the strength to go to Mother Teresa Airport and see him off, nor did I want to speak to *his* mother. So, I stayed in bed.

We'd filled out my application for the London College of Contemporary Arts. If the answer to my scholarship request was positive, which Samuel thought it would be, I would join him in less than six months. Being accepted to a study program was the only way for people like me to get a visa to the UK. Yet, something in my stomach felt like a heavy stone. I couldn't believe I would ever be that lucky.

Life without Samuel was unbearable. Every morning, my pillow was covered in dried tears. Even the city wasn't the same. My dream of becoming a famous photographer was only sustained by my Instagram posts. I had a lot of followers, but no money and no idea how to make my Instagram account profitable. I soon realised that people who made art were all the same – penniless.

I worked with other artists, but they couldn't pay me with money they didn't have, so they sent me books or pictures instead to say thank you. By now I had over one hundred free books and pieces of art. Some of them I'd stashed under my bed, and others under Magda's. How could I ask for money from writers and painters, just for posting their work on my Instagram account? I was one of them. That account was the only place I could exhibit my photos and chase my dream. Photography was the one thing that made me feel at peace with myself. There was no money in it, but I felt energized doing it. It was all I had. But I couldn't live on dreams alone. *It's money that makes the world go round, not passion*, the voices in my head whispered in unison.

In my country, students who graduated with much lower averages than mine were now representative members of parliament. Some of them couldn't even read or write properly and were mocked in the media. Mysteriously, however, these journalists had a tendency to disappear shortly thereafter. The politicians were the ones who controlled and made decisions about the lives of others. Any time they gave a thumbs down, a newspaper, a TV station, or a person, vanished. Meanwhile, those who graduated with above average grades ended up looking for jobs in bars or restaurants, just like I did. Graduating *cum laude* was better than *summa cum laude* – the latter wound up working in call centres after graduation. Which was why, trying to escape this inevitable fate, young people ran away to any foreign country better than ours.

I didn't win the competition with the project I'd worked so hard on. As predicted, the pretty blonde girl was victorious, and she got the only job on offer. Even if they *had* offered me the first prize, I would never have slept with the dean to get it like she had.

Instead, I found a job as a waitress in a small café. It wasn't my dream job, but at least I got paid and had something to keep me busy now that Samuel was gone. He didn't approve of my lowly job, of course, but I couldn't stay in Magda's room without paying any rent.

Every morning at 7 a.m. sharp, I opened the door of the café and prepared the first coffees. There wasn't much to do there, but the salary was the same regardless. If I intended to join Samuel, I would have to work hard and put some money aside. I had to prove to his mum that I had my own money, too.

Months passed, yet I'd heard nothing about my application. I was almost certain my documents had been lost in a pile of dusty papers, classified as unwanted.

Although I was short of friends and family in my own country, I still spoke to Chloe regularly. It was during one of our chats that I came to the realisation that Albanians were still going to the UK – it wasn't forbidden, simply a matter of money and the right connections. Chloe herself worked with an Albanian at her restaurant job. According to my cousin, the girl had entered the UK using somebody else's identity.

It wasn't difficult to find someone who could forge ID's, the only problem was finding the money. I made

Chloe swear not to tell her mum. I still hadn't forgiven my aunt for accepting Helen so readily and convincing my dad that he needed a woman in his life, and I certainly wasn't going to ask her for money. It may take some time, but sooner or later I would be with Samuel.

He was busy with his studies, so we didn't speak as often as I would have liked. I never told him about my plan. I knew he would try to convince me to wait for the scholarship.

In order to get an ID card, like the woman Chloe knew, I needed all the money I could get. When I saw an announcement for a job at the Belvedere Hotel, I jumped at the chance. They needed a receptionist, preferably a girl without family obligations so she wouldn't mind working strange hours. I could do that. I fit the criteria perfectly.

I'd never heard of the hotel before, but it wasn't like I'd heard of any other nice hotels either. The working hours were 4 p.m. to 11 p.m. The pay was good too – two hundred euros per month, which was fifty more than I was earning as a waitress. A glimmer of hope flashed before my eyes.

I could work at both places. If I ate less, and saved 300 hundred euros per month, in one year I would have enough money to pay what the traffickers wanted and be with Samuel. And if I got the scholarship, I would use my savings to start my new life.

What could possibly go wrong?

I rang the number advertised in the newspaper and a sluggish voice answered. Without giving me chance to explain why I was calling, the voice said, "Next interview is on Monday at ten."

My mother had taught me that daydreaming was dangerous, but I spent the entire weekend daydreaming anyway. That evening I spoke for just a couple of minutes with Samuel, and thanks to FaceTime, I saw a bit of London. I didn't tell him I was going to work twelve hours a day. I didn't want him to worry. Now that Samuel was in London, I was growing fond of the city too. I read everything I could find about the UK.

When I wasn't talking to him or gazing at pictures of London, I was reading. I cooked myself spaghetti for dinner that night. A treat. If I got the other job, I wouldn't have time to make proper meals anymore and would be saving every penny I made.

The hospital door bangs against the wall, and I'm pulled back into the present. I hear Chloe's voice. The man has turned his back to me, and Chloe is holding my hand now. She too is asking me to wake up, but can't they see I'm more awake than I've ever been? I can see *everything* now. The machine above my bed beeps faster. They are saying it's my heart. The man calls the nurse. Everyone looks scared, but I'm relaxed. There's nothing wrong with my heart, it just aches a little from the people I miss. I miss Chloe. I think I even miss this man too.

This time I don't want to go back to my dream. I don't like it anymore.

25

I don't like Mondays. I can't remember if I was pushed under a train on a Monday, but it wouldn't surprise me at all. I don't even know what day it is today. I look around my hospital room. It's the same as always; the same nurse coming and going. She changes the bag hooked up to my arm and I float off again.

I couldn't wait for that particular Monday to arrive. The day of my big interview. Although, I was so nervous, I was scared I'd get cold feet any minute. As soon as dawn broke, I slipped out of my bed and stepped into the shower. There were no private bathrooms at the dorm, just eight showers for who-knew-how-many girls. It was nothing like Samuel's luxurious bathroom. In Magda's dorm, any of the girls could knock on the door and hurry me up at any time.

The night before, I had hung my clothes over the back of my chair so as not to wake Magda up – a black pencil skirt and a long-sleeved white silk shirt. My makeup was simple: mascara and a glossy pink lipstick.

I had no mirror, but I knew I looked the part. Having curly hair was a blessing sometimes, as I didn't need to brush or blow dry it. I knew it would look just right by the time I arrived.

All the way to the interview, I was fighting with the voice inside my head, the nasty voice telling me I couldn't do this job. When I didn't agree with its evaluation of my skills, the voice quipped: *they've probably already hired someone else.*

I haven't heard the voice once since I slipped inside my dreams in this hospital room. It's been bliss.

The bus was packed. In Albania, you never know when the next one will arrive, for two reasons. Firstly, there is no timetable, and secondly, most of the time, the electronic board doesn't work. The moment the bus pulled up, everyone ran to the door, hardly letting the other passengers get off first. There was always a war of elbows pushing to get on and off. Resting one foot on the step of the bus, I finally boarded, albeit with half my body hanging out the door. I could smell the garlic on the breath of the man I was glued to. The driver tried twice to close the door which bumped against my back. It hurt, but if I got the job, it would all be worth it.

For ten whole minutes my body was squashed. The only thing I could move was my eyelids. The bus missed two stops. I was lucky it stopped at mine at all.

The same people who had elbowed to get on were now elbowing to get off, but thanks to my cramped position by the door, I was the first one to step on the pavement. My shirt had come untucked, and my skirt had ridden above my knees. I tidied myself up and ran my fingers through my hair, looking at my reflection in a shop window. Apart from my crumpled jacket, this would do. I took the jacket off.

At 9:30 a.m. I was standing in front of the Belvedere Hotel. It was located in an expensive part of the city and judging by the lack of people going in and out, it seemed quiet. I drew a cigarette from my purse and lit up. I only took two nervous puffs before throwing it to the ground and grinding it with the tip of my shoe. I glanced at my watch. Only five minutes had passed. I didn't want to get there too early, lest the sleepy voice I'd spoken to on the phone think I was desperate.

Pacing up and down the street, I wiped the palms of my hands on my skirt, pretending I was pulling it down. Having time to think was not a good thing. The voice was still there with me. How I wish I'd left it on the bus.

The man calls my name, but there's no time to return to my hospital room. It's 10 a.m. and I have a meeting. I take a deep breath to root myself in the past again.

I took another deep breath outside the hotel, pushed the door open, and stepped inside. The luxury of the foyer overwhelmed me. Two enormous chandeliers hung from the ceiling, the crystal drops twinkling in the sunlight. There were black leather armchairs dotted around the lobby, and the marble tiles were as clean as fresh snow. I gazed down at my shoes. Thanks to all the people on the bus stepping on my feet, they were now covered in dirt and didn't look black anymore.

"May I help you?" the woman behind the reception desk asked me.

I panicked. Why was I doing this? I hated job interviews. I hated rejection.

"I came for the job vacancy. I was told to be here at 10 a.m." I looked down at my dirty shoes again.

"Ah, yes." The woman crossed her arms over her chest, as if waiting for me to say more, but I remained silent. I even considered running away. She eyed me up from head to toe. "Have you worked as a receptionist before?"

"I would prefer to speak directly with the person interviewing me."

"That's me, I'm Lizbeth Baku. The hotel belongs to me and my husband. He's over there." She pointed to a man standing at the bar with an espresso and a glass of brandy in front of him. I could only see the profile of his face, and I immediately took a dislike to him. "As I was saying," Lizbeth continued. I noticed she had a couple of gold-capped teeth in the front of her mouth.

"We need a hard worker. A serious worker. Someone who comes in on time, doesn't ask too many questions, and doesn't cause any trouble. But if you have no experience, you won't be any good to us."

"I'm a quick learner. And I promise you I won't bring any trouble and I won't ask questions." *At least, not those that aren't related to the job.* "I can work overtime if you want. I have no family ties. I have all the time in the world."

Instead of running away, I was *begging* her for the job, and I hated myself for it. But I needed the extra money so badly.

Saying she needed some time to think, Lizbeth left me alone and joined her husband. I'd never seen such a tall woman before. Her shoulders were broad, and her blonde hair was very short at the back. She was wearing simple jeans, a black T-shirt, and Gucci trainers.

Lizbeth sat perched on a bar stool, both she and her husband sneaking looks at me. I shuffled my feet nervously, aware of how scruffy I looked. After a while, Lizbeth stood up and walked slowly towards me. She didn't invite me to go to their office, if, indeed, they even had one, nor did she offer me a coffee or a glass of water; not that I would have been able to drink anything. Instead, she stepped behind the front desk again.

"The working hours start at 4 p.m. and finish at 11,

but sometimes you'll be needed until midnight. We've made a decision and…" she glanced at her husband, "we're going to give you a chance."

The lift door slid open, and a man's laughter filled the reception. A girl stepped out behind him and jogged over to Lizbeth. She placed something under a pile of papers on the front desk. It didn't take a rocket scientist to realise it was money. I knew that only dirty money is exchanged like that, but I was too desperate to care.

"I've told you a hundred times not to come downstairs," Lizbeth hissed at the girl. Her voice, even though it was a whisper, was filled with anger. "That politician thinks he owns the world."

"Don't be so angry, Ma. He asked me to have a drink with him," the girl said before sauntering away.

Ma? Lizbeth had told me not to ask questions, so I didn't. My eyes were wide with curiosity though, and Lizbeth noticed.

"I have no children myself, so the girls love to call me Ma," she said casually.

Girls? *Not asking questions might be part of my job, but I will never call her Ma.*

"How many foreign languages do you speak?" Lizbeth asked. Every time she spoke, she struck the desk with the lid of her pen. The girl had clearly distracted her.

"Two. Italian and English," I replied.

"When can you start?"

"Whenever you need me."

"Okay, love. You can start tomorrow." *Love? How can such a significant word be wasted like that?* "For the first week, the other receptionist will stay with you and show you the ropes. After that, I hope you'll be able to work on your own, otherwise I'm afraid I'll have to let you go. The first two weeks you won't get paid, that's your probation time. Oh, and before I forget. Never go upstairs until I tell you to." She grinned, her mouth like a dark cave hiding something terrifying.

For a split second, I imagined Lizbeth's two gold teeth sinking like fangs into my neck.

Lizbeth is calling out my name "Rita, do you hear me? Talk to me, please." Hang on. It's not Lizbeth at all, it's Chloe. I look around me and see that I'm back in my hospital room. The man is there too, holding a plastic cup. Coffee. He must need all that caffeine to stay awake, because every time I open my eyes, he's there, beside my bed, always calling my name and holding my hand.

I think today could be the day I see his face, which might help me remember what happened... But then the doctor comes in and the man turns to face him. I lose him all over again.

26

Hell
10 November 2019

More than a week passed, and Rita was still in hell. Along with Sumaya, she woke early to fill the buckets with water. Rita washed the children's clothes and swept the two families' tents with a small broom made of dry tree branches. The first time Rita tried, the branches broke, but then Bashir made a new one and Rita mastered the art of brushing the tent with the weirdest broom she'd ever seen. The only thing Rita didn't do was cook. She had no idea how to cook without a proper pan, butter, or olive oil.

With the money Bashir got from selling Rita's iPhone, he bought a week's worth of flour and rice. Rita watched as Sumaya made bread, confused as to how she would manage without an oven. Sumaya covered the dough with a piece of cloth and then started collecting stones. Rita did the same, even though she had no idea what she was doing. Once they'd collected enough stones of different shapes and sizes, Sumaya covered the fire with them until it formed a small oven. When the heat on the stones had reached the right temperature, she shaped the dough into a disc, used another stone as a base, and placed it inside the makeshift oven. Soon the smell of homemade bread filled the camp. Rita swallowed down the saliva forming in her mouth, afraid *the others* would smell the bread too and steal it from them.

Giving her iPhone away had been worth it just to see the elation on the children's faces at mealtime. Material things no longer mattered, just survival. She would have sold anything to make these people happy, but she had nothing left to sell.

Bashir hadn't mentioned when they would try the lorries again. It seemed as if he'd forgotten all about it. Nights sucked up days as the evenings drew in, the temperature dropped, and Rita knew that each new twenty-four hours was going to be worse than the last. They were eating as little as they could, but the food wouldn't last forever. One day they would eat only bread, and another day, just soup. When they ate soup, there was such a scant amount of rice that she could count the grains. Some days the women only drank tea made from leaves they found in the woods, so there would be enough food for the children. Rita hadn't washed again since the day she'd bathed in Sumaya's tent. She was still wearing her leggings beneath her jeans, her turtleneck, and her parka. Even when she washed clothes or brushed the tent, she kept her parka on.

How much longer was she going to live like this? Bashir had told her to wait, but she'd waited long enough.

She was no longer sleeping on the wooden stool. Fatima had made some room for her on the ground. In the morning, the children's feet poked her in the neck, but sleeping close together was the only way to stay warm.

Rita tossed and turned in her cramped space. Her body ached from sleeping on the cold hard ground, and as if that wasn't bad enough, now she needed to pee. The more she tried not to think about it, the more urgent it became. It wasn't that she was scared of the dark (not anymore, at least) – she'd gone to the bushes at night on other occasions – she was simply too tired to move. When it became unbearable to hold it in any longer, Rita tiptoed outside. She almost fell over twice before she stepped behind the bushes, dry leaves in her hand in place of toilet paper. She hadn't seen toilet paper in a long time.

Heading back to the tent, she stopped in her tracks. Shadows were roaming around the camp. She rubbed her eyes in case she was imagining things, but she wasn't.

The others, she thought with a surge of panic. She was frozen to the spot. From the flickering light of their torches, Rita could see the shadows silently entering tents. They walked back out with pots, pans, and food. Cold sweat broke out all over Rita's body. They had entered *her* tent, meaning they had stolen what little flour and rice they had left. There was nothing she could do. And now, there was nothing left to eat.

By the time Rita found the courage to return, the camp was quiet. But she sensed everyone was awake. As she entered the tent, Bashir jumped up and hugged her:

"Oh, thank God! We thought they kidnapped you!" His eyes filled with tears, and he lowered his head with the embarrassment of a teenage boy. Rita had noticed he did this whenever he didn't want his mother to see his patriarch mask falter.

"I was in the bushes peeing. I saw them, but I didn't know how to stop them."

"Nobody can stop them. They're stronger than us. I've told you that."

Tears ran down Rita's face.

"It's okay they're gone now. They took what they could, but thankfully, no one is hurt. Everything will be fine."

No, nothing will be fine, Rita thought, licking the tears from her lips.

27

Hell
11 November 2019

Rita remained inside the tent the whole day. The shadows she'd seen last night flickered behind her eyes, ghosts that would haunt her forever. Thinking she was sick, Sumaya had prepared a cup of tea and come to see her. Rita knew she couldn't have done anything, and those young men had raided the camp before, but she still felt guilty. She took the cup of tea but couldn't stop her tears from falling. Tears of fear, tears of being powerless to change things for her and the people around her, tears of despair.

Sumaya hugged her for the first time, and probably the last.

"I'm going to leave tonight," Rita said, her chin quivering. She doubted she'd see her new friend again, nor the other people who had kept her alive and safe.

Sumaya's eyes filled with tears too. "Good Luck,

Rita, and thank you for bringing some sunshine into our lives. You're a good soul. Remember that."

Sunshine. That's what Samuel used to call me.

Rita and Bashir took the same path they had the first time she'd tried to jump onto a lorry. It seemed a long time ago, but Rita still remembered the fear of that night, because it was the same fear she was feeling now. The sound of crunching leaves beneath their feet was as loud as a crow's caw. Rita had never liked crows. In Albania, a crow was thought to be an omen of bad news. She lifted her head and glanced up at the moon.

"Bashir, as the moon is our witness, I want you to know that I will never forget you. You are a real-life angel," she whispered, placing a hand on his thin arm. If she didn't manage to throw herself inside a lorry tonight, she would jump in front of one instead and finish this horror once and for all. Life in Hell had changed her. She could never return to who she'd once been.

"Angels are white, just like you, Rita."

"Have you ever seen one?"

"Only in the movies. They're all white."

"Forget the movies. Have you ever seen one for real?"

"No."

Rita stopped him and cupped his face in her hands.

"You're definitely my angel."

She saw the glint of his smile in the moonlight. "Do you think they will come back again?" she asked. There was no need to say who, they both knew what she meant.

"They always come back." He picked a blade of grass and put it between his lips. A new wave of silence descended upon them as Bashir twisted the grass from side to side in his mouth.

Rita wished she hadn't asked as she took in the look of despair on his face.

The walk seemed quicker than it had the last time. After what Rita guessed was about an hour, they came to the same place as before, and stopped to watch the lorries and *gendarmes*. Rita knew exactly what to do now, and more importantly, she trusted Bashir. During the forty minutes they waited, neither of them spoke, their eyes fixed on the street ahead.

"I hope you're lucky tonight," Bashir said after a while.

Lucky. The word followed her everywhere. She had wished on her lucky star in London when the police officer stopped her, and on the morning Andrew left. Now she was asking her lucky star for help once again. She was desperate to change the pattern of her life, and deep down, she believed she had the power to do so – if only she could learn to trust herself.

Bashir looked up. "Let's go."

They walked down a narrow lane and found themselves on the main street. The place looked much the same as it had the last time they'd been there.

"You have to move quickly, otherwise they'll take your place," Bashir said, gesturing to other small groups of people slinking out of the bushes.

"And you? When are *you* going to try?"

"The moment I find a safe way. I don't want to put the little ones at risk," he said, chewing on the blade of grass. He spat the green wad out on the ground, as if spitting on his future. Bashir talked like an old man, the burden of his family weighing on his shoulders. How Rita wished she had a magic wand and could change his life, hers, and that of everyone else back in the camp.

"When the lorry stops, I'll open the door and you jump in," he said. "Don't look back." He examined the road one more time, no longer looking at Rita. A white lorry finally showed up, and after what felt like forever, it stopped at the roundabout. Bashir had calculated everything with the precision of a Swiss clock.

"Now!" he yelled, sprinting towards the truck. Using his crowbar, he wrenched open the back door as the lorry began to pull away. Rita's hands wouldn't move, her entire body was helpless. The front of the lorry had already entered the roundabout when, running behind the vehicle, Bashir wrapped his arms around Rita's legs and hoisted her half-way in.

Panting heavily, she grabbed a handle and pulled herself the rest of the way into the lorry. Even though Bashir had advised her not to look back, she turned her head. Two boys and a woman holding a child in one arm were also clambering in, pushing Rita forwards. Her body crashed into something hard, and particles of flour filled her mouth. Other people were running behind the lorry that was fast gaining speed.

That was it. She was inside. She was on her way.

As soon as the door clicked into place, the belly of the lorry was plunged into darkness. Rita crawled to the top of the crates. It was only after the lorry began to move at its normal speed that Rita blew out a breath that she hadn't realised she'd been holding in since she'd stepped off the plane in Italy. She did it slowly, making no sound.

The torch of someone's phone bathed the darkness in light. Rita was sitting on top of some pallets, while the rest of the stowaways were twisted up and crammed into the tiny spaces between the cargo. Rita had no idea if the lorry Bashir had chosen was going to Kent. She could only hope so, although anywhere was better than where she'd been living the last few weeks.

A woman and her young son were crammed beside her. He had no shoes on, and his trousers were short, like the kids she'd left back at the tent. Someone touched the arm of the man, gesturing to him to switch off his phone. If the police saw light shining from the back of a lorry, they would all be at risk. The young man turned it off, leaving them in total darkness.

Every time the lorry rounded a bend, their bodies pressed against the pallets. It was obvious when the lorry was on the highway because it was the only time they weren't being thrown around. Just when Rita began to think they were finally out of danger the lorry stopped. There were voices outside. Rita's heart thumped against her chest so hard she was sure whoever was outside would hear it. The tiny child beside her started to wriggle and she knew he was about to start crying any minute. She heard the rustle of the mother lifting her top and the contented sigh of the child at her breast. Through the gloom, she could see the silhouette of the others pressing their heads between their knees. Rita put her hands over her ears and closed her eyes. If the police opened the door, she didn't want to hear their voices or see their faces.

Seconds stretched on for an eternity. Footsteps, murmurs, voices, a bang on the side and the rattle of the doors. Everyone in the lorry held their breath, and the woman beside Rita clutched her baby closer to her. Then, all at once, there was silence, followed by the magical purr of the engine. By some stroke of luck, the police hadn't opened the doors, and the lorry continued on its way.

28

My eyes twitched a little today and the man saw it. He was so excited, but the nurse soon dampened any hope he might have had.

"It happens all the time. It's just a muscle contraction," she told him.

I wanted to laugh and tell her that I could hear everything, see everything, just from further away. But no one can hear me. Last night I tried to ask the man to show me his face. Why is he hiding? I can see the nurse's face, always kind and full of compassion. I recognise her. She appears to feel sorry for the man, just like Magda felt sorry for me.

Back in Albania, having two jobs was normal and I was coping fine, as long as I didn't have time to think too much. Every day was one step closer to being with Samuel. How long could love endure when it was reduced to mere text messages? Out of sight, out of mind? Or absence makes the heart grow fonder?

The letter I was waiting for, confirming my

scholarship, finally arrived. I'll never forget the look on Magda's face when I opened the door to our room.

There was a curfew at the dorm. At 10 p.m., the girls all had to be indoors. I broke the rules every night. How was I going to be in my room that early when I didn't finish work until 11 p.m.? The only reason the head porter at the entrance knew me by name was because of the cigarettes I gave him every night so he wouldn't report me. I knew how things worked in my country. I wasn't even meant to be staying in Magda's dorm room! We slept in the same single bed for two months until her roommate left. It felt as if since my mum died, all I'd done was break the rules.

The thick brown envelope was sitting on the table and Magda was grinning.

Not daring to step any closer, I stood in the anteroom. I'd known that letter would come one day, but my gut was telling me not to open it.

Magda rolled out of bed, picked it up, and read the black print on the outside.

"It says it's from the London College of Contemporary Arts. Open it! What are you waiting for?"

"I'm tired." I said, taking the envelope and sliding it back across the table. "I've waited this long already, what difference will it make if I open it in the morning?"

I took off my shoes and put them under my bed where I always kept them, along with my books and unwashed clothes. The window was open. It was June, and the air was already ripe with the fervour of summer. I could hear the waves washing onto the shore.

There was a small sink in the anteroom. It was where we washed our faces, our dishes, and now and then, our clothes too. We even used the small basin to wash our feet.

I opened the tap, lifted my right leg up, and let the cold water run over my toes. When I'd finished washing every toe, I dried them off without looking at Magda or the envelope on the table. I could sense her fidgeting impatiently beside me.

"Weren't you listening earlier?" Magda cried. "Stop that!"

I froze, towel still in hand.

"I'm scared, okay? I don't want to read bad news now. I'll read it in the morning. Then I'll have the whole day to fixate on my failures!" My voice was loud. Louder than I meant it to be.

"Why are you scared? They've accepted you. Why would they send you this thick envelope otherwise? Look, it's heavy. A 'no' could have been sent by email." She picked up the envelope again, weighing it in her hand.

"Fine," I said, taking it from her and tearing it open. A part of me was dying of fear, the other part dying of hope. Maybe I would be with Samuel sooner than planned.

Dear Ms. Hanas,

Thank you for your application to the London College of Contemporary Arts scholarship. We had a large number of exceptional applicants and regret to inform you that you have not been selected…

There was no need to read any more. My voice trailed off and my mouth hung open like it had last night when I failed to talk to the man beside my bed. I can't hear any voices now and the nurse has gone. The man is sleeping, and I can feel his face on the palm of my hand. I don't want to return to my dream again, because it was with those three words, '*not been selected*,' that my life veered in the wrong direction. Maybe, had the letter been positive, I wouldn't be in this hospital room right now.

I dropped the letter on the floor, but Magda picked it up. Pacing back and forth across the room, she read the letter out loud until the very end. Every single word was like a stab in the gut.

I didn't want to call Samuel and wake him up, but I couldn't sleep. As soon as the sun came up, I texted him. I hadn't heard from him for a while, although I was so busy with work that I'd lost track of what day it was. Each morning, I awoke to find two puffy bags of desperation beneath my eyes. I covered them as best I could with makeup, but there was nothing to disguise my bloodshot eyes.

I waited for Samuel to reply. One hour passed. I tried to convince myself that it was early in London, that Samuel was probably still asleep. As soon as he checked his phone, he would call me back.

For the hundredth time, I tried to convince myself that Samuel was busy, but something inside my heart had already cracked. I was so scared of those cracks turning into gaping holes. I found it impossible to concentrate at work. I used my five-minute bathroom break to call Chloe. She tried to calm me down and said she would visit in October and bring some savings I could use. I suppose I should have been happy, but I was consumed by dread. Where was Samuel? Why didn't he pick up the phone?

By the end of the day, the stupid voice inside my head had convinced me he'd been in an accident.

An entire month passed, and he didn't answer any of my texts or calls. He'd disappeared. Buying a visa now seemed more urgent than ever but saving all the money I needed for my plan to work was going to take time. If only that damn school had accepted me, I wouldn't have been forced to deal with criminals and cheat my way into the UK. But since when had anyone handed me anything on a silver platter?

I can hear Chloe's voice as clearly as I had when we'd

spoken on the phone then. I'm back in the hospital room and I'm looking at her, fragments of memories returning. She told me something about Samuel. *What was it?*

29

Winter has gotten even colder while I've been lost in the past. I don't know the exact date, but I've noticed that the visitors to my room are wearing thicker coats now. Auntie Angela was here yesterday, and she'd had a woollen shawl draped around her neck. Every time I see her, I want to cry. She looks so much like my mum.

All these people want me to come back to them, but I can't. I need to find Samuel first.

For more than three months, I kept calling him only to hear the mechanical voice of a strange woman telling me I'd dialled the wrong number.

I'd stopped writing to Mum. I had nothing positive to tell her.

The only good thing was Chloe and Auntie Angela's visit, but because of my long working hours, I hadn't been able to see them yet. I'd been avoiding my aunt for years, but now I had no choice but to see her since I needed to talk to Chloe.

I still had two hours of work left when Lizbeth

entered the lobby of the hotel. I knew it had to be something serious, because Lizbeth never dropped in at that time of night. In my mind I was constantly calculating the money I'd saved so far. It was nowhere near what the traffickers wanted, but I hoped Chloe had more.

"Go upstairs tonight. Two of my girls didn't turn up and I don't know where they are. If either of them have done something stupid, I will cut their heads off like a chicken." No 'hello'. No 'how are you?'

These threats weren't new to me. Lizbeth always said she would kill someone or other if they didn't do what she wanted. All bosses used the same language, and all the employees gave the same nonchalant response.

"Upstairs? But I'm not allowed."

"I know, stupid. But today you have to. Anna, take Rita to room six, and show her what to do," she said.

A redhead called Anna appeared from behind Lizbeth. I recognised her as one of the cleaners. I had no friends at work, and apart from Anna and the other receptionist, who always left the moment I started my shift, I never saw anybody else. I didn't care though. I hadn't come to work to make friends. I'd come to make money.

Anna smiled at me as we walked towards the lift. She seemed friendly enough, yet an uneasy feeling coiled inside my stomach. I was forbidden from asking questions, but so many were bubbling up in my mind. I did as I was told, though, and kept quiet.

You're being paranoid, there's nothing to be afraid of. Watch Anna and everything will be fine. You know how to clean a room, don't you?

"Why do you look so worried? Haven't you been upstairs before?" Anna asked.

"No."

"Strange. I´ve been working upstairs since day one."

"Of course. You're a cleaning lady."

She laughed, a dry low sound.

"Open your eyes, Rita. These uniforms are a cover. You know exactly why we were hired. I don't understand why Lizbeth is sending you upstairs so late. Maybe she was keeping you for someone special, or she was scared you wouldn't agree."

Alarm bells started to go off inside my head. Did she mean what I thought she did?

"Scared I *wouldn't agree? Agree to what?*" I stammered, grabbing her by the arm. We'd already arrived on the second floor, and the harsh orange carpet hurt my eyes.

"Quit playing dumb and come on," she said, pulling me forward. We stopped at a door with a big shiny six on it.

"We're here. Don't give all the money to Lizbeth, but don't tell her I said that. You'll learn and you'll get used to it. I can't complain, it's how I feed my kids and pay rent. You must have your reasons too."

She leaned over and opened the adjacent door to room number eight. Of course I was working here for a reason, I was saving money to join the love of my life, but I wasn't desperate enough to do what she did for a living.

"Don't worry," she said. "I'll be next door."

My pulse pounded in my neck, and my entire body was covered in goosebumps. But it was too late to do anything now, there was nowhere to run. I'd been so naïve. I looked around and spotted an emergency exit in the corner of the corridor.

Too risky? What if there was an alarm on the door handle? *What if the police came?*

I scanned the corridor to see if there was a security camera. Nothing. There was no time to overthink. I had to act quickly.

I touched the handle of the emergency exit and pressed my shoulder against it just as a man's arms encircled me from behind. I went to shout but he placed his huge spade of a hand over my mouth. I noticed the door to room number six was open. Was this the man who had been waiting for me?

"Shh, let's not bother the others," he said.

What others? I shivered. No clients had checked into the hotel today, which meant they must have been using a different entrance. *You idiot,* the voice hammered in my head.

I wanted to scream but his hand was clamped too tightly over my mouth. Giving the man the impression that I was cooperating, I nodded, and he took his hand away, but he was still gripping my waist. I glanced down and noted he was wearing nothing but a pair of garish Happy Socks and his underwear. My legs were trembling, and my head was spinning.

I tilted my head and looked up into the man's eyes. I knew him. His face had been all over the TV.

"Don't panic, love. I won't do anything you won't enjoy," he whispered in my ear.

He was pulling me back towards the room, his body flush against mine.

"Come to Papa, baby girl. Such an innocent face." He tried to manoeuvre me through the door of the room, but I refused to move. "Come now, don't look at me like that with those big eyes of yours. This is all your fault, you know. I've seen you behind reception, looking at me all doe eyed. That's why I specifically requested you."

Bile climbed up my throat, stinging my nostrils. He stroked my cheeks, and I turned my face away, the hair from his bare chest brushing against my lips. My stomach churned. What if I threw up on him? Could I get away then?

I looked at the exit again, calculating whether I could get away from him and run to it before he caught me. That's when I saw Lizbeth standing at the top of the stairs with her hands on her hips.

"I told you she wouldn't be any good at this." Lizbeth laughed. "But you insisted, so now you can deal with her."

"Don't worry. I like a challenge. It'll be like breaking a horse."

Their exchange lasted all of twenty seconds, but it was still enough time for me to think. Feeling the weight of my phone in my pocket, I felt a spark of hope. I let my body relax and the man beamed, so sure that I would surrender to him.

"Let me go, please. You're hurting me. I can walk into the room by myself," I said.

"There we go, baby. That's more like it." The man raised his voice so Lizbeth could hear. As soon as he released his grip, I lurched away from him and yanked my phone out of my pocket.

"If you don't let me go…" I yelled, pointing my phone at the man with the Happy Socks and then angling it at Lizbeth. "I'll go live on Instagram right now. Thousands of people will see you. The police will be here immediately, not to mention what your wife will say about your underwear." I directed the phone to the man's lower body, and he threw his hands up in the air, as if I were pointing a pistol at him. I wish I were. Lizbeth's face turned ashen, the grin frozen on her face.

The door of number eight beside us banged open.

"Lizbeth, what the hell is going on out here?" a man with a big beer belly appeared in the doorway. He started to say something else, but then he saw that I was holding up my phone and his mouth dropped open.

"If you don't want to join them, shut the fuck up and go inside," I screamed, with a voice sounding nothing like my own.

The man slammed the door shut and turned the key three times. My hand hovered over the Instagram button. "I'll count to five. If you don't let me go, I swear I will go live."

Albanian people were glued to the news. The hideous man and Lizbeth knew that if I pressed the button, they would be on every TV screen in the country, before they could move an inch. Neither of them made any attempt to grab my phone.

Lizbeth gestured to the stairs she was blocking. Scanning the narrow corridor, I realised I was trapped; she could grab my phone and push me down the stairs.

"Switch off your phone first. How do I know you're not recording all this?" Lizbeth kept her voice neutral, although I could tell she was trying hard to contain her anger.

"You're right." Without taking my eyes off my boss, I pressed the record button. "Great idea, Boss. I'm recording this and it will save on my cloud. If you hurt me, it will be found. If you let me go and you don't come after me, I'll say no more. You'll never hear my name again. Deal?"

We looked each other in the eye. Lizbeth finally nodded in agreement. "You're free to go," she answered, gesturing again to the stairs. "Get your useless arse the fuck out of here."

"Don't worry, I won't be back," I cried, opening the emergency door.

Lizbeth's expression changed from frozen to one of rage as I ran down the stairs, holding the banister to stop myself from falling. Once on the first floor, I looked up and saw her leaning over the banister, glaring at me.

"I'll make sure you die poor and desperate," she yelled.

I ran. Once out of sight, I caught my breath and smoothed down the fabric of my jacket. People were staring at me, but I didn't care. In the distance waves crashed against the beach, the air thick and salty. The sea was calling to me like it had the night Samuel saved me.

"Rita. Rita. Rita."

I hear someone calling my name. Has Lizbeth caught up with me? Then I realize it's the man's voice and I'm in my hospital room again. I'm beginning to look forward to hearing his voice because it pulls me back from my nightmares.

30

The middle of nowhere
12 November 2019

Every time the lorry braked, Rita's heart sank. Even in the darkness, she knew exactly where her travelling companions were. Just like her, they couldn't lie down or stand up, so they sat on their haunches or curled up in a ball. The cold seeped into their flesh as they shielded themselves in the lorry's belly. The little boy nestled into his mother's lap. Her arms were the only thing she could cover him with. Time after time, the woman brushed his downy hair and kissed the top of his head. It was so heartbreaking to watch them curled up together, using their bodies to keep warm. Rita took off her coat and handed it over to the woman. The woman's eyes shown with gratitude. She hugged her child and kissed his cheek.

Rita wrapped her arms around herself and shut her eyes. While thinking of the hours they had been inside the lorry – which felt like being swallowed up by a beast – and trying to guess where on Earth they were, she dozed off.

The dim light of a new day crept inside the lorry through the tiny cracks in the door's hinges, and when she opened her eyes, Rita could see the faces of the others. They were still asleep, their heads resting on their chests. Rita tried to stretch her legs and accidentally touched the woman. She opened her eyes with a start.

"Sorry," Rita mouthed. She'd said sorry so many times since leaving Albania, it was as if her vocabulary had shrunk to just that one word. She pulled back her legs, and a fierce cramp made her wince in pain. Her fingers were numb, and she couldn't stop her teeth from chattering. The only thing she could do was rub her palms against her outer thighs and try to keep her hands and legs warm.

The lorry started moving again, and the others opened their eyes. Rita stared at their drawn faces. One of the boys furrowed his brow and tapped on his phone. The woman had her eyes closed but kept rocking the young toddler in her arms. As long as he slept, they were safe. Rita understood that now.

Before long, the lorry came to a halt once more. Every time this happened, they held their collective breath. Again, voices came from outside. The boy turned his phone off and Rita's jaw tensed to the point that she felt as though it was cutting through her skin. She couldn't see her own face, but considering the pain in her jawbone, she was probably making the same expression as the woman beside her.

"Yes. No." Loud words from outside pierced the deadly silence inside the lorry.

If we were in France, they wouldn't be speaking English, Rita thought, hope kindling inside her. The voices got closer, and they could hear them loud and clear. One of the boys slit a sack nearby, and they spread the flour all over their bodies. At any moment, the door could open. The mother beside her lowered her head and whispered to her child. Nobody breathed.

What if the child starts crying? The thought of them all being exposed chilled Rita to the bone. The light coming from outside hurt Rita's eyes and a gust of cold air tickled her face, sending shivers through her body. From her hiding place, she could see the British officer's uniform through the crack between the tarpaulin and the truck. Her heart lurched.

Thread from the ripped sack she was pressed against tickled Rita's nose. She was going to sneeze. *I can't sneeze!* She bit down on her lip and tasted blood, but the urge to sneeze passed. The only thing she couldn't control was her heart which was pounding so hard she thought it would betray them all.

The British officer glanced over the truck, but

thankfully didn't enter. During the entire time he was talking with the lorry driver and checking his documents, the officer kept the back door open, the five stowaways crammed behind the cargo and covered in flour. Whether or not they were discovered rested purely on luck. The child beside Rita wasn't moving. Was he still alive? His mother was skin and bones, so if she hadn't been eating, Rita doubted there was enough milk to feed her baby either.

Finally, the officer slammed the door shut. Fearing it could be a trick, none of them moved. The driver started the engine, and only after another five minutes had passed did Rita let out a breath. There was no doubt they were in England now.

The moment the lorry stopped she would get out.

Peering at the others, it was clear they were thinking the same thing. Using hand signals, they decided which of the young men would open the door. The mother pulled the coat off her child and handed it back to Rita. She shook her head. Rita had her turtleneck; the kid was virtually naked.

The lorry swerved as if pulling into a parking lot, grinding to a halt. The engine died down. It was time to act. Using the same knife that he'd used to split the flour sack, one of the boys sliced through the truck's tarpaulin above their heads and they all jumped out. They hadn't said hello to one another and now there were no goodbyes. In silence, they all scrambled away, running without any idea where they were headed.

Spending the night twisted into an awkward position had numbed Rita's limbs. She managed to tumble out of the truck, but it was a struggle to move her toes inside her shoes or bend her fingers.

Cold air wrapped around her body. This wasn't the cold she was used to; this was bitter British cold. She missed her coat, and she had no idea what to do next.

She hadn't planned this far.

Hoping an idea would formulate in her mind, Rita shuffled between the other lorries in the bay. She wandered aimlessly, struggling to brush off the flour from her clothes. It had started to drizzle, turning the flour into a white sticky paste on her already filthy clothes. As if all this were not enough, she also needed to use the toilet.

You'd better go in the bushes, said the voice in her head.

She ignored it and dragged her feet towards the service station in the distance where she could see a shop and a café. Her legs were cramping so much it was impossible to put one foot on the ground without her limbs shaking with pain. She had no choice. Rita crossed the road, but she wasn't concentrating. Her head was full of panic and pain. The sound of a car horn made her jump, the vehicle stopping inches from her. A man stuck his head out the window and shouted. Rita was just about to yell back, telling him he was an idiot for driving on the wrong side of the road, but then she saw other cars behind his. A row of angry faces glared back at her.

The British drive on the left, Rita, you should know this!

She had no chance of surviving in England if she didn't even know how to cross the road.

"I'm sorry," Rita muttered, breaking into as fast a jog as her legs could manage, ignoring the pain. The second she stepped into the shop, warmth engulfed her, and her body began to thaw. After such a scare, she was more desperate than ever to use the toilet.

To her left was a long passage, a tunnel linking the Spar shop with a Subway restaurant. Didn't Subway mean Metro in English?

The clock showed 6 a.m. and the restaurant was already packed. Thankfully, no one was paying attention to the scruffy girl staggering about. Rita gazed at the glass window counter. A picture of a sandwich with cheese melting between two slices of bread made her mouth water. She tried to swallow down her hunger, but her mouth filled with saliva again.

A public phone caught her eye, but it wasn't red like she'd imagined the phone boxes in the UK would be. People might be addicted to their smartphones here – as they were in many countries – but clearly, there were others who still liked or needed these old-fashioned relics. Rita watched the man who was currently talking and laughing on the phone, a twist of envy in her stomach. He was in a world of his own, one hand in his right pocket, until he fished around it to pull out yet more coins which he put in the slot to prolong his call. He was so engrossed in his conversation, that he didn't notice one stray coin which fell to the ground and rolled away. Trying to look as casual as she possibly could, Rita walked to the fallen coin and put her right trainer on it. The need to use the toilet was pressing like mad on her lower belly, but she also needed to stay put so she could grab the coin without anybody seeing. When the man finally finished his call, Rita bent down and seized the coin. Paranoid that someone might be watching her, she closed her fingers into a fist.

Rita headed for the toilet.

She went inside the first stall and latched the door behind her. Dropping her trousers in one swift move, she sat down, her knees crying out in pain.

As her breath returned to normal, she studied the coin with the queen's face on it. *Fifty pence.* She had no idea if it was enough for what she was about to do, but it would have to be. Holding the door handle to help herself straighten, Rita got to her feet.

Who could imagine that she would so quickly turn into a thief? She closed her eyes and let a tear run down her cheek.

Back in the hall, Rita dropped the stolen coin into the slot of the pay phone and dialled Chloe's number. Laughter erupted from the restaurant behind her, making it impossible to hear the dial tone. She put her finger in her left ear and cradled the handset between her right ear and shoulder.

"Hello?"

Relief flooded through her. "Chloe, it's Rita." She glanced up at the machine, imagining it devouring her coin like a ravenous beast. "Listen, I don't have enough money, but I think I'm at a BP service station. From the signs I saw, it's in Dover. How long will it take you to get here?"

"Eh? Huh?" Chloe hadn't had the chance to construct a proper sentence before the phone started beeping, signalling the end of the call. Rita put down the phone, unsure whether Chloe had understood where she was. She couldn't risk stealing any more money. That was her one and only chance.

She fished about in her jeans pocket, as if money would magically appear, but the only other thing she possessed was Andrew's business card. She contemplated throwing it away but after a few seconds, put it back in her pocket. It was the only proof she had that he even existed – this man who, for a few moments, had shown her another world.

A map of the UK was stuck to the window by the phone. Rita put her right thumb on the dot where Dover was and skimmed the map, trying to find London. When she located it, she put her little finger on it. Looking at the space between her two fingers, the distance didn't seem that large.

You're crazy, the doubt in her mind screamed. *Maybe Britain is no bigger than an egg on a map but that doesn't mean it's a small country!*

Rita smirked defiantly. She had nothing better to do. Maybe she *could* walk to London? She once read a book where a couple decided to walk 630 miles of the South West Coast Path. But they had a backpack and some money, noodles, and tea. Rita had nothing.

No, that wouldn't work. Chloe had to come.

A man who had been eating at a corner table of the restaurant got up and headed for the exit without clearing his plate away, and Rita hurried over to claim his place. She would sit there all day and wait. The chair was still warm when she sat down. On the tray there were only empty paper bags, but Rita could smell the food that had been in them. Her granny used to say one could fill themselves up with the smell of food alone and, come to think of it, Maria had said something similar. However, that wasn't going to work this time. Rita only felt hungrier. Even the paper coffee cup was empty. She picked it up anyway and let the last drop wet her chapped lips.

She had to find a way to distract her mind from food. With her elbows on the table, she buried her chin in her cupped hands and stared out the window. Big fat drops of rain landed on the glass, and trickled down slowly, leaving a trail of water behind, a rivulet the size of her little finger. Soon it began to fall harder, hammering against the window and obscuring the outer world from view.

Large drops were also falling on Rita's hands, and she wiped her eyes. Some days she was convinced that all she knew how to do was cry and apologise. She looked towards the ceiling and tried to blink back her tears. She needed something to distract herself.

Samuel. Think of Samuel.

Yes, she would think of him. He was going to be so surprised when he saw her. She tried to imagine their reunion and take comfort in the fact that soon, they would be together again. Yet, there was a cloud of doubt hanging over her, casting a dark shadow on these happy thoughts. The story Maria had told her in Italy had left behind a bitter taste. She shook her head. *No, Samuel isn't like the others.* He wasn't Antonio or Andrew. He wasn't everyone who had entered her life then disappeared without a trace.

Andrew didn't even say goodbye, the voice of doom reminded her.

Rita lifted the empty cup to her lips again. There wasn't so much as a drop left, but at least it gave the impression to anyone watching that she was still drinking. She set the paper cup on the table and collected all the crumbs of bread left in the small paper bag. Chewing the tiny pieces of bread made her even hungrier.

Maybe she would call Andrew when she got to London. He had asked her to in his note. Once again, she checked for any crumbs left in the bag. None. She wouldn't call him. She crumpled the paper bag into a tight ball and fought the urge to throw it.

Outside, the clouds had grown darker. Rita was looking at them from her vantage point behind a gigantic Christmas tree. Wait. *Christmas!* Tears coated her eyelashes. Was it already that time of year? It had been over two weeks since she left her city. What date in November was it? She didn't know. The Christmas lights flashed on and off, just like Rita's life: illuminating for a second, then dimming, her hopes turning flickering, one by one.

Someone sat at a nearby table. The smell of food wafted over, snapping her back to reality. Her stomach growled with hunger. She closed her eyes.

Chloe would be there soon.

31

On the night Lizbeth tried to sell me, it was Chloe who opened the door of her home to me. My handbag was still under the reception desk, so it had taken some doing to get to my aunt's house.

"Rita, *shpirt!*" Auntie Angela cried, and judging by her tone and her alarmed expression, maybe I looked worse than I thought. Suddenly, I felt bad for all the angry things I'd said to her. I felt bad for having gone so long without talking to her, for hanging up the phone on her, for accusing her of taking Helen's side.

Tenderly, as if they were afraid that I might break, they pulled me indoors and I collapsed to my knees in the hall.

"What did that bitch do to you? I'll kill her with my own hands. Chloe, bring some water. Quickly."

Bitch? Who did she think had made me this scared? Auntie Angela put her hand behind my neck and held up my head. The water wet my lips. It took ten minutes for my heart rate to return to normal, though I was still shaking.

Mother and daughter lifted me under the arms and ushered me over to the couch. I sank into the cushions and hugged my knees to my chest, trembling like a scared bird. Auntie took my shoes off, while Chloe wrapped a blanket around my shoulders. I closed my eyes at the touch of my aunt gently stroking my hair.

In my aunt's house, nothing was said or done without a cup of tea. Chloe dashed to the kitchenette and put the kettle on.

"I thought Helen…" her voice trailed off. "I swear I'll kill her." My aunt looked at her hands, as if checking they were capable of doing such a thing.

I struggled to sit up. "It wasn't Helen this time."

Auntie Angela raised an eyebrow. "What happened?"

I took a deep breath and began telling them my story. I told them everything, and when I'd finished, my aunt clapped one hand over her mouth and placed the other on her heart.

"I know it sounds crazy. Even I can't believe it. I might have the video, but I'm not sure." I took out my phone and found the recording I'd made.

"Oh, you poor love," she murmured.

They both wrapped their arms around me. No words were needed, their hug was the best medicine.

I saw how similar Auntie Angela was to my mum, and for a moment I choked up with grief.

"It's over now. They can't hurt you anymore. We'll wait for it to die down and I'll stay with you, cancel my flight back to London." Auntie Angela kissed the top of my head, like she would a small child. "I won't leave you alone, again. I thought Helen was going to be a good friend to you. None of this would have happened if she'd been there for you."

"Wait. Die down?!" Chloe exclaimed. "What are you talking about? We should go to the police!" My cousin was on her feet, her hands in fists, but my aunt wore a look of utter resignation.

"We have to forget about it. Wash away the bitter taste with a glass of wine if you must, but did you not see the man in the video? He's famous. I've seen him many times on TV. The law doesn't apply to celebrities like him. They're too powerful. They will crush you if you stand in their way. If we go to the police, nobody will believe Rita. They will say she's making it up for money or attention."

There are two simple rules in my country: silence the mouth that has something to tell; shut the eyes that have seen too much. I'd seen too much, and I had something to tell. The man in the Happy Socks was famous, and well-known for being a devoted husband and loving father. In my country, the only people with rights are those with money, and those who have money push the others down. Unfortunately, I was one of *the others*.

"This is so unfair," Chloe snapped. She stormed out of the living-room and returned with three big mugs of tea. She put them on the round glass table and cracked her knuckles.

"What if I speak to a journalist?" I said. "Somebody has to believe me."

"It's no good going to the police or talking to a journalist," my aunt replied. "That woman, Lizbeth, is the only one who will get off scot-free in all this. It's a hard pill to swallow, but this is the reality. Whether we like it or not."

"But surely someone has the power to put her and her husband behind bars. If we all keep our mouths shut...," my voice was barely a whisper.

"I'm sorry to disappoint you, Rita, but this will only stop when people in this country wake up, smell the coffee, and take responsibility for their actions. Nothing will ever change unless the people learn to understand their own mistakes. We are always taking two steps forward and one step back... and three steps sideways," she added with a sigh.

"You're scaring me, Mum," Chloe said.

"The truth always hurts, my dear."

I'd never heard my aunt speak like that either, her

voice so full of rancour. My country, the land that God had blessed with three hundred sunny days a year, almost stood still.

Chloe looked at me with pleading eyes and said, "I've got to tell Mum."

"No."

Auntie Angela's eyes shifted from left to right. "Tell me what?"

For a moment none of us spoke.

"So, there's this girl who came to London five months ago using someone else's identity, and now she's working with me and Kristos. Rita and I have been making plans for her to enter the UK the same way. Since Samuel left, she's been working two jobs to save enough money to buy a card like that."

My cheeks turned crimson as my cousin told her mum about my plan. Chloe's voice was calm, as if going to London with a fake identity card was a perfectly ordinary thing to do. For me, going to London in and of itself meant passing a border between two worlds – a dead world, which I was in, and a living one, where Chloe and now Samuel lived. Could I do that, after all that happened tonight? Could I forget and just move on?

"We have to help her, Mum," Chloe continued. "She can't stay here now. What if that woman she worked for tracks her down? It's dangerous. I was going to pay, but

I've only got three-hundred pounds to spare. You need to help her!"

"You've lost your mind!" Auntie Angela shouted. She paused, looking from my face to her daughter's, then let out a long sigh. "I have money. How much do you need?"

"No, Auntie. I can't accept it."

I only had seven hundred euros. Lizbeth wasn't going to be paying me my last paycheck, that was for sure.

"I've got the number of the person who can get the ID cards," Chloe said.

And just like that, my life got darker.

My past has been like a big black hole. Every time I remember a part of it, the darkness disappears a little and I feel the weight lift. I'm beginning to see some light now, as if I've come to the end of a tunnel. The man is holding my hand again and telling me how much he loves me. He's telling me he's sorry for everything. *Sorry for what?*

I linger between my hospital room and the room in my auntie's house.

I felt safe at Aunt Angela's. Lizbeth couldn't reach me there. I remember how I dialled Samuel's number, in another vain attempt to contact him. Yet again, I was told the number didn't exist. I yelled at the automated voice and threw the phone on the bed.

Of course Samuel exists. I just had to find him.

I tossed and turned all night, unable to catch more than a few moments of uneasy sleep, before light began to slowly seep into the room. I got up, walked to the window, and lifted the edge of the curtain. It was early morning, and Durrës was still, except for an old dog ambling down the street.

If Chloe's plan works, I won't see this city again. The thought hurt.

I let the curtain swing back and headed to the bathroom. My head was still pounding. Luckily, unlike most people in my country, Auntie Angela kept a variety of medicines stored in a drawer in the bathroom: Nurofen, Ibuprofen, Flurbiprofen – everything that ended with an 'en' and was supposed to kill a headache. I grabbed two Nurofen Express, turned the tap on, angled my head, and put my mouth under the running water.

The sound of dishes coming from the kitchenette signalled that Auntie Angela was also awake. The smell of *petulla* wafted over as soon as I opened the door.

"There you are, my love," she said. She was holding a large plate filled with more than twenty small pieces of fried dough, shaped like clouds. On the table were bowls of icing sugar and honey, and two glasses of orange juice. The aroma of home lifted my spirits. It had been a long time since I'd felt such comfort. I thought I'd lost that feeling forever.

I moved closer to my aunt and hugged her. "I'm sorry," I said.

"We are always here for you. You should have told me you were working two jobs. I could have helped. Now, grab them while they're still hot."

"Nobody can cook *petulla* like you do," I said, reaching for one of the donuts. "You know, Mum used to make these when the three of us were still together."

"I miss her too, hon," my aunt said, her voice catching.

When Chloe walked into the living room, we were both wiping our eyes.

"Mmm! *Petulla.*" She sniffed the air, then dashed to the table. "I didn't sleep a wink," she said, before stuffing a whole donut in her mouth. "Rita, time to choose what country you want to be from. Considering you're fluent in Italian, I suggest you go for Italy."

"How much will it cost?" I asked.

"Well, we have two possibilities. First, buy a fake European passport, which will cost twelve thousand pounds."

I almost choked. "No way."

"Okay then," said Chloe. "There's the second possibility of buying someone else's identity for three thousand pounds."

"I don't get it." I knitted my brow.

"The traffickers will give us an ID card which isn't fake. The person whose identity card they'll use will be paid to keep her mouth shut for a week. The thing is, this is only a residence permit, and therefore it has to be associated with a guarantee... which will be fake. They say the border officer never calls the guarantor – and that's the only risk. If they do call the guarantor, well, then you're in trouble because nobody will pick up the phone." Chloe paused. "Personally, I think the second option is the best. It's cheaper, and in both cases, there's a fifty-fifty chance of things working in your favour." Chloe ate another *petulla* as if it really was as simple as that.

"Okay, let's do it," Auntie Angela jumped in, without waiting to hear my thoughts. "Give me their bank account number, Chloe. Who do I transfer the money to?"

Chloe was sitting with one leg on the chair, her knee touching her chin. She burst out laughing. "Mum, what are you talking about? Traffickers don't use bank accounts. They work with cash."

"Then how do we do it? I can't withdraw more than five hundred pounds a day, that's the limit."

"That's what you'll need to do. If you withdraw five hundred pounds every day, in six days we'll have the money we need to help Rita." Chloe wolfed down another *petulla*. That girl had an answer for everything.

"But how do you even know all of this?" I asked, narrowing my eyes.

"I love listening to people's stories. If you stay quiet for long enough, people open up and tell you everything. I know so many stories about illegal immigrants, I could write a book."

Auntie Angela had gone silent. Judging from her expression, she wasn't buying the simplicity of Chloe's plan.

"But how will we give them the money? And more importantly, *who* will give them the money?"

"You," Chloe said without a flicker of emotion.

My aunt's eyes widened. "*Me?*"

"Mum, the moment the ID card is ready, they will tell you where you have to go. You give them the envelope with the money, and they give you the card. Haven't you seen the movies where they do the big swap?"

"Is it really that easy?" she asked, glancing down at her hands. I noticed she was trembling.

When I'd first thought of purchasing a visa and joining Samuel in the UK, I hadn't imagined it would involve dragging my family into such a dangerous situation. I sighed. "Let's forget about London. Maybe it's best I just go to the police and tell them everything. Or stay indoors until things calm down. Auntie is right. It will all blow over soon."

"I will do the exchange. I can do this," my aunt said quietly, as if she hadn't registered a word I'd said.

During the following week I stayed at my aunt's house and read all the newspapers I could get my hands on. Nobody had written a single word about me or the hotel. Everything was quiet. Of course it was. The media wouldn't know anything as long as I kept my mouth shut.

My new ID card was ready five days after that dreadful night. Chloe was right. These kinds of things happened fast, or not at all. Just like in a mafia movie. My aunt delivered the money and took the card. It really was as simple as that.

She came home wearing a look of triumph and handed me the document and my one-way ticket to London. I peered at the ID card on the table, my heart submerged beneath an avalanche of emotions. The photo on the ID looked just like me – albeit a different version of me. I rarely straightened my hair because Samuel didn't like it that way, but this was no longer about my boyfriend. My safety was paramount, and I would do as the traffickers had asked so I resembled the girl in the photo as closely as possible. Once I was in the UK, I'd be free to do what I wanted with my hair – and my life.

If everything went smoothly, as the traffickers had

promised, I would be at London Southend Airport tomorrow with my cousin. Chloe's fiancé, Kristos, would be waiting for us there, and then my new life would begin. But I had to make it through passport control first.

By nightfall, I was packed and ready to go, but not before saying goodbye to someone very special.

"You're not going alone," Auntie Angela said, coming out of her room dressed in jeans and a lemon V-neck sweater. "It's not safe for a woman to visit a cemetery alone at night. I'm coming with you."

October was teetering into November, but the air was still warm. I didn't need a jacket. I watched people going out and smiling at each other as if I was looking at them for the last time – familiar faces that I would never see again. The scent of the evening sea filled my lungs. I knew I was going to miss that, but I also knew that as soon as I saw Samuel, I would happily forget it all. Especially Lizbeth.

At the cemetery, Auntie Angela respected my privacy and stayed some steps away, keeping an eye on me. I swept away the autumn leaves that had settled on Mum's marble grave. There were some fake flowers in the pot. Maybe Dad had left them there. I replaced them with three fresh roses I'd bought the moment I got out of the taxi. I pulled out some weeds from the patch where I'd buried Luk only a few months earlier.

When I'd finished, I kneeled by the grave and wept. I sobbed for my mum, for my dead dog, and for my past. Fearful of what could happen next, I shed tears for my future too.

"Mum, I'll fly out of the country tomorrow. Stay with me." I lifted my head up and looked at the sky, clasping the charm around my neck. "Be my guardian angel!"

When we arrived home that night, I stepped into the shower, hoping that the hot water would clear my addled mind. Then, without saying a word to my aunt or cousin, I went straight to their spare room, where I had spent the last of my days in Albania. Gently, as if afraid I would brush the letters away, I ran my fingers over the other girl's name on the ID card one more time.

The books Chloe and Magda had brought from the dorm for me were piled up next to my bed. It hurt when I hugged Magda goodbye, but knowing she was happy for me eased the pain.

Stage one of the plan was to go to Italy using my Albanian passport. In Italy, I would begin stage two – switching to my new identity card. If the plan didn't work and the British officers didn't let me in, I had no plan B. The traffickers had said the card would serve its purpose for one week. I had no choice but to trust them.

Auntie Angela was awake early to see me and Chloe off. She would join us in London the following month as she had a work meeting to attend.

"I lit a candle for you," she said, kissing me on both cheeks. "Good luck and stay safe."

It was dark outside as we left the house and half of the city was still sleeping. As the taxi navigated through the streets of Durrës, the only city I had ever known, I thought of my dad. I'd hardly spoken to him in weeks, but I couldn't leave like this.

"Take the next right," I said to the driver, directing him to my childhood home. I glanced at Chloe. "It will only take five minutes."

I knew that at this time of morning my dad would be outside in the car already, awaiting his daily delivery instructions from his boss. I was right. His grey Volkswagen was parked on the pavement, and he was inside. The taxi passed so close to his car I could see him clearly. His head rested on his folded arms against the steering wheel. He looked like a shell of the man he used to be, his hair even greyer than I remembered. My stomach clenched painfully, and Chloe grasped my hand in sympathy. I couldn't do it. I couldn't say goodbye.

I may never see you again, Papa. I said to him inside my head. *I just want you to know that I don't blame you for what happened. I love you.*

There are voices by my ear, and I realise I'm back in my hospital room. I don't know the woman who is standing by my bedside. She's saying something, but I don't understand her. There's a bouquet of dahlias on the nightstand. I presume she brought them. The woman is tall and graceful, with some grey hair around her temples. Unlike the others, she doesn't try to hold my hand. She is not calling me to open my eyes.

I see her pursing her lips, as if she's disappointed that I'm still in this hospital room. Does that mean she's sad I'm here, or wishing she'd pushed me harder?

32

The morning air in Dover felt thick with anticipation. If only Rita had her books with her there would have been less time to think. But her books and her empty suitcase were in a tent somewhere in Hell's Jungle. She knew those people didn't need books, they'd probably been destroyed by the rain by now or more likely used to light a fire.

Through the rain-soaked window she spotted a Suzuki pulling into the parking lot. A blonde girl opened the car door and ran through the rain towards the restaurant.

It's not Chloe, Rita said to herself. *Chloe isn't coming.*

Rita had seen so many blonde girls by now, all of them with Chloe's face. Yet, she was convinced her cousin hadn't understood what she'd said on the phone. What if she never came?

Another car stopped and a couple got out. Rita had counted over a hundred possible Chloe's since she'd sat in that café. She was tired and hungry, but she needed a cigarette more than anything. Did hunger make you hallucinate?

"Rita!"

She turned at the sound of her name.

"Thank God! You're here."

But even when Chloe approached her and grasped her hand, Rita couldn't quite allow herself to believe it was her.

"Y-you made it," Rita said at last, standing up shakily.

"No. *You* made it." Chloe hugged her tight. "It's over now."

Was this it? Was it finally over? Rita didn't dare hope.

"Okay, get your things, and let's get out of here. Kristos is waiting outside."

Rita's lips quivered. "But I've got nothing left."

Chloe's face fell but she said nothing. She wrapped her arm around Rita's waist, as if worried she would blow away with the wind at any moment. "You're here now. Everything will be fine, you'll see. We'll buy you new things. Better things."

Chloe rubbed her arms as they stepped into the car park. "Have you eaten anything? I bet you haven't."

"I think I'm not hungry anymore."

Her legs shook as they headed back to the car where Kristos was waiting. Rita didn't have the strength to answer Chloe's question. Kristos smiled warmly at her.

"It's great to have you here, Rita. I've heard so much about you."

He opened the door for her, and Rita sank into the back passenger seat, her head swimming with exhaustion. Chloe whispered something to her fiancé, then ran back to the shop.

It was the first time Rita had met Kristos, and she forced a smile on her tired face. He was slightly different from the pictures she'd seen of him – heavier, with dark chocolate hair. Rita couldn't remember if he'd had a beard in the photos she'd seen, but he had one now.

Like the getaway driver from a mafia movie, Kristos kept his hands on the steering wheel and his eyes fixed on where Chloe had disappeared into the shop. Rita closed her eyes. It was warm in the car. If Chloe didn't come back soon, she'd be asleep in the next two minutes.

The car door opened, and Chloe sat back down in her seat. She was holding a paper bag similar to the one Rita had been staring at all morning on the table. The smell of food filled the car.

"Let's get out of here," her cousin said, turning back to check on her. "Here, eat this. There's a long way to go until we get home."

"Do you have a cigarette?" It was bizarre the way Rita's stomach had shrunk according to the meagre morsels she'd had access to over the past couple of weeks. Now there was food in front of her, and she found she didn't even want it.

"Not before you get something in your stomach."

Like a child, Rita did as she was told. She pulled out a bacon and cheese sandwich and forced herself to start eating. She chewed slowly, listlessly, and once she'd eaten half, she stopped and put the rest back in the bag.

For Sumaya and the kids, she thought.

Chloe turned her head. "You have to eat it all."

Rita nodded. She knew that she would probably never see those poor people from the camp ever again, but she still felt guilty with every bite.

Fat raindrops pinged against the window. Rita reclined her head on the headrest, trying to adjust to finally being safe.

"I have so many things to tell you," Chloe said. "First off: my mum has lost the plot. She keeps calling every day to ask about you. On the way here, I told her I was coming to pick you up and she cried. She's so relieved you're safe. She also blames me for putting you in this situation. I'm so sorry." Chloe chatted away non-stop, glancing at Kristos every now and then as if seeking his confirmation that she was ticking all the boxes. "Right, until you settle in on your own, you'll stay with us. Our place is small, but that's okay. Ah, Rita, I'm so happy you're here." She clapped her hands together. "I was so scared at Southend when the officer took you away. But I thought if I said anything, it would make you look even guiltier, and they might get suspicious of me too, which would make things even harder…"

"It's okay," Rita murmured.

Rita kept her eyes on the traffic outside the window, struggling to get used to being in a car that was driving on the left-hand side of the road.

"But I don't understand what happened," Chloe continued. "So many people get away with it. You were ridiculously unlucky. I knew you would make it in the end, although, naturally, there were moments when we feared the worst. I mean, your phone was dead… and we didn't know where to look for you. Mum said you never went back to Albania. We thought about calling your dad, but he was already arguing with my mum. He thinks she convinced you to leave home. Anyway, nothing else matters now. You're here."

"I was flown back to Italy and two little shits on the Metro stole everything I had."

Chloe's head swivelled to face her so fast that her hair caught on the metal part of the headrest. She gasped and let out a flurry of expletives herself.

"They took my camera, ID card, passport, and all

my money..." Rita's voice trailed off as she relived the desperate situation before sharing further details with Chloe and Kristos. "I had no money to book a hotel, so I slept in a Metro station for two nights. A woman called Maria rescued me."

It was strange to say her name out loud. It made Rita's memories more real. Important. "I had to sell the necklace Samuel gave me to buy a train ticket to Calais. I know he'll understand. I thought jumping into a lorry and sneaking into the country would be easy."

"I'm so sorry, Rita, and I know it might not make you feel any better right now, but you're not alone. Many other people have been through the same experience as you... or worse," said Kristos, his eyes on the road ahead.

Chloe grabbed hold of Rita's hand, her eyes brimming with tears. "I can't believe how much you've been through. It's a miracle you even made it. Kristos is right. A week ago, twenty-nine people were found frozen in a lorry."

So, those were the victims. They'd been trapped in a fridge lorry, as Bashir called it. Rita thought back to the French newspaper she'd attempted to read. The news filled her with dread.

"Try and leave all that behind you now," Chloe added in a soft voice.

There was no way the last two weeks wouldn't stay

with Rita forever. She also noticed her cousin hadn't mentioned Samuel once. Did she know something Rita didn't?

33

London
November 2019

The rain was still falling when Kristos parked the car in front of their home in Acton, London. Chloe stepped out first, stretching her legs. In slow motion, Rita opened the back passenger door and put her feet firmly on the ground. It was the first time she'd touched English soil without the fear of anyone following her. She stood up slowly, holding onto the car door with both hands to steady herself. The chilly air nipped at her skin, making her suddenly more alert. A bolt of apprehension flickered through her mind. Even though Rita knew she was safe, she couldn't help peering down the narrow street searching for shadows.

"Okay, girls, you need some time to catch up. I'm off to work," Kristos said.

He kissed Chloe and waved Rita goodbye. The tender way he kissed her cousin reminded Rita that love overcame anything. That her journey here had been for a higher purpose. She longed to be in Samuel's arms again, experiencing the very same thing. Just like she used to.

Chloe took Rita by the arm and led her towards a brown-bricked three-floor mansion.

"Welcome to the beginning of your new life."

Rita followed her cousin like a puppy who had just been rescued. They passed through a small alley, Chloe pushed open an iron gate, then opened another brown door. Rita put her right foot inside first – in her country, the right foot was supposed to bring luck.

The corridor was dark and small. Rita found herself craving fresh air again.

"Come inside and close the door. It's cold," Chloe said, turning on the lights.

Okay, so Chloe might live in a mansion, but her apartment was like a matchbox. After taking exactly four steps, Rita was standing at the threshold of the combined living and sleeping area. A thick white curtain hid the double bed where Chloe and Kristos slept. In the half of the room that was supposed to be the living area, there was a grey sofa bed with some built-in storage beneath it, and a small three-legged coffee table hardly big enough for three cups of coffee. Two planks of wood were screwed to the wall, serving as bookshelves and a key holder. On top sat a framed photo of Chloe and Rita when they were younger. A flat TV screen was mounted on the wall, and underneath that was a dining table with two chairs.

"Do you need to use the bathroom?" Chloe asked, pointing at the door she'd just passed on their way in.

"I'm fine," Rita replied. She hadn't had anything to drink since the service station. "The building looks so big from the outside."

"Yeah. There are six families living here," Chloe replied. "This is our galley kitchen. It's a bit small." She pushed aside a rail of wet clothes. *A bit?*

Rita's face must have expressed her concern because Chloe continued, "I know what you're thinking. We have no tumble dryer, so sometimes it takes a week for the clothes to dry, but at least they're out of the washing machine." She winked.

"Make yourself at home. Why are you standing over there? Do you want something to eat first?"

"*Erm, Chloe?* There's no space for me here. Why am I always making problems for everybody? I'm going to be a burden to you and Kristos."

"What are you talking about? Yes, the apartment is compact, but the couch turns into a double bed." Chloe flicked on the coffee machine. "Coffee?" she asked, taking a mug off the shelf.

"No, thank you," Rita said, leaning against the wall. "Are you sure there's no other way? When you said I could stay with you, I thought you had a spare room. I really don't want to impose on you and Kristos."

"Rita, come on. You have no money, no documents, so you can't register anywhere. Which means you can't afford a place to live on your own."

The truth always hurt, just as her auntie said. Rita pursed her lips, but she couldn't find a single reason to disagree. In Albania, her only goal had been to get to London, where she had somehow expected everything to just magically fall into place. She hadn't thought beyond that. At least she was here at long last.

Chloe took a sip of her coffee.

"Relax. Everything will work out fine. You'll see."

"I could really use a shower," Rita said.

Chloe put her mug on the coffee table and stood up. "You can have some of my clothes for today, then after you've had a rest, we'll go out and buy you some new clothes."

She slid open the door of a built-in wardrobe. The apartment was tiny, but it was surprisingly functional, and Rita had never seen so many portals. Behind the white door was yet another storage area where Chloe's clothes hung on wooden rails. Every available inch was crammed with clothes. When she finished, Chloe shut the door with the tip of her toe.

Rita leaned her shoulder against the doorframe, keeping one hand on the handle and her eyes on the floor. "Do you have a camp bed? I could sleep here in the galley kitchen and leave the room for you. I'm invading your privacy."

"We don't have a camp bed, but if it makes you feel better, we'll buy one."

"I'll pay you back, I promise. I know I owe you so much money, but as soon as I find a job, I'll pay you back first."

"Do whatever makes you happy. But a camp bed isn't comfortable to sleep on."

"Compared to the cardboard mattress I had in Italy, or the wooden stool in France, a camp bed will be a luxury." Rita smiled for the first time since she'd arrived in London.

After having a much longed for shower, she dried off and put on Chloe's clothes. She liked the fresh scent of lavender they gave off. With her hair wrapped in a towel, she went back to the living area and sat on the sofa, leaning back.

"I'll be with you in a minute," Chloe called from the small kitchen. "I'm making some soup. Won't be long."

Chloe wanted to keep feeding her to make up for the days she'd eaten nothing. That was very kind, but Rita's eyelids were growing heavy. As if in a dream, she felt someone cover her with a warm blanket, lifting her legs onto the sofa and helping her lay down. Rita could have sworn it was Samuel. A warm feeling ran through her body.

Finally, I've found you.

And just like that, she fell into a deep sleep.

34

London
November 2019

When Rita opened her eyes, the digital clock on the shelf read 2:00 p.m. Her head felt heavy, and it took a while to orient herself. She propped herself up on her elbows. There was no sound from the kitchen. Hadn't Chloe said she was going to prepare some soup?

The handle of the front door slammed against the wall.

"Rita, you're awake." Chloe smiled at her.

"I guess I dozed off for a bit."

"Yeah, just a bit." Chloe glanced at the clock and grinned.

Carrying two big bags of groceries, she headed to the small galley kitchen. "It's so cold outside."

She placed the groceries on the counter, took off her thick black coat and hung it with her scarf and woollen hat on a peg by the door.

"Let's get warmed up." Chloe rubbed her hands together and turned the heater on. "So, sleepyhead, do you want to eat something, or do you want something to drink?"

"I don't know. My head is spinning." Rita paused. "What time do the shops close?" She remembered Chloe had said something about clothes.

"Let's have a coffee first."

What is it with her and coffee? She asked me if I wanted a coffee an hour ago.

"That clock isn't working," Rita said, nodding at the wall.

"There's nothing wrong with the clock, Rita! It's Friday afternoon," Chloe replied, handing her a big cup of coffee and sitting beside her.

"Friday? But it was Thursday when you picked me up."

Chloe nodded and chuckled.

"God." Rita put her head in her hands. "I've been asleep an entire day?"

Chloe reached over to the shelf beside her and picked up a box of paracetamol.

"I'll get you a glass of water." She walked over to the kitchenette. "You only woke up to use the bathroom. You pretty much sleepwalked!"

Rita took the glass Chloe handed her and gulped down two paracetamols.

"You should eat something." Chloe placed a bowl of tomato soup in front of Rita. "And then, if you like, we can go out, do some shopping, or just wander around. What do you think?"

Rita's memory of the day before was slowly returning. They were meant to buy a camp bed.

"Oh, and I've washed your clothes." Chloe glanced at the hall, where her clothes had been hung out to dry. "They're still wet, so you'll have to wear mine again. I also have a coat for you."

It was half past four by the time they stepped off the Tube. A sea of people marched towards the exit, while just as many flooded into the station. So many commuters elbowing one another. It was similar to the Italian Metro, yet so different at the same time. Rita was terrified of the underground since the incident in Milan, but she was determined that London wouldn't be the same. Nobody in London talked or looked at each other. Even if they ran into one another and had to apologise, it was just one cold shoulder saying sorry to another cold shoulder before walking away.

The sign beneath the station clock said 'Hammer-smith.' Where did Samuel live? London was a big city, so she wasn't likely to bump into him.

"I don't know where to start looking for Samuel. Maybe I should go to the university where he's studying.

What do you think?" Rita asked, scanning the names of the other train stations on the map.

Chloe chewed her lip. "Yeah, maybe. Why not?"

"I met a guy on the plane," Rita said quietly. "When they deported me."

Now, Chloe looked up. "Really? What happened?"

"How much can happen on a plane? Nothing. He left without even saying *ciao*." Rita waved her hand dismissively. "It's funny, though. He left me his business card. It was in my jeans pocket." Rita laughed, although her chest ached. "The ones you washed."

"I didn't check the pockets. But it might be okay, maybe we can still read the number. You should call him."

"Why would I call him? People hand out business cards like they used to hand out cigarettes back in the day. Speaking of which, do you have one?"

"No. I quit. The last one I smoked was after your phone call. I made a promise to myself that if I found you, I'd give up smoking."

"Oh. Impressive."

"Maybe it's time for you to quit too."

"Maybe. A New Year's resolution. But first, I have to find Samuel."

Chloe's face set hard. "I've got to tell you something," she said, her tone serious.

"*Ohhhhh, it's snowing!*" Rita flung out her arms and

spun in a circle like a small child. "Snow in London! I wish I had my camera. I've only ever seen photos of this. It's so beautiful." She turned and faced Chloe. "Sorry, what did you want to tell me?"

"Later. It can wait," Chloe said, pushing open the door of H&M.

Meandering around the shops was not for Rita. She wasn't the kind of girl who could spend two hours looking for a coat and then walk away without buying a thing. Within an hour, Rita had bought two pairs of jeans – one black, and one light blue – three sweaters, socks, underwear and a heavy anorak. She also got a diary. She wasn't going to write to her mum anymore, but she would make a note of every single day of her new life. A new diary for a new start.

Chloe paid with her card and Rita's eyes narrowed when she checked the receipt. They shouldn't have gone shopping at H&M. Primark would have been a cheaper choice, from what she'd read online, but Chloe never listened. Rita folded the receipt and put it in her pocket. Now she owed her cousin even more.

"Don't worry," Chloe said, looking at Rita's face. "I got some money from Dad yesterday. Sometimes he remembers he has a daughter and transfers money to my bank account. Consider this a present from me, or from my dad, if you like."

Fumbling for words, Rita stopped in the middle of the pavement.

"Don't look at me like that, it's not that bad. When parents don't give love, they try to compensate with money. I'm used to it, and maybe it's for the best. I've learned to enjoy spending his guilt money without worrying." She pressed her thumbnail to her teeth.

Rita knew Chloe well enough to take this as a sign that it did indeed bother her.

"God, I'm tired. I've never shopped so fast," Chloe exclaimed. "Let's sit down."

She walked up the steps of a nearby restaurant and Rita followed.

The restaurant was dimly lit, and there were few customers. Chloe made her way over to a table by the window and sat down, putting the two large shopping bags by her side. Rita took off the woollen hat that she had just bought, patted down her curly hair, and made her way to the table.

She sat on the edge of her chair. Outside, the city was sinking into night, snowflakes twinkling along with the Christmas lights strung up in shop windows. The mist had engulfed every building in Hammersmith. For a split-second, Rita felt homesick. Life in her small, sunny city hadn't prepared her for this big wintery metropolis. Would she be able to adapt? Maybe Samuel would help, but first she had to find him.

"Would you like a drink, or can I interest you in something to eat?" a female voice said from behind them. Chloe looked at her watch, as if she needed its permission to eat.

"We'll eat," Chloe said.

Okay, apparently, she does.

The waitress placed two menus on the table and left.

"What would you like?" Chloe asked, her eyes focused on the menu.

"We just had soup, remember?" said Rita. "And we still have to buy the camp bed."

"Relax! Kristos got it yesterday. We only needed to buy clothes, and we did that quicker than I thought we would. We have all the time in the world. Now, tell me what you'd like."

Rita gave up. "I'll have whatever you're having."

She looked around and noticed another girl sitting on a bar stool, legs crossed, swirling the liquid in her glass. Rita swore she could hear the ice tinkling. Her blonde hair covered her face, and Rita couldn't make out her features from where she was sitting. Half the women in London seemed to be blonde. She recalled the picture Andrew had shown her in Italy, his Rachel had hair like that woman, too.

Two minutes later a man walked out of the kitchen. "Hey, Annie, nice to see you here."

"Yeah, same," the girl replied without raising her

head to look at the man. Holding her phone with one hand, she sipped a mouthful of whatever was in her glass and took a selfie.

Rita dropped her eyes to the menu and hid her trembling hands under the table so that Chloe wouldn't notice. The girl's name was Annie, not Rachel. Of course, Andrew's girlfriend wouldn't be in the same restaurant as her. What was her problem?

"What's wrong?" Chloe turned to see what Rita was looking at. "You've gone pale."

"Nothing. That girl reminded me of someone I thought I knew. Which is stupid, seeing as I don't know anyone in London."

Thankfully, Chloe seemed convinced and started studying the menu again, taking her time like Andrew had done in Italy. After five minutes of reading everything listed, Chloe ordered spaghetti with *frutti di mare* and a bottle of wine.

While waiting for the food to arrive, Chloe talked about the weather in London, her studies that were almost over, and the job applications she was about to send out. Her current part-time job at the restaurant was okay, but it was just a student's job, and, in the end, it had served its purpose because she'd gotten to know Kristos there.

With her elbows on the table and her chin resting on her hands, Rita pretended she was listening, even though Chloe's words went in one ear and out the other. This world was so unfamiliar to her, she felt like an alien. She didn't belong here.

The only time Chloe stopped talking was when the waitress placed two glasses on the table and filled them about a quarter-full of white wine. She set the bottle on the table and, after she'd gone, Chloe picked up her glass.

"I love Chardonnay, I hope you like it," she said, swirling the glass a few times before raising it to her nose and inhaling deeply. She took a small sip, as if she were a wine connoisseur, rolled it around her mouth, then gulped it down. "Just what we needed," she added with a sigh.

Rita had promised not to drink alcohol anymore, but she'd made that promise in a faraway land. Promises of the past belonged in the past. She needed to toast her new life.

Skipping Chloe's pomp and ceremony, Rita picked up her glass and lifted it to her lips. First, she took a small sip. The taste was sharp, oaky. It reminded her of perfume. Then she took another mouthful. The second tasted better.

"Cheers to your arrival and your new life," Chloe said, raising her glass.

"Cheers!" Rita replied. "Thank you for everything you two are doing for me."

"We're like sisters, remember that. You would do the same for me. Now, let's take a selfie. This is a special moment."

Chloe posted the selfie on Instagram and they both laughed at how flushed Rita's face looked in the photo. It felt so good to be back in a civilized world again, where people used phones and social media. Rita wondered if Sumaya had ever taken a selfie, let alone posted it on Instagram.

"I need the loo," Chloe said, leaving her phone on the table as she stood up.

Rita picked it up and studied the photo of them again, then went to her own Instagram profile to take a brief look at her stats. Her last post was in Albania. It seemed so long ago, yet only a couple of weeks had passed. She hopped back to Chloe's account and scrolled down her newsfeed, looking at the posts from the other people Chloe followed. People shared cats, scenery, fancy lunches. Then she stopped at the image of a couple. Rita had never seen the girl before, but there was no mistaking the boy. Her vision blurred. She enlarged the photo, squinting to get a better look. With trembling hands, she zoomed in even closer. The girl was wearing a short white dress, her hair was burnt orange, and she was kissing *her* Samuel.

This has to be a mistake!

Chloe was now standing beside Rita, staring at her phone.

"Please tell me this isn't real," Rita moaned, her heart sinking to the pit of her stomach. "This isn't—I'm imagining things. My brain is playing tricks on me. Or I'm still asleep on the couch and this is a nightmare."

She turned to look into Chloe's face, and her cousin's expression told her everything she needed to know.

"You *knew* and you *didn't tell me? *What sort of *sisters* are we?" Rita yelled, her chair crashing to the floor as she bolted to her feet.

People were staring at them, but Rita didn't care. They didn't know her. She didn't know a soul in this city. Nothing mattered anymore.

"Rita, I'm so sorry," Chloe said. "I was waiting for the right moment."

35

"I should have guessed," Rita said, her voice dropping to a hoarse whisper. She'd been so naïve. So certain that Samuel would wait for her. She picked her chair back up and sank into it like a rock. She buried her face in her hands, wanting to scream loud enough for the whole of London to hear her pain. Her chest was rising and falling so quickly she thought her heart was about to explode.

Chloe had run out of words, too.

Rita drained her glass and poured another one.

Wine will make me forget. Dad drunk raki to forget Mum. It worked for him.

"I'm sorry I didn't tell you. I only found out myself when I got back to London two weeks ago. A friend of mine told me her best friend was seeing an Albanian guy, but I never imagined it could be Samuel. When she showed me the wedding pictures..."

"*Wedding?*" Rita yelled.

He'd gotten *married?* But Samuel loved *her*! He'd

said borders didn't matter. Tears were streaming down Rita's cheeks, but she didn't wipe them away.

"Where's the girl from?" she snapped.

"She's English," Chloe confirmed. "Does that change anything?"

"Nope." Rita drained her second glass of wine and rubbed her eyes, attempting to make sense of Chloe's words. She was already a bit tipsy, and all this information was too much for her brain to process. It couldn't be true. Samuel was hers. They were supposed to start a new life in London. Together. Even if she hadn't been able to speak to him in months. She did the math. It had been six months since she'd last heard from him, and clearly, he'd made a brand-new shiny life for himself. God, she'd been stupid.

"Pass me your phone. I want to check my Instagram account. Maybe he sent me a private message while I was trying to get here and was cut off from the world." She was talking in a calm voice, as if nothing had happened, while her heart was shattering. She was deluding herself thinking he'd sent her a message. What would he have said? 'Hey, Rita. I got married to a girl who is nothing like you and totally not my type… but I did it to stay in the UK?'

Chewing the non-existent nails of her left hand, Rita hovered over her Instagram account with her right hand. One hundred thousand useless followers. They were only interested in Rita's digital footprint for the idyllic pictures she posted, for the life she pretended to have. But all of it was fake. If they looked at her now, they would see nothing but an illegal immigrant crying over a boy who'd dumped her – a boy who'd not even had the decency to tell her he'd gotten married behind her back, a boy who had strung her along from the get-go. Was she going to show that to her followers? Of course not.

The red flag in the corner of the screen showed that she'd received a private message. Her heart skipped a beat.

It was Andrew. The absolute cheek!

"So?" Chloe asked, leaning over the table to catch a glimpse of the message. "Did Samuel send you an explanation?"

Rita handed the phone back to her cousin, shaking her head. "It's that guy I met on the plane. He found me on Instagram."

"Well, that's nice of him to write to you! What did he say?"

Rita raised her hand to stop Chloe getting carried away. "I don't need to know. I never even told him my full name. How the hell did he find me?" She let out a bitter, dry laugh. "Oh, of course. We were sharing dog photos and he must have remembered my handle."

"Are you going to tell him you're here?"

"No." Rita bit her lower lip. "Fuck, Chloe. What am I going to do now? I went through hell to get to Samuel, only to discover he's *married*?"

Rita's dry laughs quickly turned into sobs. She rubbed her eyes again with the palm of her hand.

"Maybe the universe is leading you to someone else."

"That's bullshit." She said it louder than she'd meant to, and the people seated at the table beside them turned their heads. Rita was too drunk to care.

She pushed her plate away and took a gulp of her wine. Andrew's message was just a hello. He wasn't flirting, he wasn't asking for anything. All she had to do was delete his message and tear up his business card and he would vanish just like that. No hard feelings. All she cared about was Samuel. He'd always been a part of her life, her right arm, and now she felt like a piece of her was missing. And Samuel wasn't so easy to delete, because if she cut him off completely, she would be wiping away the best thing to have ever happened in her life.

36

London
November 2019

Somewhere in the depths of her slumber, Rita heard
a noise. It sounded like someone was drilling inside
her head. She forced her eyes open, the lids seeming to
weigh a ton. She closed them again. She remembered
falling asleep on her new bed, yet somehow, she was
now on the couch. The room was spinning. She was
wearing a T-shirt that was definitely not hers, and for
some reason, a wet cloth, which still had pieces of ice
inside it, was pressed against her forehead.

Married.

The nettlesome word swirled inside her mind.
She couldn't remember who was married or why the
word was yo-yoing in and out of her dream.

"Good afternoon, sleepyhead," Chloe said, pushing
open the living-room door.

She was holding a big mug. A grey, oversized

sweatshirt covered her bare legs, reaching down to her knees.

"My head is exploding. Do you have anything stronger than paracetamol?"

"Take these." Chloe put two Nurofen Express and a glass of water on the table.

"Maybe you should just give me the entire packet."

"Do you want me to make a coffee?" Chloe gestured with her mug. "It will sort your head out."

"I'm going to need as much of it as you can give me," she groaned.

"This is my magic cup. It will cure your headache, you'll see." Chloe placed a mug with a picture of a big teddy bear holding a bunch of flowers on the table.

"Weren't you supposed to be at school today?" Rita asked quietly, scared of the answer she might get.

"It's Sunday." Chloe smiled again and drank her coffee. Rita glanced at the digital clock on the wooden plank. It read 16:00.

Shit! I did it again. It's like I came to London just to sleep.

"Do you want to tell me why I'm sleeping on the sofa again, and why I have this wet cloth on my forehead?"

"Chill. You were a bit tipsy."

"What? I got drunk? I'm just like Dad. I'm sorry," Rita mumbled. She looked at Chloe, puzzled. It wasn't just the wine, there was something else. Chloe was pacing the room now. There wasn't much space, so she was using the small hallway too.

"It's okay. I drink too much myself when I'm in hurting." Chloe came over and sat down by Rita's feet.

"Did I get hurt? That's why you put the ice on my forehead?"

"No." Chloe laughed. "I wish a wet cloth would take the pain away. You bumped your head against the wall. After we finished drinking in the restaurant, we came home. I thought you were asleep, but you drank half a bottle of wine from the fridge."

"I did *what*?"

"It was my fault. I probably would have done the same in your situation."

"What do you mean?" Rita asked.

"I mean, if my boyfriend had married an English girl the moment my back was turned."

It all came flooding back to her. *Samuel had got married.*

Rita's heart throbbed again. She lifted her mug to her chapped lips. The bear on the cup was cute, but not cute enough to make her smile.

"You know, Rita, I've been thinking about what might help. I told Kristos last night, and he thinks the same." *I knew they'd get tired of me soon.* "You've been through a lot, and you can't handle this alone. Maybe you should see a therapist."

"A what?"

"A shrink."

"Shrimp? No, thank you, I don't like them. I gave you my prawns last night, remember?"

It took Chloe a while to stop laughing. "No, silly. *Shrink*, it's slang. It means psychologist."

"What for?" Rita hesitated. "I mean, even if I *did* need a psychologist, it's expensive. They're for rich people. I don't even believe in shrinks, or whatever they call them here."

"You're wrong about that. A psychologist helps a lot. Mine is good."

"Yours? Why do you need to see him?"

"First of all, he's a *she*. It's not always men who fix things, you know. We're all humans and we all need to talk sometimes. It doesn't mean we're crazy just because we consult a shrink, or a shrimp… Call them what you like, they can help."

"I have a lot of problems, sure, but I don't need a doctor."

"That's exactly the point. Their job is to help you overcome your problems. You were talking to Auntie Luna all night. It was like your mum was in the room. You laughed and cried to the wall, Rita! You scared me half to death."

I did? Well, they do say wine brings out the truth.

"Oh, I don't remember. But listen, it's no big deal.

296

I have to talk to *somebody*, and in this case, I spoke to Mum. That doesn't mean I need help."

"Rita, your mum is dead. People don't speak to the dead."

Rita started fidgeting with the charm of the necklace her mum bought her.

I don't speak to her all the time...

But Rita didn't say it out loud. Chloe looked concerned enough.

"Okay, you have a point. I need to work on myself. And I will. I will get through this shit and come out the other end. But it's only me who can do that, not a therapist. Besides, I told you I don't believe in them. They have their own problems. That's probably the reason most of them are attracted to the job in the first place. The moment you open up to them, they're thinking about their own life, their own marriage, their own fears. You're literally spilling out all the secrets buried in your heart, and she – because in your case, it's a woman – is thinking about the socks her husband leaves under the bed. Or wondering what to eat for lunch, or if she's going to have sex tonight, or if she can get away with faking a headache."

"Okay, maybe some therapists are like that. But trust me, that's not how it is with all of them."

Rita wasn't listening anymore, but Chloe carried on, enjoying her rant. At some point Rita realised she had stopped talking and was staring at her expectantly.

"Look, in my case, I used to talk to Mum, and when Mum passed away, I had Samuel." She swallowed. "And now Samuel's gone, so apparently I've gone back to talking to Mum again." She nibbled on the edge of her fingernail.

"A therapist would help you understand that relationships often do go wrong."

Yeah? Well, mine was different. My relationship was meant to last.

Neither cousin spoke for a while. A vein pulsed in Chloe's jaw. She kept swirling her coffee with her spoon, making an irritating tinkling sound.

"I've got to tell you something else," Chloe said. She walked over to the window and moved the curtain aside. Outside, the sky was murky. It had been Friday evening when Rita got drunk and fell asleep, only to wake up late on Sunday. An entire day of her life had passed by. But when she was asleep, nothing hurt. Her waking life was like a continuous frontal assault.

Rita remembered the snowflakes that had fallen the night she'd drunk too much, a night she wanted to erase from her life. Even if the snow had piled up to the windowsill, she would have been too tired to turn her head and look. She didn't want to move. If Chloe let her, Rita would lay down right now and fall back asleep, praying never to wake up again.

"What more could there possibly be to tell?" Rita asked, slurping her coffee.

Maybe Samuel has a child on the way, the happy family complete, sneered the voice.

Rita gritted her teeth, bracing herself.

Chloe took a box off the shelf above her head and placed it on Rita's bed.

"I got you another phone."

"I don't need a phone. I already owe you too much."

"Don't worry, it's a pay-as-you-go contract. You can pay the bill yourself if it makes you feel better. I added my number." She took a sip of her coffee. "And Andrew's."

Rita almost chocked. "*Andrew's*? How did you find his number?"

"You left your Instagram account open when we were in the restaurant. I couldn't help but memorise his details. I told him you were here, but that you're feeling a bit unwell. I also gave him your new number. He's called twice."

"Just because I'm staying in your apartment doesn't give you the right to do that, Chloe! Maybe I should leave." Rita put the phone on the table and tried to stand up. But the room spun, and she had to sit down on the bed again.

"Rita, don't be so petty! I'm only trying to move your life along in the right direction."

"Well, you shouldn't have. I'm not going to talk to him, or to anybody else for that matter. Don't you think I've been through enough?" Rita pressed the tips of her fingers to her temples. Her head was on the verge of exploding. How could Chloe do this? She sighed heavily. A few moments passed in silence, but Rita's curiosity got the best of her.

"What did he say anyway?" She asked.

The nasty voice snorted inside her head. *Why do you want to know?*

"That he'll call you again," Chloe said.

37

A phone is ringing, and a man starts talking. For the first time since I've been trapped in this strange perpetual dream, I realise that my past is over. There is nothing more to tell.

The nurse opens the door. She's wearing the same white coat and the same white slippers that she wears every day. She says good morning to the man and checks the chart at the foot of my bed. My eyes well up as she changes the bag of liquid above my head and strokes my hair.

So much kindness. So much love. I have to wake up!

38

London
November 2019

The following morning, Rita woke up before the alarm clock went off. The ambulance and police sirens outside Chloe's building never stopped. But the loud noise wasn't the reason she'd woken up early. Today, she had a plan. With a bit of luck, she was going to see Samuel. She couldn't let him go just like that. Maybe he'd had no choice but to marry this girl. It couldn't be real love. Samuel was hers, and he'd promised to be with her forever.

She knew Chloe would try to stop her, so Rita pretended she was asleep until her cousin left the house. When she was sure Chloe wouldn't come back, Rita rolled out of bed and put on jeans and her new sweater, instinctively braiding her hair the way Samuel liked. Holding her compact mirror open with one hand, she applied a light layer of makeup. Samuel preferred light makeup. *His bride was wearing a lot of makeup in that Instagram photo. He must have hated that.*

There was a chance she'd have to wait all day for him, so she put on her trainers. If she wasn't lucky today, she would return tomorrow. You don't just give up on love.

At 8 a.m. she left the house. A dark cloud obscured the sun, while an icy wind whipped at her cheeks. She wrapped her woollen scarf around her neck and face, leaving only her eyes uncovered.

According to the navigator on her new phone, bus number 207 would take her to Shepherd's Bush. Rita wasn't ready to take the Tube on her own just yet. Every time she tried to forget her experience in Milan, it came back to her in a bigger and more terrifying flash, like someone setting off a bomb right beside her. No, she would hop on the bus instead. Besides, she'd always wanted to travel on a red double-decker. Surely it had to be more exciting than traveling on any other bus. Why else were they featured on every postcard of London?

Five minutes after leaving the house, Rita was standing at the bus stop. Number 207 appeared right on time, just when the GPS had said it would. Weird. She would never get used to buses arriving on time. It was packed, but Rita was lucky to find a place. She sat down next to a young girl wearing a pair of sunglasses that covered most of her face. Even though Rita couldn't see her eyes, she had the distinct impression the girl wasn't happy about Rita sitting next to her.

As usual, Rita breathed as silently as she could, trying not to disturb her. Rita was a foreigner, while the girl was clearly a local. Rita wasn't meant to be there, and it felt like everyone on the bus knew that just by looking at her.

By the time she arrived at her stop, Rita realised she'd been so engrossed in breathing quietly that she hadn't noticed the girl had fallen asleep.

Next time I'll breathe normally, Rita thought as she stepped off the bus.

Samuel's campus was somewhere nearby, close enough to walk to, according to her GPS. Holding her phone in her right hand while her left stayed toasty and warm in her pocket, it took Rita over an hour to get to the London Business School. But if she hadn't walked, she wouldn't have seen all the interesting sights along the way. Maybe when she had her own money, she could actually do the tourist thing.

She stopped on the corner of the street and blew warm air onto her freezing cold hand that had been exposed to the elements. No sign of Samuel.

Rita looked around at the large white buildings and shiny cars. The street smelt of money and rich people.

What if he's sick or busy and didn't come in today?

Then she would return tomorrow, and the next day, and the day after, until she got to talk to him. He'd feel differently once he saw her. He was the reason she'd come to London, after all.

But what was she going to say to him when she did see him? She had no idea.

The street was quiet. Rita wandered over to a flower shop on the other side of the road. Maybe she could learn the English names of some of the blooms – a good way to kill the time.

"That's a perfect bouquet for a wedding day," a voice said from behind her. The female florist gestured at the large bunch of white lilies Rita was admiring. "It's called a cascade teardrop. It's made of purple Singapore orchids and lush green tropical leaves."

"It's beautiful," Rita replied.

A wedding bouquet. Pfft. That was the last thing she wanted to see. *As if you'll ever get to hold one of those now. Samuel has chosen his bride, and it's not you.* She could always count on her cruel inner voice to chime in at the wrong moment.

Distracted by the flowers, Rita hadn't noticed it had started to rain outside. The snow at the edge of the road had already melted away. She couldn't hang around the shops opposite the campus any longer, and even if she had money for an umbrella, there weren't any for sale. Panning the street for options, she spotted a café called

Moulin Rouge two doors down. Perfect. She'd wait it out there until Samuel decided to make an appearance.

Rita ran to the French-themed café, brushing the rain from her shoulders as she entered the small steamy room. People ate sandwiches and sipped coffee. Nobody batted an eyelid at the illegal immigrant sitting in the corner. Rita ordered a coffee. Coffee was cheaper than a hot chocolate. She paid with the pocket money her cousin had given her and made a mental note to add it to her IOU bill. She drank her coffee while gazing out at the street, nothing in particular catching her eye. When she finished it, she ordered another. At this rate, she was going to give herself a caffeine overdose, but she would worry about that later.

The rain had finally stopped, and Rita was ready to leave the café and find Samuel. She looked both ways as she crossed the street, still uncertain of where she should be searching. A whiteboard hung on the fence wall displaying the message: "The main entrance and reception to the right. Delivery area to the left." Rita read the notice on turned right, positioning herself in front of the main entrance. If this was the main entrance, it would also be the main exit.

She'd promised herself she'd stay there until the last student left. There was no way she was going to miss Samuel. Rita's eyes were so focused on the door of the main entrance that she didn't see the car parked on the opposite side of the street, or the girl who came out of it. If she had seen her, Rita would have recognized the other woman instantly.

Instead, she urgently scanned the faces of the students leaving the large building. Just when she was convinced that she'd missed Samuel, she spotted him. He was wearing jeans and a black V-neck sweater. The zip of his Armani winter jacket was undone as usual. Rita's heart lurched and her knees buckled. She pressed her back against a streetlamp to steady herself, fidgeting with the charm on her necklace.

Samuel looked up and froze. His eyes darted from Rita to the girl who was now approaching him. The girl wrapped her arms around Samuel's neck and kissed him on the lips.

In another life, Rita would have had a heart attack, but now she only bit her lip hard to control her emotions. In the past few weeks, she'd seen what it was to truly suffer – she could survive this.

The girl wore faded jeans and a big parka. As she got closer, Rita could tell that the girl's Instagram pictures had all been edited. In the photos, the girl's hair had been a burnt orange colour, but now she was blonde. The rest of her looked different too, a lot less model-like. This British girl wasn't Samuel's type at all.

Now they were walking towards her, hand in hand. After spending all day waiting – not to mention weeks planning and months yearning – for this very moment, all Rita wanted to do was run.

"Rita!"

The sound of Samuel's voice made her body start to tremble. But she had to get herself together. She was not going to cry in front of him or his new British wife.

"Hi!" He leaned over and kissed her on both cheeks. It took all the strength she had not to brush her lips against his as she'd done a thousand times before. "So great to see you. This is Megan," he said, as if Rita were nothing but an acquaintance. He didn't say Megan was his wife.

The girl stretched out her hand and Rita shook it, as if in a trance.

"Nice to meet you, Rita." She emphasised her name. Maybe she knew it, or maybe Rita was imagining things. "Sammy just told me you're a friend from back home. I know how difficult it is for you people to come to London."

You people? Sammy?

"It's so nice to meet someone from his past. Why don't you come over to our place? I'm sure Sammy would love to catch up, wouldn't you, honey?"

"Yes, of course. But maybe Rita has other things to do," he added quickly.

Oh, hell no. Rita wasn't going to make this easy for

him. He wasn't going to get away with what he'd done to her just like that.

"Oh, I would love to!" she said, giving them what she hoped was her most pleasant smile.

"Perfect. Let's meet up on the weekend. I'll cook. Is that okay with you, hon?"

Samuel nodded but couldn't seem to bring himself to meet Rita's gaze.

"Great! Then it's settled. I'll have Sammy message you with our address." She beamed at Rita like a child, reaching over and giving her arm an affectionate squeeze. "It's about time I met one of Sammy's friends, none of them were able to make it to our wedding. I'm so glad you're here, Rita."

There it was. *Our wedding.*

"Let me know if there's any food you don't eat."

"I'm not picky. Maybe I'll bring some *byrek*," Rita said. "*Samuel* loves it."

"Oh, Albanian cuisine! I love exotic food, and I'm so curious to try everything from my hubby's country." Megan turned and faced Samuel. "Darling, I got stuck in traffic and I couldn't buy flowers for my mum. You know how she loves flowers. I'm just going to pop over to the flower shop."

Smiling brightly, she turned and enveloped Rita in a big hug. It was a warm embrace, but Rita felt nothing but chills.

Megan left and a dead silence hung in the air.

"Well, it's certainly a surprise to see you," Samuel said at last, shifting from one foot to another. He kept his eyes on Megan, watching her back as if he was afraid that she would turn around and say: *Gotcha*. "Look, Rita, I know you're angry with me right now, but I can explain everything. It's not what it looks like."

Just like in the movies. It's not what it looks like... yeah, it's even worse.

Samuel was talking faster now. "Can we meet somewhere, another day? We're going to Megan's mother's house tonight." Oh, how very convenient. A nice quick getaway. "But any other day you want, we can meet. Let me explain. Where are you staying? Actually, how did you get here? I thought they didn't grant you the scholarship."

Rita let out a long, slow breath. Rage flowed from her core like a river of lava, threatening to engulf everything in its path – including Samuel and his new British wife.

He saw my messages and he let me go, happy in the knowledge I couldn't follow him.

"Why Samuel? *Why?*"

"It's a long story. Basically, it was the only way I could get a full residency permit."

"You lied to me! You disappeared when I needed you most! Why?"

"Honey… You know you're my sunshine."

Samuel reached out for Rita's hand, but she snatched it back.

"Don't you dare! How many sunshines do you have in your life?"

"Look, Rita, I'm sorry, okay? Give me some time and I can fix everything."

Including my broken heart?

"You know what we say in Albania: a broken piece of bread can't be knitted back together."

"Rita, I'm just asking for some time. You owe me that."

"I don't owe you fucking shit!" She shouted so loudly in Albanian that two girls walking past turned their heads.

"Please."

Rita laughed pitifully.

"And how much time exactly do you need?"

"Three years."

"*What?*" Rita cried. "Why?"

"If I divorce her before then, I'll lose everything. The Home Office won't extend my residency here. I depend on her, and she *is* nice. Once you get to know her. She really does love me. I did it for us, Rita. The moment I divorce her, I'll marry you. I promise. Then you'll have your residency permit without having had to do a thing and we'll start our new life together."

"You make me sick, Samuel. Are you telling me you don't love her back, and you married her just for a piece of paper?"

"Of course! I love *you.*"

Her stomach sank. Those were the only words she'd been longing to hear for the last six months. This very moment was what had made her break the law, sleep rough, enter a country illegally, and risk her life. But now, after hearing those words, all Rita wanted to do was spit in his face. Did he really think he could abandon her completely, marry another woman, discard that woman, then pick Rita back up like an old toy? She swallowed down the acrid taste his words left in her mouth and raised her hand. Would all this anger inside of her vanish if she slapped him?

"Stop, please," she said, her throat tight with oncoming tears. "You have no idea what it took for me to get to London. I thought you were sick, or that you'd had an accident. I thought you were dead, for God's sake... and this is the reason you didn't reply. You lied to me from the very beginning, and I believed you. Well, not anymore, Samuel. I went through hell to find you. And now that I have, I wish I hadn't. You're worse than Antonio."

An image of Maria living on the streets of Milan flashed before Rita's eyes and she willed away her tears. No, she was not going to cry in front of Samuel.

"Who's Antonio?"

He came closer to Rita, a new look of alarm etched across his brow.

"It doesn't matter."

"Do you have a boyfriend?"

A tiny spark lit up inside Rita. Was he jealous?

"You're married. Why do you care?"

She felt her phone vibrate in her pocket. She glanced down at it and winced. *Andrew.*

God had a great sense of humour, and for the first time that day, she was thankful to Chloe for having given him her number. The timing was perfect.

Without apologizing to Samuel, she snapped her phone open.

"Hi! Yes, can't wait to see you. Eight this evening is perfect," Rita said in English.

Maybe she was being the tiniest bit unfair to both men – okay, mostly to Andrew – but at least agreeing to see another man proved to Samuel that she wasn't pathetic and lonely without him. His betrayal hurt, and it was only natural that she wanted to retaliate.

"And was that this Antonio calling? Did I miss something?" Samuel asked, a slight tremor in his voice.

Rita smiled coldly, enjoying the way Samuel was looking at her, as if he'd never truly known her.

"Oh, you've missed a lot. But it doesn't matter now. Your wife is waiting for you. You don't want to keep her waiting too long or she might divorce you before your three years are up. Oh, and tell her I changed my mind about dinner. I've got better things to do with my weekend."

"Rita, this isn't like you! Who is this guy? You know Englishmen only want foreign girls for one-night stands! Especially Albanians. They think our women are sluts. He doesn't care about you the way you deserve to be cared about... the way I do."

Samuel got even closer and for a moment Rita thought he was going to take her in his arms. Did she *want* that? No. All she felt now was hatred and disgust. The love she used to have for him had burned to ashes. He wasn't Samuel anymore. He was Sammy. He was someone she didn't know.

"The way you *did*!" Rita quipped. "Ha. I was the longest one-night stand you'd ever had. Now, if you'll excuse me, I need to go. Say goodbye to Megan for me."

And with a wave of her hand, which was no longer trembling – so very satisfying! – she turned and walked away, determined they'd never cross paths again.

39

London
November 2019

Rita had no other option but to meet Andrew now. She had to follow through with this petty revenge. *What was wrong with her?* She was no different than Samuel, using a nice, unsuspecting English person for her own agenda.

When she arrived home, neither Chloe nor Kristos was there, so she took a quick shower, attempting to warm her cold, numb body. Filled with anger and wishing she still had her makeup bag, she opened Chloe's built-in cabinet above the sink and picked up a glossy lipstick. She didn't bother with anything else. She wasn't trying to impress this guy. She squirted some of Chloe's Channel N°5 perfume on and she was done.

Next, she opened the small wardrobe door and stood there for a while, trying to figure out what to wear. Burrowing through her new clothes, she found the diary she'd bought when she was shopping with Chloe. She was not going to start the first page writing about Samuel and his British wife. But it probably wasn't the best idea to start with Andrew, either. She stashed the diary in one of Chloe's many shoeboxes then put on her jeans and new purple sweater.

The doorbell rang. He was early.

"Rita!"

"Andrew."

They both spoke at the same time, their voices colliding mid-air. He'd trimmed his beard. It suited him better than the one she remembered in Italy.

"I told you, my friends call me Andy," he leaned over, gave her a light peck on the cheek and handed her a bouquet of flowers. Twelve purple orchids.

Goosebumps flecked Rita's arms. How could he possibly know she liked purple and loved orchids? This bunch was almost identical to the one she'd admired at the florist!

"I'm so sorry I had to leave so suddenly in Italy," he began.

Rita waved his words away. "It's no problem." She laughed for no reason at all. "Let's go." Her behaviour was odd, and she knew it, but she just couldn't stop herself. All she had to do was turn back, lock the door, and stay away from Andrew, but she followed him to his car.

Outside, the sky had grown darker. Rita had already been in London for five days, although four of them she'd spent sleeping. And on the fifth day, she'd found the boy she'd loved all her life… and his wife. Oh well, now she was going out with someone she'd met on a plane. Why was life so weird and stupid and totally unexpected?

The voice in her head kept repeating the conversation she'd had with Samuel. She had to get rid of it, but how? It was wrong of her to accept Andrew's invitation. All the things Rita did on a whim turned out disastrously. Panic rose in her chest, but she blinked her tears away.

This was fine. They had got on well in Italy. Why shouldn't they be friends?

The label of her new sweater was irritating her neck. Then again, every part of her was itchy with anxiety.

Andrew sat to her right in the driver's seat (which was still confusing her) and started the engine. He took the first right turn and they merged with the sea of cars flooding the dual carriageway.

"I booked *Chicchetti* for tonight," he said. "I hope you'll like it. It's near Piccadilly Circus, which is slightly inconvenient as it's such a busy area, but we'll get there on time."

Rita kept her eyes on the road ahead. The longer she carried on with this story, fooling herself that she was hurting Samuel, the more she was hurting herself – and now maybe Andrew, too. She needed to tell him to stop the car, but she couldn't muster the courage, so she bit her nails instead.

They passed Hammersmith, the Victoria and Albert Museum, Buckingham Palace – names Rita had, until now, read only in books – and a chill ran down her spine. She was making a big mistake. She was not a fraud; she was not Samuel.

Eventually, they reached their destination, and Rita still hadn't found a safe moment or the right moment to jump out of Andrew's car. She couldn't bring herself to leave his side and run away into the darkness. She was too tired of running away.

They drove around Piccadilly Circus a few times and finally found a parking place.

Andrew opened the car door and the cold air hit Rita in the face like a slap. The same cold, foreign, unwelcoming air she was still unaccustomed to.

"*Chicchetti* is one of my favourite Italian restaurants. You'll feel right at home here," he said, helping her out of the car.

I'm not Italian. I'm not English. I'm not even from my own country anymore. I'm just floating. No roots, no home.

The restaurant was warm, and the lights were dim. A waiter walked them to a table by the window. The place was packed, but the best table had been reserved for them.

If she'd known he was bringing her to a fancy restaurant, Rita would have put on something smarter. Maybe even one of Chloe's dresses. But it didn't matter that Rita didn't own any fancy outfits, because this would be her first and last dinner with Andrew.

The waiter brought a small basket of bread and two little dishes filled with herb butter.

"What would you like to drink?"

"Just water for now, please." Rita rubbed her forehead. "I have to tell you something..."

"Me too," Andrew said, tripping over his words. "But not on an empty stomach."

The waiter came, holding his hand behind his back, he poured some water into Rita's glass and some white wine into Andrew's glass.

"Let me show you something," Andrew said the moment the waiter left. He opened his bag. "This is for you." He put a large box wrapped in colourful paper on the table.

Rita's face flushed. She pushed the gift away. "I'm sorry, but I can't accept this. It's too much!"

"I won't be going back to the shop again, so it'll go unused and unloved if you don't open it," said Andrew sadly.

Struggling with her emotions, Rita took her time pulling off the paper. It was a brand-new camera! And it was even better than the one she'd had before.

She clasped her hand over her mouth and gasped loudly.

"Oh, my God! How did you know I lost mine?"

"It's my welcome gift to London," Andrew said, lifting his glass of wine in a toast. "Chloe told me what happened to you in Italy." His face fell. "I'm so sorry I wasn't at the hotel when you came. You know I would have helped, but I had my reasons." He ran his fingers through his hair and looked up at Rita. A warmth lingered in the space between them, the same indescribable feeling she'd had in Italy.

She lowered her eyes, avoiding his gaze. Her heart had only ever been reserved for Samuel, but now, when she thought of her ex, there was nothing but heaviness. Whereas this man sitting before her had seemingly, dangerously, unchained a piece of her heart...

Maybe we can just be friends?

The voice in her head laughed. She cast it and her thoughts aside and stared in a mixture of disbelief and awe at the camera in her hands.

"Your Instagram fans are waiting for you," Andrew said, taking a sip of his wine.

"Yeah, I guess I have a new fan now." She smiled.

I can't believe you're smiling at him! The irritating voice persisted.

"I hope you don't mind that I messaged you on Insta. I felt so bad about rushing off. My father was ill. H-he passed away." Andrew leaned over the table and cupped Rita's hands again. She swallowed hard and tears sprang to her eyes. She knew all too well the pain of losing a parent. Poor guy. So, it hadn't been about Rachel at all.

"I'm sorry for your loss."

Andrew gave her a sad smile. "It's okay. I'm so glad your cousin called and told me everything. I thought you hated me."

The waiter came again, and Rita pulled her hands away, as if she'd been caught doing something illicit. Pretending he hadn't seen that he'd ruined a special moment, the waiter placed a big dish of grilled king prawns, scallops, mussels, clams, and langoustines on the table. The seafood made Rita's stomach churn. She couldn't face anything except water.

"Chloe didn't tell you everything," she whispered. Andrew nodded but stayed silent, patiently waiting. "My name is Rita Hanas and I come from," she paused and took a deep breath, "I'm Albanian."

Andrew shrugged. "Cool. I've never met an Albanian before."

Is that it?

"It's not that hard to find us. But when people do, they think we're thieves, drug dealers, working girls… you know."

Her cheeks burned. What if Andrew thought the same about her?

But Andrew's expression remained blank, as if he didn't know whether to apologise, explain, or disagree. Now that she'd started, Rita had to continue with her backstory and tell the whole truth.

"I tried to enter England illegally, using the identity of another person. It's a long story. Anyway, it didn't work. That day on the plane, when we met, I was being deported. I'm ashamed to say that when I first saw you, I wanted to use you to get myself into the UK. I would have paid you – not that I had any money, or even knew if you'd agree. When everything was stolen from me in Milan, I decided to tell you the truth, but you'd already left."

Rita shrugged and let out a long sigh. She didn't mention Samuel because he no longer mattered. *There. Now he knows everything. He knows I'm a cheating, untrustworthy, lawbreaker.*

"I'll understand if you hate me, if you tell me to leave, or call the police."

Why did you tell him everything? What if he does report you?

She ignored the fear screaming inside her mind. No more lies. Now that the truth was out, she felt lighter. And sick.

The waiter had returned, again, with impeccable timing. He topped up Andrew's glass again before walking away. Andrew remained silent, his elbow on the table, his thumb under his chin.

"I'm so very sorry you had to go through all of that," he said finally. He fell silent again, seeming to be looking for the right words.

Rita fidgeted in her chair. She went to stand, but Andrew put his hand gently on her arm, urging her to stay seated.

"Please, don't go. Don't disappear again."

"Even after all the lies I told you?"

"It wasn't all lies. I'm pretty sure your fear of turbulence was real," he said with a smile.

He chewed on a large shrimp and washed it down with a mouthful of wine. He put his knife and fork on his plate, wiped his mouth with a cloth napkin, then folded it.

"So, what are your plans now that you're in London?" Andrew steered the conversation in a totally different direction, and Rita was both confused and grateful for it. Was this one of those polite British things she'd heard about? Did it mean he'd forgiven her, or that they were going to avoid talking about her story ever again while he silently judged her?

"By the way, I like your curly hair. Suits you."

"Thanks," she said in a soft voice. "I need to find a job and move out of Chloe's tiny place. The thing is, I'm here illegally. It's as if I don't exist."

"I see."

"I know I'm not the first or the last to be in this

situation. I'm sure I'll find something."

An awkward silence hung between them.

"A friend of mine is looking for a childminder. The one they had left unexpectedly. Alessia is a really cute toddler. I could ask them to meet up with you. Do you have any experience with young children?"

Okay then. He couldn't have been disgusted by her story if he was looking to help her! Rita's face lit up, thinking of Daniel. "Yes. Lots. Do you think they would consider me? I mean, I don't have any references or anything like that. Just my word."

"I'll talk to them. I'm Alessia's godfather. I'll tell them a friend of mine is looking for a job and she has experience with children."

There. He'd said it. A friend of mine. It suited Rita perfectly that he wanted nothing more. Having an Englishman as a friend was a good thing, after all.

Rita was just opening her mouth to thank him when his phone rang.

"I have to take this. It's my mother."

Rita couldn't hear the voice on the other end of the line, but she could work out the gist of what Andrew's mother was saying.

"Sure, Mum, I guess I could come. Rachel, why?"

Andrew listened, then added, "Yes! Okay, see you tomorrow."

Rachel. Of course. He'd gone back to her.

40

Rita didn't tell Chloe about meeting Samuel or Megan. She wasn't going to tell anyone. But she did tell her about the flowers, the dinner with Andrew, and the job interview she might have secured. Chloe was happy for her, and Rita apologised for her initial outburst.

Deep down, Rita couldn't believe Andrew was really going to ask the parents of his goddaughter to meet with her. She was still a stranger to him, for goodness' sake! And even if he did ask them, they would likely say no, because she never had any luck when it came to jobs.

The next morning, Rita was woken up by the sound of her phone beeping. Andrew said Alessia's father, Oliver, had taken the day off and wanted to meet her.

Shit! What am I going to wear?

Rita wasn't really a breakfast person, so she flicked on the coffee machine instead. Since the first day she'd arrived in London, Rita had started drinking her coffee in the big bear mug. She grabbed it now and took a sip as she stood at the window. *Imagine if I do get this job!* This could change her whole outlook because nothing gave you confidence like being employed. Not to mention, she would be able to pay back the money she still owed her aunt and cousin.

She got herself ready, applying her makeup as neatly as possible and feeling a twinge of guilt as she sprayed on some more of Chloe's perfume. It wasn't only her job interview that made her nervous, she was going to meet Andrew's friend, so she had to make a good impression. Considering how cold she'd been the day before, waiting for Samuel, she decided to put on a pair of black trousers, then pulled her thick, pumpkin-coloured jumper over her head.

The interview was at 11 a.m. at the family's house. At least the sun was shining, and Andrew had agreed to accompany her. That had to be a good omen.

By the time he pulled up in his car to give her a lift, Rita was pacing the pavement, biting on her nails. Today Andrew was clad in jeans and a black sweater. Perhaps it was a trick of the sunlight, but the sandy-haired Brit looked more handsome than he had the night before.

"Oliver and Chiara are excited to see you."

Chiara, an Italian name. I hope she accepts me and thinks I'm good enough to look after her child. Rita crossed her fingers behind her back.

"I don't know how to thank you, or how I'll ever repay you for your help."

"Easy. Have lunch with me afterwards. I can show you a bit more of London."

"Will Rachel be okay with that?"

The words blurted out of her mouth and a blush crawled up her neck.

"Hey." Andrew turned her head gently to face him. "Rachel and I may have been together in the past, but I promise you we are nothing more than friends now. After that trip to Italy, it took me just twenty-four short hours to realise I'm not in love with her anymore." He stopped for a beat and looked Rita in the eye. "We still talk to each other, we still go to the same parties and mix in the same circles, but that's it. She has her life and I have mine."

Rita chewed her lip. *God, I'm so stupid.*

"So, back to my question," said Andrew. "Lunch?"

"I guess that's the least I can do. But on one condition."

He raised his eyebrows quizzically.

"Only if they hire me."

He laughed. "It's a deal."

"What about your work? Shouldn't you be trading?"

"I don't have to do a thing today. I'm all yours."

Rita remembered he'd told her about BTC. When Chloe had gotten her a new phone, she'd looked it up and read all about this digital money Andrew had talked about. She still didn't understand it.

"And how is your job going?" she asked, as she did up her seatbelt.

"Great. I'm closing on a new house at the end of the month."

Buying a house! Rita was shocked. The idea that he could afford a house with the sort of job he had, which seemed to her like no real job at all, was ridiculous. Lovely as he was, Andrew was not from her world. He knew what he wanted and how to get it, while Rita was desperately looking for any job she could find, just to get by.

The ride to Alessia's house didn't take long but finding a parking space was a mission. Rita was on edge, as usual. Every time she left Chloe and Kristos' apartment, she was constantly scanning the streets for others who looked like her, for thieves, for the police. Andrew had told her not to worry, that there were so many illegal immigrants in London the police hardly bothered. They had bigger issues to worry about. Nevertheless, she couldn't seem to relax.

They reached the door and Andrew knocked three times. Rita looked around at the smart neighbourhood and park in the distance. A man in a light jacket darted behind a parked car. *Samuel? Was he following her?* She blinked but there was nobody there.

Her nerves were getting the better of her.

Oliver opened the door with a big smile and led them through the entryway to a bright and spacious living room. Andrew immediately made himself at home, while Rita perched on the edge of the cream-coloured couch, pulling at the charm on her necklace. Everything in the house was clean and neat, no clutter or toys. Had Andrew not told her there was a two-year-old toddler in residence, she would never have guessed it.

Chiara and Oliver were in their thirties. They sat on the couch opposite Andrew and Rita, their hands folded on their laps. Oliver, in his white button-down shirt, had a casual charm about him. His fair hair was similar to Andrew's. Chiara, on the other hand, was dressed like she was on her way out. Her silk aquamarine shirt was tied at the side and her neat hair, with expensive-looking chestnut highlights, was styled in a wavy bob.

Rita was so tense she couldn't look Chiara in the eye, so she kept her gaze on the woman's black pencil skirt. Chiara's posture made Rita feel like she was at an interview for a position at Westminster – not a job looking after a kid. Based on the outfit Rita was wearing, she was sure they were going to say no to her on the spot. As intimidated as she was, Rita took a deep breath, hoping no one heard her erratic breathing.

There was a light pattering of feet and Alessia toddled

into the room like a little wind-up toy. She was dressed as Disney's Elsa, and was holding a doll in one hand. She stood in front of Rita and stared up at her with big sparkling blue eyes. "How do you do, little one?" Rita said, gently shaking her chubby hand and making her giggle. Alessia turned her head and squealed with excitement as soon as she saw Andrew. He scooped her up into a big hug, making her laugh even more.

"Room. Look!" Alessia exclaimed.

"You want me to look at your bedroom? I would love that," Rita said, feeling her heartbeat quicken. The little girl took Rita by the hand and led her down a hall to her room. From the corner of her eye, Rita saw Chiara watching them leave, a small smile tugging at her perfectly lined lips.

Alessia's room was fit for a tiny princess. There was a small pink bed covered with a floral pink duvet, a white wardrobe, and lots of stuffed toys. Without saying another word, Alessia sat at a small pink table on a small pink stool and started drawing, deep in concentration as Rita watched on.

She left Alessia drawing and returned to the adults.

"Well, it looks like Alessia likes you. Anybody want a drink?"

It was the first thing Oliver had said since they'd arrived. She was glad that he'd highlighted Alessia's approval. Rita only hoped Chiara had heard.

"Not for me, thank you."

Rita was too scared to drink anything in this gleaming house in case she spilt it.

"A coffee for me, please," Andrew said.

Oliver stood and poured some coffee from a pot on the small table in front of them.

"As Andy may have already told you, we need a new nanny," Chiara said. "The one we had left without notice, but we won't go into that now," she added, her lips pursed. "We're looking for someone to take care of Alessia three days a week: Monday, Wednesday, and Friday. These are the days I work, and I don't want our daughter at the local nursery school. There are all types of children there and you never know what she might catch."

Chiara grabbed a bottle of hand sanitizer and squeezed some into her palm. She'd done the same after shaking Rita's hand earlier.

"I'm a critical care nurse at Charing Cross hospital."

There's plenty of germs in hospitals too, Rita thought, but didn't say out loud. This was neither the time nor the place to express her opinion, especially not as an illegal immigrant looking for work.

"My job is almost an hour away, so I need to leave the house early and I come home late. Oliver leaves the house early as well." Her mouth set in a straight line. "We need someone to fit in with our schedule and we need them to begin tomorrow, if possible. Andy has told us something about you, but I… we," she looked over at her husband, "want to hear more from you."

Rita blushed, her heart pulsing in her throat. It happened every time she had a job interview, and it was happening again right now.

Your accent, Rita! They'll know immediately where you're from and never hire you, the incessant voice in her head warned her.

"My name is Rita," she began shyly.

Chiara's mouth set in a grim line for the second time in the last minute. If only Rita could stop trembling, she knew she could do better.

"I love working with kids. I've been childminding for four," *no, better make it five, Chiara couldn't check,* "actually, five years now. The thing is, as Andrew has told you, I've just arrived in London, and I have no references with me. But I can start tomorrow."

"Where are you from? I can hear from your accent that you're not British."

You're not British either, Rita wanted to say. But she and Chiara were clearly not the same type of foreigner. Andrew had told her she could tell them she was any nationality she wanted, but Rita had already decided she wouldn't lie again. If they wanted to hire her for who she was, great; if not, she would have to find something else.

"I'm Albanian," she said, in a calm voice. Chiara's face blanched a little and her cheeks reddened. She coughed but said nothing.

"If you trust me to take care of Alessia, I promise to work my very hardest. I can even teach her Italian," Rita said, hoping her suspicions about Chaira's nationality were right. "I speak Italian as well as my mother tongue. My grandmother was Italian."

Chiara's eye twitched. With every word Rita uttered, the expressions on the woman's face flickered, while Oliver didn't move a muscle. There was a lengthy pause after Rita stopped talking while Chiara stared down at her smooth nails. It felt like a century had passed when she finally turned to her husband:

"What do you think?"

"Could you give us a minute?" said Oliver. He had kept quiet until now, observing Rita while Chiara did the talking. Now he wanted time alone with his wife, probably to express his disapproval.

The couple left the room and Andrew put some more coffee in his cup. He offered to pour some for Rita, but she wasn't going to be drinking anything in this house. She wanted to leave and forget she had been here at all. Ignoring Andrew's attempt at conversation, she fidgeted with her lucky charm. *Why did I come here? How did I think I had any chance? I'm not like Chloe, and I'm definitely not like Andrew.*

Oliver coughed, bringing Rita back to the present. He and his wife had returned and they were both looking at Rita. From the heat on her face, Rita knew her cheeks had turned scarlet.

"Okay. This is the first time I've ever hired anyone without checking their CV first and thinking it over, but time isn't a luxury we have, and we trust Andy like he's family. I need you to be here tomorrow morning at six-thirty. I'll leave you a list of things to do – which includes reading, so try to work a little on your accent," said Chiara.

Prejudiced bitch, Rita thought, but she managed to plaster a smile on her face.

"However, now that you mention the Italian, I think it's a good idea to focus on that too. My family is Italian but… well, I haven't had the time to teach my daughter a second language. I guess I'll have to revise my own to-do list." Chiara pressed her fingertips to her temples, as if trying to keep everything she had to remember inside her head. Rita didn't understand most of what the woman was saying but nodded anyway. It seemed Chiara wasn't Mary Poppins perfect, after all…

A to-do list for a two-year-old? Seriously? Had she understood that correctly?

Oliver stood up, and with that, the interrogation was over. Rita couldn't understand how Oliver was Andrew's best friend. They didn't appear to have anything in common. Was Andrew the same as these people she had just met? Were all British people this cold and sterile?

The front door closed behind them, and Rita breathed a sigh of relief, wiping her sweaty hands on her trousers.

"What did you think of the family?" Andrew asked.

"Alessia is a sweetheart, and I am sure we'll get along just fine. Chiara scares me a little... But I have a job and that's all that matters."

She couldn't tell him that for some reason, both husband and wife had made her feel uncomfortable.

"Yes, Chiara is a bit uptight, but deep down she has a good heart. Even if she is something of a control freak." He laughed. "Right then, now you've found a job, do you have any other plans?"

"Eat lunch with you, I suppose."

"Perfect. We'll be tourists for the day. After all, it's your last day off before work tomorrow." He winked at her. "The best thing to do is start with Covent Garden, then on to Embankment, we'll cross the Thames, take a spin on the London Eye, stroll along the Southbank to the Tate, St Paul's and the Square Mile. How does that sound?"

She had no idea what any of those places were but seeing Andrew's face lit up like a child at Christmas, she found herself saying, "sounds great."

The morning slipped into the afternoon, and without warning, the evening started gnawing at the daylight. Rita took her first selfie with Andrew at the top of the London Eye. She didn't want to admit it, but she was enjoying her time with him. The voice in her head was quiet for the first time since she'd arrived in London.

The higher they went, the more amazed Rita was at the breathtaking view. Andrew played tour guide, pointing out the Houses of Parliament overlooking the river, and the historic Tower of London. The double-decker buses looked like ants on the bridge. It turned out that Andrew had arranged everything in advance. Rita couldn't decide if that was noble and romantic, or a bit presumptuous. Either way, it was a rare treat.

Andrew had booked a private capsule at the London Eye, complete with a bottle of Pommery Brut Royal champagne. He could clearly afford the good life. With her pay check from childminding, Rita would just about be able to buy herself the bottle opener (or a decent pair of winter gloves). Rita took a sip of champagne and wondered if this was what being swept off your feet felt like. *Someone like you doesn't deserve all this!* Uh-oh. The voice was back.

Every time Rita had a bit of fun and let her guard down, the voice couldn't resist whispering to her, trying to spoil her mood by reminding her of what she'd come from and how far above her station she was getting –

which, at her current elevation, was quite literally true. Rita shook her head, hoping her negativity would fall out of her mind and into the river below.

She gripped Andrew's arm tightly. Maybe it was the champagne, maybe it was the view, maybe it was all the crazy experiences of the last few weeks, but she felt like she was floating through the sky.

The negative voice was wrong. She did deserve this, after all she'd been through.

She turned her focus to the marvellous view of London, feeling Andrew's eyes on her. Then, in a sudden and unexpected rush, her present collided with her past and everything seemed like it was too much. Too good. She was certain it would be taken away from her. Girls like her didn't get moments like these.

You're falling in love, a softer voice whispered in her mind. *How can you do that? How can you forget Samuel so easily?*

Rita shivered. *No, I'm not! Andrew and I are just friends. And Samuel was the one who forgot me, remember?*

Perhaps you *need to remember he asked for more time?* the voice insisted, its dulcet tone of moments ago an illusion as it berated her so loudly, she feared the entire Ferris wheel would hear.

That's bullshit. He wants to cheat on Megan, the way he cheated on me. Stop playing cruel tricks on me.

And what about Andrew? The voice teased.

Why, oh, why couldn't Rita just enjoy the moment and stop thinking?

As if to silence her racing mind, Andrew leaned over and gently kissed her lips. Light and soft as a feather, and so quick that she wondered if she'd imagined it. His touch didn't scream wild passion so much as it whispered protection. He looked at her, nervous, as if he thought he might have overstepped the mark. With a little smile on his face, he moved closer. Cocooned under the crook of his arm, Rita blushed.

Using her new phone, she took a picture of their champagne glasses against the London skyline and added it to her Instagram account.

#London #backtolife

Would Samuel see it? Did she even care?

41

I'm in my hospital room again. I'm tired and I have nothing more to say about the past. I just want to wake up. The man beside me is sleeping. The nurse comes in wearing the same white outfit she does every day, the same expression on her face. Calm, focused, kind. Today she's using the same glossy lipstick I used to admire when she went off to work. I bought one like it too with the bonus she gave me, *and* a new coat.

The nurse pats the man on the shoulder, and he wakes up. My vision is clearer, but my body is trembling. Will I finally see his face today?

I try, but then he turns his back to me because the doctor has come in. It's the usual morning routine. The same procedure since day one. They keep their voices low as if they might wake me up, even though that's exactly what they want.

I'm so tired. Just like I was on my first day of work.

42

The following morning, Rita woke up covered in sweat. She'd been dreaming that she was having a picnic with Samuel, but then Megan appeared and started chasing them. Running hand in hand, Rita and Samuel came to the edge of a cliff. The sea was crashing against the rocks below. Samuel was holding Rita's hand as if he were afraid that he would lose her forever. She turned her head to see Megan laughing from behind them, pointing a gun at them both. Who was she going to shoot first?

When she opened her eyes, Rita was relieved to find herself in her camp bed.

It took her some time to choose the right clothes for her first day at work. Chiara's preferred dress code was probably a secretarial skirt and a blouse.

I'm just a babysitter, who cares? Rita grabbed the warmest sweater she had. *I'm not wasting money on a fancy blouse, especially not before I get my first pay check.*

Out on the street, a wild wind nearly blew her off her feet.

She shivered and thrust her hands in her coat pockets. She still hadn't bought a pair of gloves and was thinking of that smart shirt she should probably be wearing.

It was still dark, yet people were already out, hurrying to work or wherever they were going. *This city never sleeps,* Rita thought, heading for the bus stop.

Her phone vibrated. It was a text from Andrew. 'Good luck today!' Those three words, *and* the fact he'd woken up early to catch her, melted her heart. She touched her lips, the lips he had kissed yesterday. Was that wrong? Was it too soon to have let him kiss her? In her homeland, you would be considered easy for kissing a guy so early in a relationship, or as Samuel had said, a one-night stand. But Andrew had only kissed her with lightest of pecks on the lips. Nothing more. Even though yesterday had been the happiest day of her life since her mum died, it was probably best if she stayed away from Andrew. For now.

Once on the bus, Rita found the courage to text him back. 'Thank you!' She pressed send. No more, no less.

It was 6.20 a.m. and Rita was already outside Chiara's pristine white front door. She inhaled deeply and was about to knock when Chiara flung it open, leaving Rita's hand hanging in the air. She was smartly dressed in a dark coat reaching down to her black ankle boots.

I'm going to buy a coat like that one day.

Rita looked at the rest of the woman's outfit, increasing her shopping list to include a satin blouse, a pair of gloves, and a pair of heels.

"Rita, thank God you're on time. I wrote down everything you need to do on the piece of paper over there on the dining table." Chiara pointed vaguely inside the house. "Alessia is still asleep. If anything is unclear, please call me. I've left you my number. Now, have you seen my car keys?"

How could Rita tell her they were in her hand without humiliating her new boss on day one?

"Oh, here they are! I've been looking for them for the last five minutes. Okay, I've got to run. Just follow the schedule and call me if you need anything."

As soon as she entered the house, Rita went over and looked at the list on the table. She read it out loud, hoping it would help each word stick in her head.

8 a.m. Wake Alessia up. Bathe her, then give her breakfast: toast with peanut butter or cornflakes. NOTHING SWEET.

9 a.m. TV time: Peppa Pig.

*10 a.m. One bottle of milk: 200 ml, and not a drop more! Warm the milk in the microwave for **30 seconds**. When she's finished the milk, take her to the bathroom, even if she says no.*

11 a.m. Read a book. The first row of the bookshelf is

Alessia's. She loves Guess How Much I Love You.

12 p.m...

A cry cut Rita off. Alessia stood barefoot in the doorway, her thumb in her mouth. It was 6:45 a.m.

Oh God, there was nothing on the schedule before 8 a.m.!

"Hi, sweetie!" Rita said, attempting to sound as friendly as possible.

"Wet." Alessia's blue eyes were teary. She lowered her head, looking at the damp patch on her nightie.

"Oh, don't worry. I'll find some dry clothes for you. It's okay."

"Mummy no like." She stood still, like an angel trapped in a cage.

Rita kneeled and cupped the girl's face. "This happens to all little girls and boys when they're sleeping. It's not your fault. I had a little brother who loved playing games. He used to think his games were more important than going to the potty, and he wet himself even during the day." Rita smiled at her. "Do you want to know something else?" The girl nodded and Rita lowered her voice to a whisper. "Sometimes, even grown-ups have accidents, when they're worried, or when they don't get to the bathroom in time, or when there's a long queue for the toilet in a shopping mall."

Rita didn't know if the child had understood what

she said, but Alessia was giggling now, so her words must have worked. Finding Alessia dry clothes was easy, as everything was neatly folded in her wardrobe. After changing the little one, Rita prepared her bottle of milk. She removed the sheets and let the bed air before putting on clean ones. As she put the wet clothes in the washing machine, a voice made Rita jump, and for once, it wasn't the one inside her head. Oliver had come into the kitchen, looking flustered. "Good morning, I have to run," he said, blowing a kiss to his daughter and bolting out the door before Rita even had a chance to return the breezy greeting.

She hadn't even known he was still in the house.

At 8 a.m., Alessia fell asleep on Rita's lap. According to the list, this was the time when she should have woken her up. Rita sighed. She'd failed already and she was only as far as the first instruction.

She kissed Alessia on the top of her head and put her down on the couch to sleep, placing two big pillows by her side and a chair close to the sofa to make sure she didn't roll off.

The house was clean. Still, to justify her presence and her pay check, Rita wiped the almost non-existent dust off the bookshelf and the coffee table. There was nothing written on the list about what or when Rita could eat or drink, so she assumed she had to take her opportunities when she could. She made herself a mug of hot chocolate and sat down next to Alessia. The girl sucked her thumb even in her sleep. Rita sipped her chocolate as quietly as she could – there was nothing worse than waking up a sleeping toddler. She studied the bookshelf but didn't dare take a book off it. What if Chiara saw her fingerprints?

At eleven on the dot, which was supposed to be reading time, the doorbell rang. Her to-do list didn't say if Rita should open the door. Pretending she hadn't heard the bell, Rita picked up Alessia's book and sat next to her, stroking the girl's hair in an attempt to wake her up.

Her phone pinged with a message. 'It's me!'

Rita sighed in relief. She ran to open the door and Andrew entered along with a gust of fresh air. He lowered his head and kissed Rita on the edge of her lips as if it was the most natural thing in the world. He did it quickly, though, as if he realised that he may have over-stepped the mark again.

A squeal signalled that Alessia had woken up.

"It's such beautiful weather outside and I know a playground nearby," he said, ruffling the little girl's hair. She jumped into his arms; her legs locked around his waist.

The curtains of the house were thick and grey, and still closed. Rita hadn't dared to open them. She could have checked the weather on her phone, but it hadn't occurred to her.

"Oh, but we can't. It's reading time now. Plus, I haven't done half the things on the list Chiara made me."

Andrew turned to Alessia. "Do you want to stay at home, or do you want to go to the playground?"

What a question!

"Swings!" The little girl clapped her hands, her eyes shining brightly.

Great. Would Chiara have a problem with this spontaneous change in plans? She felt a pang of worry and frustration but managed to keep herself in check. Andrew was the one who had found her this job, after all. Not to mention, he was Alessia's godfather, and as Oliver had said, they considered him "like family." She supposed he naturally outranked her in this situation, and she couldn't be blamed for deviating from the schedule Chiara had set out if the child's *godfather* insisted. Nevertheless, it made her nervous. She was a stranger in a place where she didn't belong, and she couldn't afford to make any mistakes, lest she find herself jobless and alone. She let out a deep sigh, deciding that the best thing to do for now was to go with the flow.

Time flew by in the playground. Andrew left to buy some coffee at the corner shop. When he returned with the drinks, he handed Alessia a bag of fried fish fingers that he'd picked up from the fish and chip shop en route. Rita raised her eyebrows. The day's to-do list was majorly derailed. She sighed in defeat.

"I'm a terrible influence," said Andrew. "But she loves them. Everything in moderation and all that. Besides, I don't get to see my goddaughter very often." He gave Rita a mischievous wink, but she stayed quiet. "Oh, all right. I'm incorrigible and you have every right to be angry with me. First, I take you both outside and stop you from following the list." He handed Rita her cup of coffee. "And now this."

"It's just... Andrew, I want to do this job properly. I *need* this job," Rita pressed her fingers to her temples. "Now I will have to clean *everything* before Chiara comes home. She'll fire me on the spot if she finds a grain of sand in her pristine house."

When they had left the house, Alessia's flowery dress had been beautiful and clean, her rose-gold glittery boots complementing her crocheted hat. Her outfit wasn't at all suitable for a playground. But then again, none of the clothes in her wardrobe were. Dressed like that, she looked like a doll in a display case, rather than a child playing in a sandpit.

"I would never let that happen," said Andrew. "And I will take all the blame if she finds even half a grain of sand. None of this is on you. But look at her," Andrew added, beaming in Alessia's direction. "She is *so* happy out here in the fresh air."

"Yes, she is," Rita had to agree. Alessia was in her element. "But we have to respect Chiara's wishes, she's the boss... and there's a to-do list which needs completing."

"I'm sorry, Rita. I am just so excited to have you in my life and I wanted to surprise you. Let's get back to the house. I will help with the cleaning."

Really? Rita was gobsmacked. A man helping a woman with the cleaning? What world did Andrew come from? *Dad never helped Mum –and he loved her very much. Samuel never helped me.*

Andrew wrapped his arm around Rita's shoulders.

"It's my birthday on Friday and I'm having a little party," he said. "I'd love for you to come."

Their conversation was interrupted by a loud cry, and Rita looked over to see that Alessia had taken a tumble. Rita ran over to her, but before she could reach her, the little girl had already stood up and brushed herself off, as if nothing had happened. Alessia picked up two stones, walked over to a little boy playing nearby, and gave them to him. Alessia said something to the boy, whose mother was watching the interaction, smiling. When the boy gave no response, Alessia marched off to go play with some other children, her golden hair bouncing behind her.

She was clearly quite the little social butterfly.

Back at the house, Rita put Alessia in the bath again and washed the dirt from her face and the sand from her hair. When she returned to the living room, Andrew had cleaned up all the mess. He picked up the bag they had taken to the playground, emptied its sandy contents into the kitchen bin and swept up the excess that fell to the floor.

"Thanks for your help, but it's probably better if you leave now," Rita said apologetically. "It's getting late, and we really need to tick at least something off her long list..."

Andrew kissed Alessia on the top of her head but looked undecided as to whether Rita would appreciate a kiss, too. His phone pinged. Taking the opportunity, he gave Rita a quick peck on her cheek and took the call on his way out of the house.

Rita sighed, but she wasn't sure if it was from relief, stress, or frustration.

Once Alessia was snug and dry, she sat her on the couch and the toddler's thumb was soon back in her mouth as she demanded to watch Peppa Pig. Rita peered at the list. It wasn't Peppa Pig time, it was drawing time. But surprise, surprise, the little girl refused to draw, throwing her crayons around the room instead.

Rita really needed a picture to show Chiara.

"If you do a nice drawing for me, I will give you a lollipop."

NOTHING SWEET. The words popped up in her mind. *But Chiara only specified nothing sweet at breakfast time,* she told herself, taking a lollipop out of her bag. She normally ate them to get rid of the cigarette smell on her breath, but this would serve as the perfect bribe. Nobody needed to know. It was a one off.

Alessia quickly collected all the crayons she had thrown about and sat down. Magic.

For the first time since they came back to the house, Rita had time to think about Andrew's invitation. Friday. That was just a few days away. Things were snowballing, and she was doing nothing to stop them. This British man kept popping up in her life when she least expected it, and she wasn't sure if she liked it or not, although she could hardly deny their chemistry. But if Andrew's company was still revenge of a kind towards Samuel, then this was all wrong. What should she do? Could she say no? It was his birthday for goodness' sake. How could she not show up after all he'd done for her?

In Albania that would be pure disrespect. It was so difficult to fit into another culture when you didn't know how things were done, and perhaps more importantly, which things shouldn't be done under any circumstances.

Alessia tugged on the sleeve of Rita's sweater, demanding her attention. She handed Rita her drawing – a happy flower and a smiling sun – one thumb still plugged in her mouth.

"Thank you, my love! I've never seen a smiling sun before. I'll hang it on the wall above my bed. This sun will shine for me every day, even when it's raining outside." Not that Rita even had a proper bed right now, let alone her own bedroom. "Here's your reward." She tentatively handed Alessia the lollipop. "Should we make another deal?"

Alessia nodded, the candy already in her mouth.

"If you don't suck your thumb for a week, I will buy you another big lollipop. And, if you keep the promise until the end of the month, I will buy you the biggest ice cream ever. What do you think? Are you in?"

Alessia gave her a thumbs-up, the same thumb she always put in her mouth.

Soon after their deal, the front door opened. Rita heard Chiara wipe her shoes on the doormat and step inside. She threw her key on the white shelf in the corridor, shrugged off her coat, and walked into the living-room.

"I called the home phone, but no one picked up." Her voice was like ice just before it cracks.

Shit!

"Mummy!" Alessia jumped in her arms. "I went swings."

Chiara stared in puzzlement at her daughter, then at Rita.

"*Zio* Andy," Alessia added.

The Italian word softened the frown on Chiara's face. "Oh, I see. I'm glad you had fun, even though…" She went to say something but stopped.

"I'm really sorry. Andrew insisted, and seeing as he's Alessia's godfather, I didn't know what to—I'm so sorry, it won't happen again." Rita's apology came spilling from her lips, her cheeks warm and crimson. Chiara remained silent, and Rita began gathering up her belongings, feeling defeated. She was probably going to be fired, and it was all Andrew's fault. Scratch that: it was all her own fault. She was a grown woman. She knew her responsibilities. She didn't have to behave like a lovesick teenager, hanging on Andrew's every word and doing whatever he said.

As she put on her parka and headed for the door, she heard Alessia running after her.

"*Ciao*," she said again in Italian. Rita turned and her eyes met Chiara's, whose mouth betrayed a tiny smile. Maybe the to-do list wasn't her top priority after all.

"See you next time," Chiara said and closed the door.

Well, it appeared that she still had a job.

The last few hours had been so busy that Rita hadn't noticed that night had fallen. Mist hung close to the ground, making everything even gloomier. She took a deep breath, dug out a much-needed cigarette and struck a match. *What a day!* She inhaled and blew out a cloud of smoke. The cold air stung her nose and ears during the five minutes it took to walk from Chiara's place to the bus stop, which was enough time for Rita to finish her cigarette and check her phone.

A private message on her Instagram account popped up. It was in Albanian.

"I saw your post with the champagne glasses. So, you think that this man who lavishes you with expensive things actually likes you? Wake the hell up, Rita! He's buying you. Like they buy all the Albanian whores."

Rita's heart surged with anger, and her finger shook as it hovered over the message.

It was Samuel. It had to be. She scrolled down to his account. It wasn't in his name of course, because everything in his name had ceased to exist a long time ago. But Rita knew it was him. Who else would message her in her language? The same language Samuel had written her love notes in, a million years ago.

Rita thought back to everything she'd suffered just to get to London. To find him. While she'd struggled to survive, he'd simply waltzed into the UK on a visa and shacked up with the first woman he'd met, then dropped Rita like she didn't exist. Like she'd never mattered.

A bus came and went, but Rita remained rooted at the bus stop. Snowflakes fluttered in front of her. She lifted her head, watching them drift to the pavement. The weather was strange in England. On the same day you could experience sun, rain, and snow. This never happened in Albania. If it was summer, you put your winter clothes in a box where they would stay for months.

She stuffed her phone back into her pocket and gazed at the snowflakes.

Poor you, she told them silently. *You're just like me. The moment you think you've settled, people will crush you. Oh, first they'll use you – take some nice pictures, post them here and there. But when they're done, they'll shovel you away to the corner of the street and forget you existed.*

She had loved snow as a child. On the rare occasions it snowed in Durrës, she'd drag her dad out for snowball fights while her mum watched them from the window, smiling and cheering. Now that she'd found her feet, it would be the perfect time to call her dad.

She hadn't done that when she'd arrived in London because she hadn't wanted to worry him. But she had a job now. Something that would make him proud. Without any further deliberation, she took her phone out again and punched in his number. She waited, so many emotions welling up inside her at the thought of speaking to him again. Finally, after the fifth ring, he answered.

"*Rita?*"

Oh, how she'd missed that voice.

"Dad! I have some great news—" she began, but he cut her off.

"How could you bring shame on our family? Only delinquents run away from home! The whole city is gossiping about where you went and what you're hiding from. As for that irresponsible, stupid aunt of yours, don't even get me started…" He continued to shout, furious that Rita's kind aunt Angela had paid for her to escape, swearing that if he saw her in the city again, he would throttle her.

Rita regretted making the call. Her dad had never been the same since Helen moved in. She was about to shove her phone back in her pocket when another message popped up.

"If I can't have you, then nobody can."

Samuel again. Was he threatening her?

Rita let out such a high-pitched hysterical laugh that a woman waiting with her toddler at the bus stop, pushed her buggy further away.

"Fuck you!" she texted back. "You're dead to me."

She thought it would hurt to fight back, but the

sinking feeling in her stomach dissolved instantly and she felt lighter than she had in a long time. She smiled up at the black sky, snowflakes kissing her numb cheeks.

People like destroying the things they once loved – but the thing about snowflakes is that as pretty and delicate as they are, when there are enough of them, they become an avalanche.

Rita texted Andrew.

"What time is the party on Friday?"

43

It was never a good idea to make impulsive decisions in Rita's experience, especially when it involved a Friday night party and a man she barely knew. Two days had passed since she'd accepted Andrew's invite, and now all she could do was look for excuses not to go. Maybe she could say she had the flu, or… diarrhoea?

Part of her wanted to see him again, but another part of her was nervous about Samuel. He was texting her multiple times a day, telling Rita he didn't love his wife, that he just needed time and he'd divorce her, that all of this was because of the damn residence permit. What if he was keeping tabs on Rita and followed her to the party?

Rita couldn't accept Samuel's explanations, but she didn't block him either. She simply read them all, but never replied. Samuel might be angry, but he would never physically hurt her.

If I can't have you, nobody will.

He was angry and embarrassed that not only had he

been caught, but Rita was living her life and happier without him.

He'd stop eventually, she thought.

Maybe I should block him...

But she didn't.

Rita shook her head and tried to return her attention to the episode of Peppa Pig that Alessia was watching on TV. Today, however, she just couldn't muster her usual enthusiasm for the cartoon. All it was doing was giving her too much time to think.

I'll go to Andrew's party. He has an ex – who may not even be there and might have another man in her life by now – and I have an ex, who does *have another woman in his life. It's perfectly normal. People find themselves in these situations all the time.*

Rita wrote down some Italian words and drew a picture next to each of them so Alessia would find it easier to remember them. Rita's mum had been a good teacher. She recalled her doing the same, marvelling at the way it sounded like her mum was singing when she spoke Italian, the words dancing on her fingertips as she wrote them down.

At the end of her shift, Rita left Chiara's house in a rush, forgetting all about Samuel's latest text message. She didn't want to be late for Andrew's party. She knew his friends would be there, including Oliver. Would it be awkward, with him being her boss?

No, Chiara was her real boss. Oliver knew that as much as Rita did.

On the way to the bus stop Rita bought a bottle of Pomerol wine. It cost her thirty pounds. She would have preferred a more personal gift, but she didn't know Andrew that well yet. At least it was a good bottle, more than she could really afford.

Holding the carrier bag in one hand and burrowing the other in her pocket – she still didn't have any gloves – she opened the door of Chloe's apartment, which seemed to be getting more cramped by the second.

Chloe was excited that Rita had a party to go to.

"Calm down, you have plenty of time," she said.

"I have nothing to wear," Rita replied despondently.

"You need a black dress. That's what London women wear to parties."

Rita didn't have one of those, but, reliable as ever, Chloe did. Her cousin made a big deal out of helping her get ready, and Rita found she sort of actually enjoyed all the fuss. She didn't want to be late, but Chloe was right – she didn't want to be the first one to arrive either.

She applied her usual light makeup and put on Chloe's glossy lipstick. She'd used it so many times it practically belonged to her now anyway.

Chloe's black dress fit perfectly. Rita didn't like

black, as a rule. It was for funerals. But if Chloe said she should wear black to a party, Chloe knew best. This brand-new world was too difficult for Rita to keep up with at times.

She had no option but to travel by Tube this time, the buses were too slow. *What happened in Milan is never going to happen in London,* she kept saying to herself, but her body wouldn't stop trembling when she stepped inside the carriage.

At that time on a Friday evening, the Tube was packed, which would be most people's idea of a nightmare. But Rita sighed with relief. There was safety in numbers. No one even looked at her.

When she got out, it was snowing yet again. The thick snowflakes beneath the streetlights looked like falling pearls. She'd never seen it settle though. She decided the snow was a good sign and took a picture on her phone, posting it on Instagram. There were two new messages in her inbox, but she chose not to read them. They were from Samuel. They had to be.

Rita checked the name of the pub Andrew had given her. It was an eight-minute walk. If she had worn trainers instead of these uncomfortably high boots, she'd be there in four minutes.

The pub was small inside with wood-panelled walls and wooden floors covered partially with vintage rugs.

Andrew was propping up the bar and grinned from ear to ear when he saw her. He wore a black short-sleeve T-shirt, and a pair of faded jeans. Rita looked at her dress. *Was it too much?*

"I'm so glad you're here," Andrew said, draping his hand around her shoulders.

Rita handed him the gift. "Happy birthday," she said, smiling.

"Ah, thank you." He opened the bag and pulled out the bottle of wine. In her country, people would put the gift somewhere safe and open it only when the guests had left. Not everyone could afford to buy a nice present, and it spared them from the shame of comparison. But here, everything was different, and she was glad she'd splashed out.

"*Pomerol!* I'll save it for a special occasion," he said, kissing her lightly on the lips.

"Did I miss anything?" a female voice behind her interrupted their moment.

She sounded just like Megan. Rita swung around and blinked. She'd knew this woman from somewhere, but where? Then it dawned on her – the picture of Rachel she'd seen in Milan. Except this woman was more beautiful in the flesh, in her cherry off-the-shoulder shirt that revealed her belly button, and a pair of skinny jeans. Her hair was cut in a sharp blonde bob, just like the picture, but today, she'd added some waves. She held an almost empty glass of wine in her hand.

"Ah, Rachel, meet my friend Rita," Andrew said.

Why is she here? Rita's heart skipped a beat. *We go to the same parties,* Andrew's words replayed in her head.

"Ah, the Albanian girl." Rachel stretched her hand out and shook Rita's. She said *Albanian girl* like she was telling Rita she had spinach in her teeth. Instinctively, she rubbed her tongue against them. Why had Andrew told her where she was from?

"So, Rita, what would you like to drink?" he asked.

But drinking was the last thing on her mind. Now all Rita wanted to do was disappear. This was a mistake. She didn't belong in this world. She didn't belong anywhere. She was trapped somewhere in-between countries and loves, a dust mote floating in the air.

Rachel ordered another glass of wine and swanned off to join a group of friends, but Rita couldn't take her eyes off her. She was so beautiful, so elegant. She was what Andrew deserved, and she was everything Rita wasn't.

"Water, please," she stammered at the bartender.

"You do realise they don't serve water in London pubs?" Andrew said with a wink. Was he joking? She no longer knew what was real or not.

"Okay, fine, wine then. Just a small one."

She'd have a few sips of wine, wash down the humiliation, and leave.

"Make yourself at home," said Andrew, handing her a glass of wine.

Rita looked around and her eyes landed on Rachel, "I, erm... I didn't know Rachel would be here too," she said.

"Honestly, Rita, she's just a friend. Despite our history. Nothing more. I wish I'd never brought her up in Milan. She's been to all my birthday parties so I couldn't not invite her to this one." He put his arm around her shoulder again. "Whereas you are a VIP, since it's your first time at my birthday party – hopefully the first of many." Andrew's face lit up and Rita couldn't help but hope he was right. "Come and meet the rest of my friends. I've told them so much about you. They all want to say hello."

Rita let him lead her to the back of the pub, but for all Andrew's words of reassurance, all she could think about was Rachel and the derogatory way she'd referred to her. Rita's female intuition knew Rachel still thought she had a hold on Andrew. Why else would she have inserted herself between them like that?

Could you really remain friends with someone you had once been in love with? Samuel and Rita could never be friends again.

"Do they all know I'm Albanian?" she asked,

looking over at a group of men who were laughing. "I thought that was a secret between us. Now half of London knows."

Rita took a sip of wine and swallowed down her impending tears. Under no circumstances was she going to cry in this pub.

"Rita, listen, I don't care where you're from. And neither do my friends. I'm just happy that you're in my life. That's all. I didn't mean to offend you."

She hushed him, scared the others would hear. Everyone was already sneaking furtive glances at them. Her dress hovered above the knee, yet she felt completely naked. She couldn't tell if she was angry because Rachel was there, or because she knew that Rita was Albanian. There was nothing wrong with being Albanian, she didn't want to hide it, it was just the look on people's faces that she loathed.

But, as usual, she'd over-reacted and most human beings deserved more credit. As soon as they approached Andrew's friends, they welcomed Rita like they would any woman, and no one showed any interest in her accent or where she was from. Oliver was there too, and he gave her a wide smile, raising his glass in greeting.

The men were friendly enough and thankfully, Rachel kept her distance, although Rita could definitely feel her eyes on her. After a while, she relaxed a little, but her stomach was still in knots, not to mention empty.

She should have eaten before she left the apartment, but she'd been too nervous.

She wasn't sure if she needed the loo, but she knew she needed a few moments alone. She excused herself and followed the signs to the bathroom. In the small cubicle, she lowered the toilet lid and sat down with her chin in her cupped hands.

Maybe two people that have been in love before can be friends. Maybe eventually even Samuel and I could be.

She opened her phone and saw three more messages. She had time to read them all now.

Samuel was still saying the same thing, accusing her of being naïve and saying men just wanted her for sex. London had changed him. He'd never used language like that before. What did he expect? That Rita would stay in a strange city alone and wait three years for him? If only Megan could see the way he was talking about her, calling his new wife fat and ugly and saying he could never love her. He may have used Megan, but they were married.

Rita heard voices outside and quickly stood up, flushing the toilet to show she was in there.

"I think you're jealous," a voice said.

"Me? Jealous of some immigrant? As if Andy could ever love that peasant!"

Rita froze with her hand on the door handle. It was Rachel.

"She is pretty, though," said the other woman.

"You think so? I think she has a plan. All of them do. But she's not tricking my Andy. He's got too big a heart. That's his problem. He just wants to help her, and she's got it all wrong if she thinks he's going to fall for her. People like her just want to use us."

Rita's heart thumped in her chest. She knew what Rachel meant by *people like her*. Immigrants. Albanians. Rita waited until it was quiet outside before opening the door. Filled with anger and humiliation, she studied herself in the mirror. Her face had paled, and her legs felt too weak to carry her, but she couldn't hide in the toilet all night.

Back at the bar, Andrew was nowhere to be seen. She scanned the rest of his friends in case he was in their midst. Rachel was deep in conversation with another woman.

It must have been the same friend she'd been discussing Rita with in the restroom. Feeling trapped, Rita pasted a fake smile on her face and sat down in a free seat. As soon as she saw Andrew, who was probably in the loo himself, she'd tell him she didn't feel well and head home. Rachel's words were still ringing in her head. She wasn't welcome here.

She chanced to steal a glance at Rachel, horrified when their eyes met. *Oh no!* Rita quickly lowered her gaze to the rim of her glass where her lipstick was imprinted. But the damage had been done. Out of the corner of her eye she could see Rachel making a beeline for her. Rita swallowed hard and wrapped her hands around the glass. Her mouth had turned to sandpaper.

"So, Rita, tell me something about yourself," said Rachel as she perched on a bar stool. Her eyebrows arched so much that they almost touched one another. "Remind me again. How *did* you meet Andy?"

"On a…"

But she didn't let her finish. "You must think I was born yesterday," she said in a low whisper. "But I know your game, sweetheart. I'm on to you. Your lot are all the same, sniffing out a nice guy to help you stay in our country."

Rachel was careful to spew her vitriol so quietly that only Rita could hear it. The others were so drunk they wouldn't care anyway. *Your lot.* Rita lifted her wine glass to her lips with shaking hands.

"You have me mistaken," she said, taking an unsteady sip. The wine tasted awful. Rita wanted to spit it in Rachel's face.

"Don't play dumb with me. Do you think Andy really cares about you?" She smiled, then knocked over Rita's glass of wine. "Oops!" she cried out so dramatically that her friends turned around in the distance. "I'm so sorry. You're a bit tipsy, aren't you? Let me clean that up." She pulled some paper tissues from her bag and rubbed viciously at Rita's dress. Tears of shame streamed down Rita's face. *You're the one who's drunk, bitch!* thought Rita, but as usual her words were stuck in her throat. Rachel was a Londoner and Rita was an illegal immigrant.

Rita couldn't let herself be humiliated for a moment longer, even if it meant not saying goodbye to Andrew. She ran out of the pub, people staring and muttering in her wake, and headed, mortified, to the Tube station. *Stupid, stupid, stupid!* the voice in her head drummed. Why did she think she could be accepted? The men thought she was a slag, and the women didn't trust her. Why hadn't Chloe warned her? Why did she think London would be some magical city where she could start anew?

She stumbled to the station, tripping over twice, steadying herself before falling face-first on the ground. Her phone buzzed. She glowered at it, put it on silent and thrust it in her bag. She didn't want to talk to Andrew. She didn't want to talk to anybody.

Rita cried all the way home, filled with shame and anger. The wine on her dress had dried, but her spirits were still damp. What was she going to say to Chloe? Luckily nobody in the carriage paid her any attention. At this hour on a Friday night in London, there were plenty of people in a worse state.

Rita got off the Tube and hurried back to the

apartment. She was not going to leave its safe haven until Monday morning. Yes, she still had to go to work, but she wouldn't take Andrews's calls.

She pushed the small iron gate open, relieved that she could soon lie on her camp bed, shut her eyes, and try to forget about all of tonight's hideous events. Just then, she heard somebody call her name. *Andrew?* Rita turned, slowly and tentatively to see who the male voice belonged to. *Shit!* Samuel got out of a grey Mini Cooper.

What is he doing here?

"Are you crying? Did that bastard do this to you?" he shouted in Albanian, coming so close to Rita as to try to wipe away her tears. She pushed him away, astounded that he had sneaked up on her like this.

"Don't touch me! H-how did you find me?"

"Some of our friends back home have Chloe's address." He gave her that lazy smile of his and a wink, the same look that used to drive her wild. When he used to look at her like that before, she would kiss him, turn to putty in his hands. But now all she wanted to do was run away as fast as she could.

Funny how he can find you so easily now, after ignoring you for six whole months.

"Samuel, *it's over*!" said Rita. "I've got to go." She turned towards the house, and the lights were on inside the apartment. What was she going to tell Chloe and

Kristos? Why could she never stay away from drama?

Samuel grabbed her arm.

"Hey, you're hurting me!"

"Rita, listen to me. Please."

Snowflakes had turned to rain and a cold wind slapped Rita's face.

"Let me go, Samuel, or I swear I'll show your wife all your messages. If she sees what you really think of her, you can say goodbye to England forever."

"Are you threatening me?"

"Interpret it how you want to," said Rita, pulling her arm free.

She ran to the apartment, let herself in, and slammed the door behind her before bursting into tears.

44

London
December 2019

Rita was getting better at keeping her promises. She ignored all of Andrew's calls, yet still he texted her, apologising for Rachel's behaviour. He told her Rachel wanted to say sorry in person, but Rita knew it was a meaningless trap. The woman despised her, and Rita was not going to let Rachel humiliate her again. Andrew could keep Rachel and the life he had before Rita showed up in it. *He can keep it and shove it where the sun doesn't shine.*

Samuel kept sending messages too, but Rita deleted all of them without reading. Every now and then she swore she saw a grey Mini Cooper following her, but how many Mini Coopers must there be in London? Plus, she knew that Samuel wouldn't dare come close to her. She meant every word she'd said to him. His wife was his ticket to stay in London, and no way would he jeopardise that golden ticket for Rita.

All she had to do to stay safe and sane was keep away from the only two men she'd ever cared about.

On Monday morning, she made Oliver a coffee as usual but avoided making eye contact.

Alessia was the only thing Rita wanted to focus on right now, although she didn't take her to the playground again in case Andrew looked for her there. The bad weather was a blessing, alternating between rain and snow until Rita wondered if she'd ever see the sun again.

It was the middle of December when Chiara replaced her to-do list with a small envelope containing a fifty-pound bonus. Alessia had stopped sucking her thumb. Rita now had *three* smiling suns, and an extra fifty pounds.

Thanks to Chiara's generosity, Rita planned to buy a black double-breasted knee-length coat on her day off. Her gut instinct told her that it was going to be a good day because it was the first day that she hadn't received a new message from Samuel. She closed her eyes, relieved that he'd finally let her go. She had a missed call from Andrew, and another text message from him too. She would read that later when she was on the bus.

While she had no intention of seeing Andrew again,

she couldn't quite bring herself to ignore his messages. The last thing she wanted was to prove Rachel right by being a rude Albanian girl who'd been using *her* Andy.

The chilly wind bit at her ankles the moment she closed the small gate and stepped onto the pavement. She wrapped her scarf tightly around her face, then walked down the hill. It was late afternoon and the cloud around the sun resembled a big woollen blanket.

With money in her pocket and a large coffee to go in her hand, Rita arrived at the bus stop. She didn't need to use her GPS anymore; she was turning into a local.

Once on the bus, she felt warmer and removed her scarf. Sitting on the top floor, where the view was better, she sipped her drink and picked up a newspaper someone had left behind. Rita wondered who had last touched it and whether they had washed their hands. There were so many people in London, so many germs.

Oh, my God! I'm turning into Chiara.

Rita shook off her paranoia and flicked through the pages of the newspaper, unable to focus on anything in particular. And then, a headline caught her eye:

'Another tragedy in France.'

Her stomach twisted, memories flooding back to her. Life in London had been so busy that she'd forgotten all about her Jungle friends.

It was only a small story on page seven, no big

headline, the caption printed in tiny letters: 'Eight bodies were found frozen inside a lorry. The police believe they were illegal immigrants trying to enter the UK.'

Rita's chin quivered as she struggled to make out the rest of the caption. 'French police discovered the bodies during a routine check near *Rue Mollien*. The driver claims to have been unaware that the people were in his lorry.'

Rita felt hot and queasy. The bus began to spin.

'The investigation continues.'

Fresh tears sprang to her eyes. There was no need to read any more.

But it couldn't be Bashir! He knew how to recognize a freezer lorry. Or had they finally gotten that desperate?

Teardrops blurred the words on the newspaper.

"Are you okay, dear?" a woman beside her said.

"I'm fine. Thank you," she muttered.

I'm fine, but they aren't. And I'm only fine because they saved me.

She took a deep breath and glanced at the photo again.

'Illegal immigrants,' it read.

They were *human beings!*

Her mind was reeling, thoughts splintering like shattered glass. She thought of everyone else who had read the same article as her today. Had they cried too?

Busy commuters skimming over the headline

thinking to themselves: 'Who cares what happens in France to a bunch of strangers? Not our problem. We have enough on our plate with Brexit and our own immigration issues. One or two dead immigrants, or even eight, it's all the same. No big deal. What can I do about it anyway? I still need to buy Christmas presents, and I'm running late for a meeting. I have enough going on in my own life!'

The bus pulled up at the stop and Rita got out, taking the newspaper with her, legs shaking so much she had to sit on the pavement.

A burning desire to yell at everyone that passed by flared up inside her. She wanted to scream against all the injustice of the modern world, but she knew better than to attract attention to herself on the streets of London. She couldn't change what had happened, nor could she bring those poor souls back to life. For illegal immigrants like herself, even if their bodies were burnt to ashes, no one cared. Staying in her spot on the pavement, she fished in her pocket for her pack of cigarettes, pulled two out and struck a match.

In her motherland, when a loved one died, you lit two cigarettes – one for you, and one for them. She lit a second. *For you, Bashir, the young man who would never got to be a child.*

In the absence of a marble tomb, Rita stuck the

cigarette into a crack in the pavement and watched it burn slowly.

A woman tapped her on the shoulder. "You can't leave lit cigarettes near that bin. You'll start a fire!"

Rita turned her head and watched the woman's red high heels walk away.

"*Ik pirdhu*," she whispered in her mother tongue. Because 'fuck you' was better said in your native language.

She waited until Bashir's cigarette had burned down before getting back to her feet. Her world was spiralling fast. She felt faint and lowered herself back onto the curb just as a grey Mini Cooper passed by. The person inside looked like Megan, or maybe it was Rachel?

Does every girl in London have blonde hair and drive a Mini Cooper?

The pavement was filthy, but she felt too weak to stand.

She reached for her phone and called Chloe, but it went straight to voice mail. She didn't want to talk to a robot, that would be like talking to herself. And she did that enough already. She needed somebody to hug her, to tell her everything would be okay, even if she knew that it wouldn't be.

She called Andrew.

45

Rita could have died, she could have been in that refrigerated lorry, but fate had spared her. Her heart might be broken in a million places, but she was alive and that was all that mattered. It was her duty now to make the most of her life – for Maria, for Bashir, for Sumaya and those poor children. Cuddled up against Andrew's chest, she inhaled deeply, breathing in his familiar aftershave.

"I've missed you," his voice was soft and full of concern.

Rita didn't say a word. She didn't want to tell him she'd missed him too. The thing she liked most about Andrew was his patience. She wasn't used to men letting her talk in her own time without interrupting or advising – without mansplaining.

They stayed in silence for a while, both of them sitting on the cold curb of the pavement where he'd found her five minutes earlier.

"They didn't make it."

She pulled out the crumpled newspaper from her bag, pointing to the bottom of page seven. "They didn't make it," she said it again, her chin quivering. She took another deep drag of her third cigarette and stared into the distance. "Isn't it weird that the world goes on after you die, as if you never existed? The sun rises the next morning, even though you're not there to witness it. We make absolutely no difference to this world."

"I think we all make a difference, no matter how small." Andrew closed the newspaper, tucked it under his arm, and cupped Rita's face in his hands. "First of all, you don't even know if those were your friends. There are no photos of the victims. Even if they were, there's nothing you can do or could have done to change it. Cry as much as you need to or talk to me, tell me when you need a hug, but please..." He stroked her cheek. "Don't blame yourself. There was nothing you could have done to change their lives."

Rita pointed at the only photo there was, a close up of an empty lorry full of debris and a few items of clothing. "I gave her that bracelet. It has the letter S. She was so happy that day."

Snowflakes landed on her wet cheeks. A kiss from the heavens.

"Come on," Andrew said, looking up at the sky.

She nodded. *Life goes on.*

Andrew draped his right hand around Rita's waist

and with his free hand, he opened the car door. They sat in silence, as if they were both searching for the right words. Rita recalled the coat she was going to buy that day. If it hadn't been for that coat, she would have spent the day in bed, reading her book, completely unaware of the newspaper on the bus and the story inside it. She'd have missed today's news, which would soon have been replaced with other news, other tragedies. Rita would have lived her life certain that Bashir and Sumaya were somewhere in England leading happy lives. If it hadn't been for that coat, she wouldn't be with Andrew now. Had calling him been a mistake?

"Do you want to hear good news?" Andrew said, after several minutes, his voice rising an octave as if he was trying to cheer Rita up.

"Yes. I could do with something to smile about."

"I bought that house I told you about. It still needs a lot of work, but all the furniture is new and… Would you like to see it?"

"Of course!" Rita said, listening to her heart instead of her sceptical mind.

Andrew's smile widened.

It was a half-hour drive to Andrew's new home and night had already fallen. Rita still wasn't used to how dark the winters were in this country. She gazed out at the streets whizzing by, not recognising where she was.

Another reminder of her foreign status, forever trying to settle into a country that wasn't hers.

Life is like flowers. You buy them in a pot, where they are perfectly happy, and then you transfer them to new soil in your garden. Some of them blossom, some of them die. Rita was a flower, searching for the right soil in which to spread her roots again. Was it possible to put down roots in a land that wasn't your own?

Andrew made small talk as the car wound through the busy, narrow streets of London. "Turn right onto Forest Gate," the GPS instructed, bringing Rita back to the real world. Two minutes later, he cut the engine off, and opened the passenger door for Rita, ever the gent.

She stepped out and took in the row of houses standing proudly in front of her. Her eyes stopped at a Victorian three-story house with the number ten on its door. Next to it, on the left, was a brown door with the number eight. She squinted to the other side of the road where the houses were numbered nine, eleven, and thirteen. How strange that the odd numbers were on one side and the even on the other. Not that any of that mattered, but she preferred to focus on house numbers rather than think about the poor family trapped inside a frozen truck. Or what might now happen between her and Andrew behind that glossy new front door.

Trapped by her own emotions, she stood on the threshold.

Nothing good will come from this, her mind told her.

"Make yourself at home," he said, letting them in and pushing open the door of the living room. A small Christmas tree festooned with lights twinkled beside the dining table. It was a real tree, the expensive kind. There wasn't much furniture, but Andrew had still gone to the effort of putting up a tree.

Archie, Andrew's dog, jumped up at Rita.

"Look at him. He loves you already! He's normally a shy boy," said Andrew, patting the dog's head.

Rita was nervous. Not because of Archie, but the avalanche of emotions cascading inside her. Since Luk died, she hadn't dared get close to a dog, let alone stroke its fur. She thought it would be impossible to care about another dog after Luk…her poor Luk, buried in a faraway land. It turned out that she was wrong.

She kneeled down and rubbed Archie's ears.

"Give me a minute to rustle something up," Andrew shouted from the kitchen. "Archie, be a good boy and show Rita around the house."

Rita smiled and threw her parka and bag on a chair, then sat on the chestnut leather couch and looked around. There was a large colourful rug on the polished wooden floor, with what appeared to be a vintage coffee table in the centre, with a tray of candles on top and a shelf of books underneath. A small desk with a computer sat by the window, and to her left, there was a bookshelf, although it wasn't completely full yet.

"Can I help you?" she called to Andrew.

"I'll just be a minute."

Soon, he returned to the living room carrying a bottle of wine in one hand and two glasses in the other. He placed them on the coffee table, picked up a lighter and lit the candles. Then he turned on the TV.

"Let's pretend there's a fireplace, until I get the real one cleaned and working again." He winked at her as flames crackled on the TV screen and jazz music played in the background.

The flames on the screen warmed her face, even though they weren't real. Or perhaps the heat was coming from somewhere deep inside.

She removed her woollen scarf and Andrew took it, along with her parka, and disappeared.

"I'll be right back," he called out, leaving the door ajar. "So, what do you think of the house?"

Rita gazed at the flickering flames of the candles and the two glasses on the table. "It's nice." She wanted to say, "I love it," but it was better to delete that word from her vocabulary. *As if he'd love that peasant!* Rachel's words rang through her mind.

She shook her head. Being with Andrew was like the tide ebbing and flowing. She tried her best to stay away, but somehow, she always drifted back to him.

Andrew appeared again, pushing the door with the tip of his shoe, his hands full. He placed a big tray full of French bread cut into bite-sized pieces, steamed broccoli, slices of apples, strips of steak, and diced potatoes on the table.

When did he prepare all of this?

"I hope you like cheese fondue," he said, lighting another small candle beneath a pot of something yellow. "It's the quickest thing I could make."

Rita guessed she would, although she'd never heard of it.

She gave Andrew an uncertain smile as he sat down beside her. He poured some wine into her glass, then topped up his own. Spearing a slice of apple with a small prong, he dipped it in the melted cheese, which was now steaming, and ate it.

Okay, so that's what you do.

She figured it was better to start with the food she was familiar with. Rita had never eaten apples and cheese together. She dipped a piece of bread in the cheese, then popped it into her mouth. "Mmm!" she said, unable to hide her delight.

It appeared she was a cheese fondue convert.

Leonard Cohen's *Dance Me to the End of Love* surrounded them from hidden speakers, and Archie sat at Rita's feet. She took another sip of wine, reminding herself not to drink too much. The room was growing unusually warm. This was all a bit too perfect.

"Listen, Rita. I'm really sorry about what happened the night of my birthday."

"I only ignored your calls because I didn't want to get between you and Rachel."

"What do you mean? How many times can I attempt to reassure you? She's just a friend."

Rita sighed and Andrew took her hand.

"I've known her all my life, since we were kids, but if you don't want me to see her again I never will. I know she was drunk, but she shouldn't have said, or done, what she did."

"It's okay. Let's just forget about it." Did Rita really mean that?

She reached for a slice of apple and finally felt brave enough to dip it into the cheese. It was strangely delicious.

"I have to stop turning up at Chloe's half drunk," she said with a laugh.

"I have a spare room." Andrew cocked a brow.

She smiled, her head resting on his shoulder.

"Maybe I'll stay," she replied coyly.

"Do you remember, back in Italy, when we were talking about crushes?"

Rita giggled. "I'm still embarrassed for confusing the words crush and crash."

"Well, it's probably obvious… but I've got a *huge* crush on you."

Rita put a finger to Andrew's lips. A crush was enough for tonight, she didn't want him to say anything else and ruin the magic.

He pulled his arms tighter around her and she leaned into him, forgetting her day, her sorrows, and her pain. She had found a warm, safe place. With her head on his chest, she listened to his breathing. She wanted to say something but, as always, she lacked the right words in English. Then again, neither of them needed words.

Andrew ran his fingers through her hair and down her neck, tenderly kissing her earlobe.

"I'm so glad you called me today," he whispered in her ear.

Rita looked up, her lips brushing against his, and kissed him.

46

Rita opened her eyes, finding herself enveloped in Andrew's arms. But for the first time in a long time, she didn't doubt her decision. Carefully, so as not to wake him, she slid out of his embrace. Her phone showed it was 5:30 a.m. Not wanting to switch on the light, she tiptoed to the window and pulled the curtain aside a little, revealing a view of a small garden. *A garden.* It was a typical city garden with a paved patio, but there was still enough space to plant some flowers and put a table and chairs out there. Apart from a single oak tree, the grass and everything else was dead. Rita had always wanted a house with a garden.

Using the little light there was from outside, Rita searched for her clothes and threw them on quickly. She had to get to work. She grabbed her bag, took her parka, and wrapped her woollen scarf around her neck, kissing Archie on the top of his head before leaving the house.

Outside it was still dark, and there wasn't a single star

in the sky. Rita shivered, unsure if the cold sensation came from the darkness, or waking up in an unknown neighbourhood. She checked the route on her phone and headed for the nearest bus station.

Rita was only a few minutes late, but Chiara looked furious. "You're late. Where on Earth have you been?" She threw her hands up and stormed off to work, leaving the door open behind her.

"I've been in Heaven," Rita whispered, a faint smile tugging at the corner of her mouth.

She closed the door quietly behind her. Alessia was still sleeping, and Oliver had gone. She sighed with relief and went to the kitchen to pour herself some coffee. With her mug firmly in both hands, she walked over to the window. Her mind was a whirlwind of confusion as raindrops pattered on the glass.

She had no idea how long she'd been staring out the window when she heard the little one run in. Rita kissed the top of her head and prepared her bottle of milk.

Her phone pinged with a message.

"I didn't hear you leave. I forgot you had to work today. I would have made you breakfast in bed. Last night was amazing. I will pick you up after work."

Rita was in great spirits, and had she not been at Chiara's house, she would have started dancing.

That day, Rita followed Chiara's list. She also did something that she'd never done in Chiara's house before: she got onto the H&M website and ordered the coat she was supposed to buy yesterday. If she was dating Andrew now – and she guessed that she was – then she wanted to look the part. She was no peasant.

By the end of the day, Alessia was bored, and Rita couldn't wait to leave the house. How could she explain to a two-year-old that she was distracted because she was in love, when she was scared to believe it herself? She kept thinking about last night. Was it a mistake? Even if it had been, she would still do it again a million times over. And that had to be a sign that it was right. Right?

As soon as Chiara arrived home, Rita left the house shouting a speedy goodbye behind her as she ran. She wanted to see Andrew, but not before having a shower and getting changed. She texted him to meet her at Chloe's apartment, and, as usual, he agreed. Rita had to get used to Andrew's way of thinking. He was a man who agreed with what a woman said.

Rita might have overcome her anxiety about getting on the Tube, but as always, the train was packed. She looped her arm around the pole and checked her phone. Another message but this time it was from a different Instagram account.

Rita frowned.

'It's me again. Megan found all the messages I've sent to you and fucking translated them on Google. She knows everything. She's gone mad. If you see her, tell her the truth. Tell her I never cheated on her!'

The message went on and on, but Rita decided not to read anymore. Not her problem.

Rita blocked Samuel's new and old Instagram accounts. She was no longer the old Rita that Samuel thought he knew.

47

If somebody had told Rita that life would be kind to her one day, she wouldn't have believed them. But now, she was spending every day with Andrew and her life had never felt so wonderful. He'd asked her to move in with him! As much as Rita wanted to give Chloe and Kristos back the privacy she'd stolen from them, it was a little early for that, but the thought made her glow from the inside out. For the first time since her mother died, Rita's future looked happy and bright.

Thankfully, Rachel and Samuel had kept their distance. She saw fewer grey Mini Coopers nowadays, and Rita convinced herself that she'd imagined them all in the first place. Everything had been in her mind. It always was.

When Andrew asked her to spend Christmas with him, she'd agreed on the spot. But when he'd said that this was his family's first Christmas without his dad and his mum wasn't coping very well, Rita reconsidered her decision. She couldn't spend Christmas with his mother! What if she reacted the same way Rachel had when they met?

Just wait until you tell her where you come from, the voice in her head laughed. *She'll think you're only with her son for his money. She likes Rachel, remember. She won't accept you.*

That's for Andrew to decide, Rita silently fired back.

She kissed Alessia on the top her head. The little one was watching Peppa Pig and the house was spotless.

As if she was scrubbing the thoughts from her mind, Rita wiped down the already clean table and kitchen worktop.

Chiara finally came home and the argument in Rita's head stopped. She had two more days to decide what to do in any case. Today, she was going to surprise Andrew. He wasn't the only one capable of grand gestures. She had stuffed a spare change of clothes in her bag. They were going to watch a movie and she was going to cook him a traditional Albanian dish.

Chiara eyed the red shirt that Rita had just changed into. Rita knew she could tell straightaway that it was an online bargain, but she simply smiled. Then, she handed Rita the envelope containing her weekly pay check. Rita's face lit up.

True to the shopaholic she was fast becoming, she stopped at a shop near Hammersmith Tube station. She'd seen a vase that would look perfect in Andrew's new house. It was going to cost half her salary, but it was worth it. The sales assistant wrapped the vase carefully and put it in a paper bag. Rita would start saving in January. Another New Year's resolution.

Happy with her purchase, she stopped at Andrew's front door and rang the bell. She'd wanted to surprise him but hadn't considered the possibility that he might not be at home. Impatient to see his face when he opened the gift, she rang the bell again.

The vase was heavy, and her hands were freezing. She still hadn't bought any damn gloves. She would make another resolution to finally buy some in January. She set the present on the doorstep and rummaged around in her bag for her phone, having to put everything on the ground just to find it. She was still busy fumbling with her things when Archie jumped up at her. Rita patted his head and looked up. Her smile froze on her lips. Rachel stood at the door. Rita blinked but the other woman was not a mirage. Rachel was topless, aside from her black bra!

"Ah, the peasant's here," Rachel shouted, grabbing her jacket hanging on the rack by the door and stepping outside.

Andrew appeared at the top of the stairs. At least he had his shirt and jeans on. Should Rita be relieved? He held another shirt in his hands.

"Rita, what are you doing here?" he asked, failing to

hide the tension in his voice.

"I clearly chose the wrong time. I just wanted to surprise you, but it looks like somebody beat me to it."

"Come inside. It's cold out there." He looked at the shirt in his hands. "Where's Rachel?"

"She just left. Sorry I interrupted your time together. I guess I really am just another stupid Albanian slut. I also guess you're done with me now?"

Andrew's eyes widened.

"No, Rita! Please, get inside. I haven't seen Rachel since my birthday. She came here drunk… again… I ordered her a taxi home – it's on its way – and I gave her a glass of water to try to sober her up, but she spilled it on herself." He held up the shirt in his hand as if it was courtroom evidence. "I was getting her one of my clean shirts, so she wouldn't look in quite such a state when the taxi arrived. Please, let's talk inside."

Archie was now standing between them, barking and wagging his tail. Rita kneeled and stroked his ears. "Goodbye boy," she said, kissing the top of his head.

She turned to Andrew. "And fuck you."

How could he possibly expect me to buy this?

Stupid, stupid, stupid! her dark voice hammered inside her head as she ran away as fast as she could. This time the voice was right. Hatred rose in her chest like a tide, her pulse pounding in her neck. The words of the Albanian poet, Migjeni came to mind:

In tears have we found consolation...
Our heritage in life has been
Misery...

Outside the Tube station entrance, Rita stopped and lit a cigarette, her fingers trembling, tears soaking her face. Why was she always crying around public transport? And why did she always break her promises? After Samuel betrayed her, she vowed she would never fall in love again, knowing it would only lead to more heartache. Yet, that's exactly what had happened. She'd fallen hard. Not only that, but she'd made love to Andrew and discovered a part of herself she'd never known before. But it had all been for nothing. Like Maria, she'd been blinded by love, and it had destroyed her. Crushes turned to crashes eventually.

Rita looked out at the icy street, a veil of mist shrouding the city. This was not her city. It was a mistake to think she would find a life here, let alone true love.

She blew out a cloud of smoke, watching it mingle with the millions of snowflakes whirling through the air. Her thick jeans and black double-breasted coat weren't protecting her from the cold. She'd worn her new coat purposely today, but Andrew was too busy getting inside Rachel's bra – and who knew where else – to give a shit.

I bet she has matching underwear. She's not an

immigrant peasant like me.

Rita took another puff of her cigarette and checked the time of the next train. The small automatic doors that separated the underground from the outside world were expelling huge crowds of people and letting seemingly bigger crowds in. London never stopped. It was almost time for everyone to gather around their dining tables in their beautiful warm houses — everyone except Rita. She was nobody, and nobody cared about her.

Rita threw the cigarette butt on the ground and stepped on it with the tip of her shoe. That's when she saw the grey Mini Cooper. She was definitely not imagining it this time.

But it wasn't Samuel inside. Rita sighed with relief when she saw a woman behind the wheel. *What kind of car does Rachel have?*

Without thinking twice, Rita mingled with the other passengers until she found herself on the correct platform. She was no longer scared. Away from the street, nothing could happen in such a crowded place. Yet a feeling of unease grew inside her. Every time she turned her head, she felt eyes upon her. Had Andrew run after her? Maybe it was Samuel? What about Rachel?

A blonde girl glowered at her through the crowd, her eyes like a bird of prey ready to attack. Rita took a deep breath and fumbled for her phone to call Chloe, but once she managed to punch in the number with trembling hands, it kept cutting out. Mobile phone reception wasn't great on the underground. Rita turned her head, but the girl was no longer there.

The platform display showed her train was delayed. She needed to talk to somebody to distract herself and calm down. She needed a silly word game like the one Andrew had foisted upon her on the plane. But Andrew wasn't in her life anymore, and he never would be.

Rita looked around, but everyone was engrossed in their screens. There was no one to talk to because nobody talked to strangers in London. She took out her own phone again and checked her Instagram. Maybe she should go live?

And what the hell are you going to say? the voice in her head screamed, the only voice willing to talk to her right now. *That you're an expert at falling in love with the wrong person? Or that you're scared you're being followed? You're losing it, Rita!*

Rita ignored her fear and pressed the live button. She was not sure if she would get any reception, but she had to try. Yes! It worked. Thousands of people were watching her online within seconds. She'd tell them the truth: London wasn't all it was cracked up to be.

A figure appeared behind her on her camera and Rita gasped.

Then came the scream.

48

London
January 2020

There's no screaming now, just silence. I'm back in the same room I've been in for days. Maybe weeks. The man stands, watching over me, and I can finally see his face.

"Rita, can you hear me?"

I feel his tears dripping on to my cheek. I try to move my hand, but my arm is hurting from all of the tubes connected to it.

My eyes flicker open, and this time, it's for real. The man is looking at me. He is unshaven, his hair a mess.

The light hurts my eyes and I shut them again, just for a second. I'm scared to keep them closed for too long in case I'm sent back. I thrash about, almost choking on the tube in my mouth. Where did that come from? I've seen this room so many times, yet now that my eyes are finally open it looks different somehow.

Andrew's face comes into focus again and a tear runs down my cheek, landing on his hand which is gently cupping my face.

"Hey, don't cry. It's over now."

But he's crying too.

The nurse and the doctor enter the room immediately. I know the nurse and my heart swells. She removes the tube and dabs my mouth with a wet sponge. So, it's Chiara who's been looking after me all this time. She's not wearing the high heels or the silk blouses I'm used to seeing her in, just a boring white uniform like all the rest of the staff. She gives me another big and reassuring smile. I've never seen Chiara like this.

I try to say something, but my throat is dry, and everything hurts. *Water* I finally manage, or at least I think I do; what comes out of my mouth is just a strangled noise.

"Take it easy, Rita," says the doctor.

The way he says my name it's as if he's known me for ages. What day is it? How long have I been here? I want to ask, but I can't say the words.

"Give yourself time. We're lucky to have you back. Somebody up there must love you very much."

She does. She really does. I can't help but think – *know*, actually – that my mum has played a part in sending me back to this room, to this life, for good.

The doctor looks at me over his glasses and consults the chart Chiara has handed him.

"You have a broken leg, and two cracked ribs on your right side."

Oh, that's why it hurts to breathe.

"But thankfully, no damage to the brain."

The doctor smiles kindly and nods to Chiara who is scribbling something down. I hear the sound of her pen - scratch, scratch, scratch.

"And this young man here," he turns and looks at Andrew, "has been by your side since we brought you in. I'll give you some space."

They leave the room and I'm finally alone with Andrew. The man who has not left my side the entire time. My vision is clearer now. I glance at the flowers on my bedside table and remember the woman who brought them. I've never seen that woman before.

"My mother brought those for you," Andrew says.

Does that mean she likes me?

"I'm so sorry, Rita. I should have run after you, and maybe none of this would have happened. I had no idea that crazy woman was after you. They caught her. I don't know how, but apparently it was live streamed."

Megan. It was Samuel's new wife who had tried to kill me then! I remember it now. The twisted snarl on her face as she approached me on the platform, watching her on my screen, trying to understand what

399

was happening as she came up behind me. The train hurtling towards us, but I was too close to the edge, so I tried to step back, then she pushed me. She pushed me. People screamed and my world went black.

I try and say something, but my throat is still too dry and there seem to be tubes coming out of every part of me. Megan must have seen the messages Samuel had sent to me, just like he'd warned me she had. Did she think that if I was dead, he'd love her more? I nearly died trying to reach Samuel, only to discover he'd betrayed me.

Whereas Megan was prepared to kill for him.

I look up at Andrew. The only human being who hasn't left my side since I've known him. Despite being a relative stranger.

"I love you, Rita." He swallows hard, his Adam's apple bobbing up and down. "And I promise I will never let you go again. You belong here, with me, together. This is your home now."

I give him a shaky smile. Incredibly, my mind stays silent. Not a single negative voice dares to contradict him.

He says I belong.

I am home.

Acknowledgements

I would like to take a moment to express my deep gratitude to all the wonderful people who have supported me in the creation of this book.

First and foremost, I want to thank my dear friend Natali Drake for her unwavering support and encouragement. I am so lucky to have found such a caring and supportive friend in you.

Eternal thanks to my friends Samantha Curtis, Helen Pryke and Jane Harmon McFarland for their love and support throughout this journey.

I am also incredibly grateful to my beta readers: Saras_mystery_bookclub, Dorina Koliçi and Kria, for their invaluable feedback and help in shaping this book. Your insights and suggestions were integral to the final product.

I am endlessly thankful to my husband for believing in me, long before I believed in myself. Thank you for your love and support.

I also want to thank my two amazing boys Joël Amadeus and Ayden Maximus, for giving me the space and time to write.

Lastly, I would like to thank my little sister, Arilda, for reading and believing in everything I write. You are a constant source of inspiration.

To all of you, I offer my heartfelt thanks. Your support and encouragement have meant the world to me and this book would not have been possible without you.

About the Author

Teuta Metra is an Albanian/Dutch writer based in Rotterdam. Through her fiction books, Teuta advocates for women's rights in her home country. With a background as a former journalist, she believes in the power of literature and words to make a positive impact. By day, Teuta works as a librarian in Rotterdam and by night, she dedicates herself to writing, weaving stories that inspire and empower.

Visit her website, www.teutametra.com, to stay updated on her latest projects, events, and appearances.

Printed in Great Britain
by Amazon

19312048R00236